"You okay?
look a little

"I'm fine." And I was, until I saw the airport security checkpoint.

"Be calm," Griffin said. "We're going shopping in Paris. Remember that." He squeezed my hand and laughed as if I'd said something funny.

I giggled in response, but shut my mouth when the sound edged toward hysteria. We're shopping. Just two people going shopping. I chanted the words like a prayer in my head.

We went through the metal detector without a hitch. I breathed a sigh of relief. Perhaps events were turning in our favor.

I was putting my shoes back on when something hard jammed into my side. A firm hand grabbed my elbow. "Please come with us, Ms. Palmer. Quietly. We have a few...questions."

I looked down. The something hard wedged into my flesh was the barrel of a gun.

Dear Reader,

Two years ago, I found myself at a writers' conference, standing on a sky bridge and talking to Evelyn Vaughn. Conference packets in hand, we discussed writing, laughed—and that's when she asked if I'd be interested in working on an author-generated series called THE MADONNA KEY. An ambitious series, it focuses on a group of seven gifted women as they race to save the world and work together in the process.

Of course I said, "Yes." I'm not one to turn down an opportunity—especially one that sounded so fun.

Working with the other authors on THE MADONNA KEY series *has* been fun. Exhilarating. Educational and challenging. I'll also cheerfully admit there were a few times I wanted to run screaming down the street, and ended up being plied with wine and chocolate in order to maintain sanity.

I hope you have as much fun reading about the amazing women of THE MADONNA KEY series (minus the screaming down the street, of course) as I had writing for it.

Sharron

Sharron McClellan

HIDDEN SANCTUARY

Silhouette®

BOMBSHELL™

Published by Silhouette Books

America's Publisher of Contemporary Romance

THE MADONNA KEY series was co-created by
Yvonne Jocks, Vicki Hinze and Lorna Tedder.

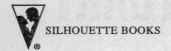

SILHOUETTE BOOKS

ISBN-13: 978-0-373-51428-1
ISBN-10: 0-373-51428-X

HIDDEN SANCTUARY

www.SilhouetteBombshell.com

Printed in U.S.A.

Books by Sharron McClellan

Silhouette Bombshell

The Midas Trap #29
Hidden Sanctuary #114

SHARRON McCLELLAN

began writing short stories in high school but became sidetracked from her calling when she moved to Alaska to study archaeology. For years, she traveled across the United States as a field archaeologist specializing in burials and human physiology. Between archaeological contracts, she decided to take up the pen again. She completed her first manuscript two years later, and it was, she says, "A disaster. I knew as much about the craft of writing as Indiana Jones would know about applying makeup." It was then that she discovered Romance Writers of America and began serious study of her trade. Three years later, in 2002, she sold her first novel, a fantasy romance. Sharron now blends her archaeological experience with her love of fiction to write for the Silhouette Bombshell line. To learn more, visit her at www.sharronmcclellan.com. She loves to hear from her readers.

To Von: For asking me to be a part of this. Thank you, thank you, thank you for this amazing opportunity.

To Jennifer: For being our "calm blue ocean" (you are an inspiration).

To Cindy: For talking me down from the metaphorical "writer's ledge" on a regular basis.

To Carol: For jumping into the exciting chaos of the MK continuity without hesitation.

To Lorna: For sharing your profusion of metaphysical knowledge.

Chapter 1

"Son of a—"

A sharp elbow in my side, courtesy of my right-hand man and lead technician, Pete Calandar, made me bite the whispered expletive in half.

It was two in the morning, and we hid in the shadows of the large maintenance tent that rested at the edge of our small, ten-member camp. I shivered in the night air, wishing I'd taken the time to slip on a pair of shoes. It was winter in the desert, almost December, which meant that while the days were hot but bearable, the nights were as cold as Massachusetts in the middle of a snowstorm.

I had bigger worries than frostbite. Beyond our hiding place and outlined by moonlight, some of the locals were sabotaging my oil rig and ruining my progress.

Technically, the destruction in front of me should not be happening. My company was allowed to drill on Nubian land due to mutual agreement—but not everyone in the local village felt we had the right to be in their desert.

Oddly enough, it was the younger people who were the least receptive to our presence. That, or they were the most bored and we were the easiest people to annoy. The distinctive sound of twisting metal clipped the air. Whatever their reason, I didn't care. A growl of frustration rose from my throat, and I raised my rifle.

"What are you doing, Tru?" Pete whispered, his deep voice carrying no farther than my ear.

"Stopping them." I took a moment to sight them through the night scope. The moon made the view as bright as midday. Not that the time of day mattered when it came to my aim. Pete said I couldn't hit water if I was standing in a lake.

I looked anyway and confirmed my evaluation of the intruders.

I was right. They were boys. Age eighteen, maybe less. Dressed in jeans and T-shirts. They looked harmless with their skinny legs and thin, adolescent shoulders.

But I knew how much harm a wrench or length of pipe could do in the hands of a teenager.

One of them kicked the oil rig's engine.

Every muscle in my body contracted as anger roiled through me, making me shake. Taking a deep breath to calm myself, I shifted my aim before I did something I'd regret, repositioning my sight from them to their Jeep.

With luck, I could take out a tire. Then there'd be no way they could escape unless they tried to run on foot, and in the southern Egyptian desert, that was a death sentence, even for the locals.

Grabbing the barrel, Pete pulled my rifle until the muzzle pointed at the glittering sand beyond us. "You can't shoot them."

I yanked my weapon out of his grasp. "Not *them*. The *Jeep*. I was getting a closer look at them, that's all."

"Oh." He had the presence of mind to look foolish as he ran a hand through his thinning red hair—a nervous gesture he'd had since before we met on the Bantha project five years ago in Russia.

Twenty years my senior, Pete had seen it all. Done it all. That experience commanded loyalty. His crews worked like dogs for him. So, when I started Geo Investigations Incorporated three years ago, I knew Pete was the one person I had to have on my team. It hadn't been easy to convince him to join a start-up company, but a generous bonus tied to our first success had convinced him.

Now, we were together out of mutual loyalty, and I enjoyed our quasi father-daughter relationship.

Except at times such as this, when he acted like I was still a pampered heiress who didn't know her head from a hole in the ground, and who was not the boss of a successful oil exploration company.

With a sigh of exasperation, I raised the rifle again and took a last, quick glance at the intruders.

"Just kids," I muttered.

Kids that were tearing my main engine apart.

Shifting, I sighted the Jeep. "Be prepared to chase them," I whispered.

"Chase them?" Pete's tone was incredulous. "You've got to be kidding. They may be skinny as rails, but they're wiry and all muscle. Athletes. I'm a middle-aged oil rig manager."

"Just do it," I said, exasperated with arguing.

"We should have brought Griffin," Pete whispered. "Let him chase them."

"He's a powerhouse, not a runner." My liaison to Dynocorp—the conglomerate that had hired me to run this project—and head of security, Griffin Sinclair was capable and calm, took everything seriously and considered his rock-hard body another weapon in his arsenal.

I considered his physique the one perk of having him around. On more than one occasion, I'd seen him half-naked, and it was well worth the stolen glance.

Unfortunately, it was the only perk. Griffin was a gorgeous specimen of the human male, but he also reported everything I said, did and probably ate back to Dynocorp's board.

I tried to keep him out of the loop as much as possible.

"Yeah, but he's still younger and faster than me," Pete insisted.

"Anyone is."

"Thanks." His voice dripped with sarcasm.

"You're welcome," I said with a grin. Pete wasn't Griffin, but he was more fit than most men, and we both knew it. "Look, I don't want Griffin informing the Dynoguys that we couldn't keep a bunch of kids from shutting us down. Not if I can help it."

A loud clanking refocused my attention on the

vandals. Someone yanked God-knew-what out of the engine.

No more talking. I sighted the Jeep's back tire and fired.

The muzzle flashed bright in the shadows, and the ping of the bullet striking metal echoed in the night.

Followed by a shriek as one of the boys cried out and fell to the ground. My gut clenched as I realized what had happened. *Ricochet.* "Damn it."

The rest of the boys froze like wild animals caught off guard, eyed their friend, hesitated, and then sprinted for the car leaving him behind.

The driver gunned the Jeep to life, and seconds later the intruders roared past us, shouting what I figured were obscenities in a combination of Arabic and possibly Nubian.

Rifle still in hand, I let them get away so I could deal with the more pressing problem.

I'd shot someone.

Pete and I raced over to the wounded boy.

"Wait, let me," I said, grabbing Pete's arm and stopping him. "I'm a girl and less scary."

"Only if you don't know women," Pete muttered.

I held back a retort and bent down, putting myself at eye level with the fallen boy.

His eyes wide with both pain and fright, he tried to crawl away from us, using his right Levi's-clad leg to push himself across the sand. I realized that I'd hit his left leg. Luckily, the blood wasn't pooling or spurting, which meant I hadn't hit an artery.

I followed his panicked gaze and realized his attention was locked on the rifle I still gripped in my hand. *Hell.*

Even *I'd* try to get away from me under these circumstances.

"Pete." I handed him the rifle, took a deep breath and held out my hand, hoping I appeared more sympathetic than I felt. "It's okay," I said in my softest voice. "It's okay. We're going to help you."

Lying on the ground, he looked harmless. Like a youth caught up in something he hadn't planned and wished he could take back. "Come on, kid. It'll be all right," I assured him, as I inched closer. "Let me help you."

He cringed.

I felt like a bitch, but reminded myself that if the little idiot hadn't been trashing my oil rig, none of this would have happened.

Suddenly, his eyes shifted, tracking past me. I followed them.

Griffin. His short, dark hair was a swatch of moonlight-silvered black. Despite the chill desert night, he only wore boxer briefs, his every chiseled muscle highlighted and defined by light and shadow. He glared at me like a reproachful Egyptian god come to earth in contemporary form to discipline a particularly wayward follower.

He looked very, very good.

Then he opened his mouth. "What did you screw up now?"

Five minutes later, Griffin had managed to do what I could not—convince the boy to stay put so we could bandage his wound.

In that same time span, Pete and I had talked to all the crew members awoken by the noise, telling them that everything was under control, the boy would be fine, and to go back to bed.

Although they all left, their obvious skepticism told me that none of them believed our assurances.

Neither did I.

"Pete, can you take our friend here to the med tent?" Griffin asked, rising and dusting the sand off his bare knees.

"Of course," Pete said. Besides being my right-hand-man, he was also a trained EMT. "Luckily, it looks like a flesh wound. He's scared more than anything. I'll give him something to drink, put him to bed and watch him while he sleeps. We'll take him home in the morning."

"Thanks," Griffin replied.

"We'll leave you two alone to discuss business." Pete helped the boy up from the ground and rushed him away as fast as his wound allowed.

I didn't miss the amused glint in his eye.

Coward, I mouthed as he backed away, wishing I could go with him. Griffin's anger bothered me more than he knew and more than I would ever let on.

Growing up, my mother had shouted at me when my actions called for it. Time-outs were the norm. The occasional missed meal. She'd even spanked me once.

As for my father, when he was mad I'd felt the back of his hand. I shuddered at memories of his fury, and then shoved them back in the part of my mind where I could ignore them. And him.

Either way, my parents' response to my misbehaving was clear. So I never quite knew how to react to Griffin's calm, controlled admonishments.

When Pete and the teen were out of sight, Griffin turned back to me, his jaw rigid. "You want to explain why you didn't come to me for help?"

"Your tent is too far away. There wasn't time to get to you," I said.

He didn't look convinced. Not that I blamed him. Griffin's tent was at the edge of our encampment, but since the only things between him and the maintenance tent Pete and I had used for cover were worker tents and a few small structures for things like cooking and communications, the far end of camp was not really a great distance off.

Still, I had to tell him something.

"It's two in the morning. If there was time to come out here and shoot at someone, there was time to stop by my tent." His hands tightened into fists. "You're lucky no one was seriously hurt. *You* could have been hurt."

He made a tsking sound, and the hairs on the back of my neck rose in response. "Does your blond go all the way to the brain, Tru? You're smarter than this."

I met his glare with one of my own. "I'll thank you to leave my hair out of the conversation."

"And I'll thank you to wake me up when my project is in jeopardy," he countered.

"*Your* project?" I sputtered like someone who'd drunk a gulp of water and had it go down the wrong pipe.

"You're a contractor. I work for the company that pays you. So, yes. My company. My project."

I crossed my arms to keep from punching him in the head. "I can break the contract if you keep annoying me and interfering with my job."

His expression hardened. "Go ahead. Do whatever you need to, but I can tell you right now that I will not stop doing my job. And *my* job is making sure you do *your* job."

He took a step closer, breaking the rule of personal space. I didn't back up.

His mouth inches from mine, he continued. "You're bluffing. I've read the report on you. You walk away from this project, from Dynocorp, and it'll be years before you get significant work. I know it. You know it."

I glared at him, indignant, but he was right. In this business, reputation was everything, and mine was good, but it wasn't impeccable. Last year, when my mother died, I'd left a project, my unexpected grief interfering with my oil-finding gift, leaving me unable to find the promised deposit. Not that the industry knew, or even cared, why I'd left.

Walking away once was excusable. It happened.

Twice in two years would do serious damage and make getting another job more difficult than even I wanted to think about. But he didn't have to be a jerk about it. "Why do you have to be such a bastard, Griffin?"

He shifted, and for a flicker, I thought it might be due to guilt. Then he straightened. "All's fair, and my loyalty is to the people who pay me."

I sighed. What did one say to a man who would do or say anything to protect what he considered his? How could you win that fight?

I knew the answer. You couldn't.

His eyes locked with mine, and the hard glint faded, replaced by something different. Something more akin to curiosity. "Why do you fight me like this? Why not admit that you screwed up? If Pete told you the same thing, you'd agree, but you seem to take pleasure in disagreeing with me. Why?"

I shrugged, but it came off more petulant than disinterested. He kept staring at me, waiting for an answer. "It's not you," I finally replied. "Not personally."

"Then what?"

"It's your job," I said. "You're an informant." If there was one thing I loathed, it was people watching me, waiting for me to screw up.

"It's why Dynocorp hired me. To keep an eye on their investment."

"That and your ability to shoot the wings off a fly at a hundred paces," I muttered.

His mouth turned up at the compliment. "I do have certain skills, which help when one is on location." Then his dark eyes bored into me, curiosity and amusement fading as quickly as they'd appeared. "That is, if one is told there is a problem."

I flushed. As much as I hated it, he was right. Griffin was an excellent shot, and asking for help would have been the smart thing to do.

Pride goes before a fall. My mother's voice rang in my memory, even though I hadn't contacted her since I left home ten years ago.

Early on, after my bitter departure at eighteen, she'd tried to talk to me. Phone. Even sent friends as intermediaries. But I wasn't ready to listen.

When I was ready to talk to her it was too late. She was gone. Still, even in death, she held some sway over me.

Worse, she was right.

I held up my hands in surrender. "You win. Next time I'll ask for help."

Griffin gave a nod of approval. "Good, but there isn't going to be a next time. Tomorrow, we're taking that kid back to his village and talking with the elders. One way or another, we're going to get this straightened out."

"I'm looking forward to it, but I'm a bit surprised you're letting me go along," I replied. To call Griffin a macho control freak was a bit of an understatement, and who knew what I might do? Or so I was sure he thought.

"No choice," he said, his mouth twisting as if he'd bitten a lemon. "I want you to apologize for shooting the kid."

"It was an accident, and besides, what he was doing wasn't a prank." I pressed a hand to my forehead. "It wasn't like he was TPing the rig. He was trashing it. He had to realize he might get hurt."

"Regardless, he's a kid, and we need to make nice with these people whether you like it or not. We're on their land only because of a piece of paper and their goodwill. Because of you and your lousy aim, this could escalate into something deadly, and we could lose more than the contract. It's my job to make sure that doesn't happen."

"Fine," I said through clenched teeth. I'd planned to apologize anyway, but now, no matter what I claimed, Griffin would think it was because of his authority and not my own volition.

And Pete wondered why I found Griffin annoying.

He turned on his heel and walked back toward his

tent. "Talk to you in the morning," he called over his shoulder.

I didn't follow. There was a rig that needed repairing. Gathering my tools, I went to work, refusing to think about Griffin or what problems the morning might bring.

"How's it going?"

Even with my head and hands deep in the engine, I recognized Pete's voice. "Good," I replied. At least, I hoped so. If I didn't repair this engine, the project was stalled.

I couldn't afford that. I was on a tight timetable to produce results, and up until now, the vandals' attempts to stop the project hadn't impacted my schedule to a serious degree.

This might.

"That hose is still loose," Pete said, leaning in and blocking my light.

I waved him away. "I know." He moved, and I could see again. As much as I liked Pete, I didn't enjoy him looking over my shoulder and kibitzing while I worked. And he knew it.

"Aren't you supposed to be watching our *guest?*"

"Griffin took over after he was done yelling at you. Did you check the belts? I was thinking about them last night. With all that was going on, they might be nicked. One small cut and they'll break."

"Yes," I snapped, then checked my tone, reminding myself that Pete was just trying to be helpful. "The belts are fine."

I went back to work. "How do you know Griffin yelled at me?" Swiping at a drop of sweat, I felt grease smear across my cheek. I hated working on engines. I hated the grease. The smell. The stink of oil.

But more than that, I hated someone else doing it and screwing it up.

"I know Griffin and I know you."

I reached for the crescent wrench I'd laid on the lip of the machine a few swear words earlier, couldn't find it, and then felt the tool pressed into my hand.

"We don't always yell," I replied as I fitted the open end around the last nut and tightened it.

"Yeah, sometimes there are those silent arguments." His voice moved closer, and he leaned in again. "Are you sure that's where that wire belongs?"

My jaw tightened as I forced myself to bite back my impatience. "Yes. I'm positive." I tilted my head and looked up.

He was grinning. *Trying to be helpful, my fanny.* He knew what he was doing. I rolled my eyes and went back to work. Just what I needed. A comic.

A final twist with the wrench and I was done. I hoped.

I extricated myself from the engine and wiped my greasy hands down the front of my jeans, leaving long dark streaks.

Pete's gaze slid to my jeans as he shook his head, reminding me of my father when he caught me climbing a tree or making mud pies in a dress.

Now I grinned. What did he expect? Sugar and spice?

I'm not that kind of girl.

He met my eyes. "Think she'll start?"

"Hope so," I said. Flicking the primer switch

on and off, I crossed my fingers and turned the ignition key.

The engine coughed. Sputtered.

"Come on," I whispered. "Start." I flicked the switch again, said a silent prayer and turned the key once more.

Another sputter, then it caught and the engine purred to life.

I breathed a sigh of relief. The vandals had done some serious damage, and around four in the morning, I hadn't been sure it was fixable.

"Good job." Pete laid a palm against my shoulder and gave a fatherly squeeze. Absently, I patted his hand.

"Sounds like all is not lost."

I turned and watched Griffin walk up to us. He wore desert camouflage pants, a tan T-shirt and military boots. Though I couldn't see them, I knew he carried an assortment of weapons.

I tilted my chin up in a brief, silent *Hi*. "How's our guest?"

"Eating breakfast with the crew," he replied.

I nodded in approval. "I'll get changed." I wanted to appear sincere, and showing up looking like I hadn't bathed in a week didn't convey *I'm sorry* nearly as well as putting some effort into appearance.

Another lesson from my mother.

A wry smile curved my lips. Would I never get away from her and my father?

Picking up my rifle, I walked past the men.

"Tru?" Griffin laid a firm hand on my arm as I passed. "The rifle, if you don't mind. You are the last person they need to see armed."

"Fine." Reluctantly, I handed it over.

"Be back in ten minutes," he said as I walked away.

I waved in agreement over my head and tried to decide which was worse, having to apologize for shooting a vandal who wanted to destroy my company and career, or spending the day with Griffin Sinclair.

Chapter 2

"When we arrive, let me do the talking," Griffin said, while I hung on to the car seat and tried to keep an eye on our guest at the same time.

The boy's village was a twenty-minute ride away, but it was over a rocky, semi-paved road that sported the occasional windblown dune. Red dust blew in through the open window, transforming my white cotton shirt into a mottled mess and gathering in the creases of my khaki cargo pants.

Sometimes I hated the desert.

"Not a problem," I replied. "Considering I don't speak either Arabic or Nubian."

For a beat, his eyes widened in surprise. "I thought you did."

"Just enough to get by," I said in between *oomphs* as we rolled through a shallow ditch and I bounced up, then landed hard on the worn, cloth-covered seat. My lack of language skills appeared to have escaped the report on me. I smiled, satisfied. It was nice to know that some aspects of my life were still mine to divulge.

I glanced back. The little vandal grinned at me, and my smile vanished. He was enjoying this? Refusing to give him the satisfaction of seeing my aggravation, I went back to watching the road.

He probably thought I'd be flogged when we got to his village.

Though most of Egypt had adopted Western ways to a degree, there were still regions that were years behind the modern world in regards to the treatment of women.

In this hodgepodge of cultures, females ranged from equals to chattel, depending on location. His community might be one of the latter. If it were, the elders might demand more than an apology.

I glanced at Griffin over the rim of my sunglasses. Would he allow me to be hurt in order to save the project?

Better question, would I?

When we drove through the village, their workday was well underway. Women chatted as they hung laundry on lines. Children ran around playing some game that I didn't know the name of but recognized as a form of tag.

All this stopped when we pulled into the barren twenty-by-twenty patch of dirt that served as the town square. I noticed that most of the houses surrounding it were built of adobe with stylized motifs, ranging from owls to a sideways eight, painted along the outside for decoration.

Griffin turned off the engine. "Put your hands where they can see them," he said, opening the door and coming around to my side of the vehicle.

I slid out, holding my hands up. Griffin did the same. The teenager I'd shot in the leg pulled himself out of the Land Rover as a woman ran past me.

She was small, not even five feet in height. Although her face was visible, a long scarf covered her hair, protecting her from the harsh desert sun.

She wore an ankle-length, golden-yellow embroidered skirt with a matching sleeveless shirt. Copper and silver bangles jingled on her wrists, and multiple chains, some as thin as thread, draped her neck.

She spoke to the boy, and for a minute they conversed back and forth. I couldn't help but notice that he looked like her. Same eyes. Same mouth. His mother, was my guess. Their talking grew louder and more animated. She made him pull aside the bandage to reveal his wound.

I didn't know what they were saying, but watched Griffin's face. His eyes widened.

That couldn't be good.

"Don't flinch," he muttered, barely moving his lips. "And whatever happens, do not fight back. Just suck it up and take it."

"What?"

That's when she hit me.

My first reaction was to return the punch, and I drew back a fist, only to have Griffin grab it. "Don't," he growled.

I glared at him for a split second, as the woman hit me again. Then I turned my back to deflect the worst of her tirade.

Screaming what I assumed to be Nubian obscenities, she slapped and punched my back and shoulders. Although she was a tiny woman, she had a mother's righteous anger, and the blows were painful.

I gritted my teeth and held still, determined to take it. She stopped, and I relaxed, breathing a sigh of relief.

Then Griffin moved, reaching past me, but not fast enough.

She struck my head. For a moment, I saw the stars that everyone talks about.

And I'd thought they were strictly metaphorical.

Despite what Griffin said, I wrapped my arms around my skull to keep from getting my brains knocked out by the petite avenger. A few seconds later, there was a flurry of activity as Griffin crouched over me, shouting something.

The beating stopped. When I uncovered my head, her son and a man whom I assumed was her husband were holding the woman back.

She clutched a large rock in her fist.

I touched the spot she'd hit, and when I looked at my hand, there was blood on my fingers.

"Damn it." Griffin turned my head so he could look at the wound. "Sorry."

"You let her hit me!" I pulled away from him.

"She's so tiny, I didn't think she could really hurt you," he explained as he gazed into my eyes, going from one to another, presumably checking for a concussion. "I didn't see the rock."

The guilt in his own eyes was stronger than any punishment I could offer. He wasn't the first one to misjudge a situation like this. "We all make mistakes," I said, glancing toward the kid I'd shot.

The boy grinned, clearly enjoying the drama. Little bastard.

"I see what you mean," Griffin replied, a hint of sheepishness mixed with his concern.

"Thanks." I knew his understanding wouldn't keep him from doing what he needed to do to solve this tense situation, but his quasi understanding was a step toward making me feel less like a clumsy idiot.

Next to me, the boy's mother glared and continued muttering under her breath.

I met her angry stare with my own, prepared to defend myself. Before she could raise a hand, Griffin spoke a few sentences. The woman clamped her mouth shut, but her gaze never wavered. Hate for me blazed in her dark brown eyes.

I turned away. "What did you say?" I asked, rubbing a sore spot on my shoulder.

"That while you wanted to apologize and make amends for your behavior, she needed to be aware that your shooting her firstborn was accidental and might even be considered his fault for being there."

I smiled at Griffin's defense of my actions, but there would still be reparations. We both knew that. "What kind of amends are we talking?" Money I could offer, but to people in the middle of the desert, money was not what was precious. They wanted water. Food. Perhaps ammunition.

Griffin shook his head. "With luck, a formal apology in front of the village elders, or some such, will be enough."

"Did you tell them that he and his friends were tearing my oil rig apart?"

"No, because it doesn't matter. Our dealings with

them have always been strained, despite their agreement to let us drill. Blaming the kids will only come across as us trying to dodge responsibility for the shooting. I think it's best not to go there."

"You think my apologizing will fix this?" I asked.

Griffin sighed. "Hopefully. We can show the villagers who are against our presence that we're civilized people. They don't like the concept of a big corporation tearing up their land, but if we can offer them humans to relate to as opposed to some faceless entity, they might stop trying to shut us down."

I hated it when he made sense. I ran a hand over the knot on the back of my skull, a hiss of pain escaping at its tenderness. "Okay, but if they decide to flog me, I'll never forgive you."

He pointed toward a small adobe building that had a cross perched on the roof. "Wait in there."

A church? I wondered what a Christian-style church was doing in a primarily Muslim country. Perhaps a relic from some past missionary's attempt to convert the village?

I raised a brow. "The traditional hiding place of saints and sinners? Are you sure that's a good idea?"

"Just go while I try to fix your mess."

The last thing I wanted was anyone taking care of my mess. The distaste must have shown because for a flicker, Griffin's mouth softened. "You don't speak Nubian, Tru."

I managed a sharp nod of agreement before he turned and left.

The red dirt was hard under my feet, packed solid by decades of occupation, as I walked a gauntlet of angry eyes.

I refused to quicken my pace. The kid brought this on himself. He trashed my oil rig.

So why was guilt welling up inside me, making my stomach queasy?

Entering the church, I shut the door behind me and sagged against it for a moment. The place was empty.

My heartbeat slowed, and I took a deep breath. "Sanctuary."

Another breath and I took a good long look at my place of refuge.

At first glance, it was a typical church. Simple stained glass windows. Rough-hewn pews on both sides of a long aisle. On the back wall, two doors flanked the pulpit.

At closer examination, the church wasn't orthodox anything, but a hodgepodge of beliefs that happened to occupy a building with a cross on the roof.

Iconic statues occupied every niche in the wall. A ceramic Virgin Mary stood next to Kali, the dark mother-goddess of the Hindu religion. Across the room was a small marble Greek statue. From the helmet on her head and the owl on her shoulder, I decided she was Athena, goddess of knowledge, war and justice.

How appropriate.

That was when I realized that all the statues were female.

"Just women," I whispered. How odd. And why?

That's when I felt it. The peace in the air changed, and energy washed over me. An intangible force, unlike anything I'd ever felt, pressed inside my mind.

Unprepared, I fell to my knees. A sharp pain, this one as solid and real as a fist to the skull, brought darkness, then dreams.

* * *

Aleta stood in the shadows, her handmaid behind her, and watched as the Romans ransacked what was once her temple. What was once her home.

"Did all escape?" Cleo whispered.

Aleta nodded, but was unsure.

When the men had arrived, bursting into the temple waving weapons and fire, the young women, the acolytes, had fled. Had scattered down the secret tunnels, leaving everything behind.

Aleta closed her eyes, listening. There were no screams of pain. No cries for help. No noise but the roar of the fire as it consumed her home, and the exuberant shouts of the men as they watched.

When she opened her eyes, it was to see the men topple the statue of Isis that guarded the base of the stairs leading up to the temple.

The ten-foot marble masterpiece landed with a crack on the paved walkway, the right arm breaking off. "No," Aleta whispered, clutching her deep blue robes in her hands.

One of the men turned toward her, peering into the flickering shadows.

He could not have heard her, could he?

Aleta and Cleo shrank back, pressing themselves against the brick wall, hiding from the flames and from view. Aleta forced herself to keep her hands at her sides even as she desperately wanted to flick the hood of her robe over her hair, worried the bright blond strands were visible in the shadows and would give them away.

Countless heartbeats later, when she dared look around the corner of the building, the man no longer faced them, but was helping to topple the statue of Ma'at.

Her beloved Ma'at. Goddess of harmony. Truth. Balance.

Aleta's stomach clenched tight.

There was no balance in the universe. Not anymore.

She could bear no more of this desecration, the metaphorical—and often literal—bloodletting as a new god took over the city and expelled the old ways.

While she understood it on a mental level, it had never made sense to her heart. Why did one spiritual belief have to destroy another so completely?

Were the old ways that much of a threat? Was this new god so insecure that all who might challenge him must die?

Or were his followers simply cruel?

Whatever the reason, it did not make watching any easier.

She blinked back a tear, knowing she had to leave before she gave herself away. Putting herself in danger was foolish enough, but Cleo was a child. If they stayed much longer, both would be discovered, and her handmaid might never see her first year as a woman.

It was time to find the others. The women who thought as she did. They would help her. Take Cleo and protect her.

"Come," Aleta murmured, clasping Cleo's delicate cocoa-colored hand, and turning away from the destruction of the only home she'd ever known.

Keeping to the shadows, she remembered how the women had come to her months ago, asking for her help.

They were creating a mosaic and needed her. Their artisan had passed away in the night, and Aleta was the only woman they felt was talented enough to finish the meticulous work.

She'd been too busy to listen. Too occupied with the everyday business of the temple. Too involved with the world of men to assist.

They'd pleaded with her for help and had even gone so far as to tell her their secret.

The mosaic was more than an object of beauty. Imbued with power that came from both the precise arrangement and the vast array of stones and ceramic pieces going into its creation, it was magical. Once completed, it would be a masterpiece with an energy not seen in the world before. It would help calm the rage that currently seemed to consume mankind.

Uncaring of their problem, she'd bid them leave, confident that her talent and reputation as a priestess would keep her and her people safe. The world of men might touch others, but it would not touch her. People needed her and her art. Kings and queens appreciated her gift and called for her favor.

Hubris.

Pride had kept her in the temple. Made her believe she was immune to the insanity that seemed to be overtaking the world, the city.

But not her world. Not her temple. Not her life.

Or so she had thought.

The memory of her arrogance was bitter in her mouth, but she swallowed it as she turned a corner and the light from the flames dimmed.

Now, her world was charred. Her friends scattered.

Her only chance at redemption was the mosaic that needed her attention. The women claimed the completion of the artwork would provide the balance to keep the scales of life from tipping too far to one side. Would help quell the insanity of men.

Insanity she'd ignored until it touched her.

With Cleo's hand clenched tightly in hers, Aleta pulled her toward a side street, and the last flicker of light from the flames disappeared.

Something inside her cried out at the dark finality and the realization that there was no going back.

She was on a new path.

When I opened my eyes, I was on the floor, the rough wood planks pressed into my back. In my mind, I still felt Aleta's desire to find the women and finish what they asked. It was like a fire in my stomach. "The mosaic," I murmured. "The women."

I had to find them.

"What did you say?" a husky voice asked.

I blinked. A woman, her features as regal and refined as a queen's, knelt next to me.

For a hazy moment, she resembled the woman in my dream. Her robe and hair covering were the same royal blue, and the same maternal concern shone in her eyes.

"Aleta?"

Her eyes widened. "No. I am Efra."

Then I noticed the gray that streaked her black hair and the fine lines that creased her skin where her brows drew together in concern.

Besides, Aleta was Roman. A blonde with blue eyes and fair skin.

Not Nubian.

I shook the confusion from my thoughts. The vision—no, dream, I corrected myself—the *dream* was so real that it seemed as if the heat of the flames still licked my face and the smoky air coated my throat.

Once again, I felt rising panic and anger as the temple burned, and I pushed Efra away.

It's not real, I reminded myself. Squeezing my eyes shut, I took a deep breath to calm myself.

A deep, smoke-free breath.

It was a dream. Nothing more.

I opened my eyes, feeling both foolish and disappointed. "Sorry," I muttered, seeing Efra sitting in front of me, looking a bit peeved but also worried. "I'm just…" I hesitated.

What could I say? That I'd panicked because I thought I was a priestess from ancient Rome who was on the run from bad guys?

"I fell asleep. I was dreaming," I finished.

Her worry lines disappeared, replaced by relief. "Apology accepted."

I shifted my elbows under me and tried to rise. The back of my head throbbed in response. Gingerly, I ran a hand through my hair and flinched when I touched the sore spot.

"Let me help you off the floor." Carefully, she slid an arm under me and steadied me as I rose to my feet. Still shaky, I sat down on one of the pews.

"What happened?" I asked.

She shrugged. "I do not know. I was preparing to assist in the discussion as to your punishment when I heard you cry out."

The energy. I remembered how it had over-whelmed me, and I shuddered.

"What is wrong?" she asked, interrupting my thoughts and resting a firm hand on my shoulder.

I shrugged her off. I needed to think about what had happened, not discuss it with a stranger. "You speak English," I commented, changing the topic. "I didn't expect to find that in an outlying village."

"I speak five languages," she said, her tone frosty. "English is simply one of them."

Heat flushed my face. "That wasn't what I meant. I didn't mean to sound so…"

"Condescending?" She finished my thought.

"Yes." The warmth in my cheeks worked its way down my neck to my chest.

She smiled. "My apologies. I know you did not mean to insult me or my people." She rose. "But it has been a trying morning, and meting out punish-ment is never an easy task."

My punishment. "We could forgo that if it makes you feel better," I suggested, half-joking but also half-serious.

Her smile broadened to reveal even, white teeth. "That is not my choice to make." She dusted off her hands. "Can I offer you water? Food? I do not like the thought of you uncomfortable while in our care."

"That's ironic." The sarcasm slipped out before I could stop it. I clamped a hand over my runaway mouth.

"It is, I suppose," she replied, not taking apparent offense at my slip. "Are you sure you would not like something to drink? Perhaps a cool compress?"

"I'll be fine." I waved the suggestion away. I

wanted to get my punishment over with. Besides, it was easier to think about my trial. That was tangible, something I could cling to. Not a vision—no, a *dream*—that overwhelmed me and left me lying on the floor.

Efra gathered her robes in her hands, lifting them off the ground. "Then I must prepare for your sentencing."

Sentencing? That didn't sound promising. "Remember, it was an accident," I muttered.

"I know," she assured me, her eyes touching me with compassion before she whirled around. She walked through the door on the left side of the pulpit, leaving me alone in the sanctuary.

What were they going to do? I wondered. In the Nubian culture, women held quite a bit of clout, dating from the period when Nubian women served as queens of Egypt. While there were no queens anymore, and the people had scattered when the construction of the Aswan Dam flooded their homes, the society remained matrilineal.

Which meant that the pissed off mama would probably get her way.

Then *it* hit me again. The energy. Grabbing my head, I cried out, but better prepared, I managed to stay lucid enough to remain on the pew, as opposed to falling to the ground.

Groaning, I battled against the unexpected pressure. Any more intense and my skull would burst.

I fought to master it. Deep breath.

I inhaled, but even as I exhaled, the pressure continued to grow.

Another breath. More pressure.

Come on. A few more breaths and I would overcome it. It was strong and unexpected, but I was
stronger.

I started to slip under.

Then it stopped as suddenly as it began.

I sat up, wiped my tearing eyes, to see Efra
standing in front of me. "I knew it," she said, her
voice triumphant. "You felt something, didn't you?"

"No." Panic at the thought of her discovering my
special abilities replaced the earlier fear that my head
would explode. "Just a headache from the fall."

She sat next to me and took my hand in hers. Her
skin was as cool and dry as parchment. "I heard you
speak of the great mosaic when I found you on the
floor, so do not lie to me. Tell me the truth."

She was serious. Dead serious.

There was nothing I could say to convince her otherwise, and even I knew that silence was stronger
than a weak lie.

"Tell me," she insisted, her eyes bright. "Tell me
how you know."

"I can't," I whispered, even as I wondered what the
mosaic had in common with the energy Efra spoke
of.

Her grip tightened, but I shook my head.

I'd had this conversation before with other people.
It never turned out well. In fact, when I was seventeen, a conversation that started out in a similar way
had ended with me spending a year in a sanitarium.

"Please," she murmured, her voice desperate.

There was nothing she could say, nothing she could
do, nothing in heaven or earth that could make me tell
her I felt the earth in ways other people couldn't.

That I could find water in the desert. Gold in a mountain. Oil in the ground.

And all without the help of the equipment I appeared to rely on.

She squeezed my fingers. "Trust me."

I pulled my hand from hers. Not even Madonna-like compassion and understanding could make me admit aloud that I was a dowser.

Or, as I'd heard growing up, a freak of nature.

Chapter 3

Lying on the pew with my boot-clad feet propped on the arm, I tapped out a rhythm as I continued my wait. It seemed like half a day since Efra had left me alone and gone to join the others to decide my fate, but when I glanced at my watch, I saw it had been only two hours.

"Two of the longest hours of my life," I muttered, wishing Griffin would hurry.

I shut my eyes, but once again, Efra's expression flashed through my mind. Her dark eyes full of joy and triumph when she'd discovered I might be special.

Like she'd discovered oil in her backyard.

But I wasn't oil. I was a dowser. And she knew it—or at least knew I was different. Covering my eyes with my forearm, I groaned at the memory of my pathetic response when she'd confronted me. Normally, I'm a good liar. A great liar.

I'd had lots of practice since I left my past behind.

Now, a stranger knew I felt *something* that most people couldn't even conceive of experiencing, much less believe.

That meant she felt the strange energy, as well.

The realization caught me off guard, and I bolted upright.

Was she like me? Was she a dowser? My skin broke out in goose bumps at the thought.

I'd searched my whole life and never found another such person. Never found someone whom I could be myself with. Had I found one now?

A sister of sorts?

Or was I fooling myself? So desperate for someone to confide in, someone I didn't have to hide from, that I'd believe anything?

If she wasn't a dowser, how did she know?

I swung my feet to the floor and sat up, not ready to deal with my own hope. The church provided plenty of potential distraction, but I curbed my curiosity.

In my time alone, I'd been tempted to snoop around to see if I could find what had caused the energy surge that triggered my dowser talent—and the vision.

Now that I'd had time, I could admit the episode for what it was. Not a dream. Not even close.

I toyed with the teardrop-shaped amethyst that I wore on a chain tucked under my shirt, the gesture a nervous habit that refused to die. Whatever the energy was, it wasn't like anything I'd ever felt before.

Generally, I tasted changes in the earth like a trained chef can taste spices in food. I rolled the molecules around my mental tongue and discerned their structures.

Silver tastes cool. Light. Like the first ice of winter. Or a snow cone. Uranium is raw, like biting into curry paste. Oil is slippery, like a mucky puddle.

This energy was different. Foreign and unexpected. Overwhelming, and leaving me a little giddy. Like chugging champagne when one expected ginger ale.

I sighed, bored. I'd never been one to enjoy inactivity. Never been the kind of girl who needed rescuing.

And most certainly was not the kind to sit patiently while someone else decided her fate. "This waiting should be considered punishment enough," I muttered. "I mean, really, how long can it take?"

It takes as long as it takes, my mother's voice in my head reminded me.

Go away, Mom.

Her pink, lipsticked mouth frowned.

I squeezed my eyes shut and saw myself during better times. I was ten and standing in front of the oven, staring through the glass and willing the cookies to finish baking. My mother placed her hands on my shoulders and pulled me way, bribing me with coffee that contained more cream and sugar than caffeine. We'd drunk the weak brew, and when the cookies were done, we'd dunked them in the dregs, laughing and giggling.

Of course, all the good times had occurred before my mother and father had me committed.

"I heard you fainted."

I whirled to see Griffin in the doorway, leaning against the jamb in a lazy, careless way. I stood up.

Lazy and careless, my ass. He never looked relaxed. Not unless something was wrong, and he was trying to appear reassuring.

I must be in deeper trouble than I realized.

He strode down the aisle, his camouflage and sidearm out of place in the quiet church. "Are you okay?"

"So far so good," I said, not daring to ask about my punishment.

"You sure?"

I raised a brow at the insistent concern. "You waited hours to check on me. Does it really matter?"

He stopped midstep. "Efra just told me. Do you always have to assume to worst about me?

I didn't know what to say, but felt like an ingrate.

He continued, "Do you really think I'd sit around and negotiate if I knew you were passed out on the floor?"

"Sorry." I ran a hand through my hair. "So, *negotiations,*" I said, drawing the word out as I sought a new direction to the conversation, and some levity. "How are they going? Is the trial over or will I get to testify?"

"I think we'll be able to keep our jobs," he said, continuing toward me. "And while this might feel like a trial, it's not. It's a simple negotiation. Who gets what. How much. Et cetera."

So much for levity.

"What do I get?" I asked the question before I could stop myself, although a part of me dreaded the answer. Now that I'd met Efra, I knew that these people, or some of them, were more educated that I'd thought, but they still lived in a quasi-primitive village in the middle of nowhere.

The flogging I'd joked about earlier suddenly seemed more probable.

"It doesn't involve you strapped to a whipping post," Griffin said, remembering our earlier conversation and answering the question in my mind. "But you'll have to issue a formal apology."

The muscles in my back loosened a fraction, and my breath came easier. "That's it?" I asked, still suspicious despite my relief.

He shook his head. "Of course not."

Figured.

"You will now employ the father of the boy you shot, and when the boy is healed, you will employ him, as well."

"Oh really?" I do not like others telling me how to run my business. I crossed my arms over my chest, took a deep breath and fought to keep my every emotion from playing across my face. Part of me would prefer a flogging to having these people on site. A flogging would be painful, but it would also be over and done, and I could go on with my life.

This would go on for months, their presence a constant reminder of my ineptitude. "What can they do that makes them employable?"

"Cook. Run errands. Sweep the sand for all I care." Griffin looked at me like I was crazy for questioning him. "It doesn't matter. The point is that if they work for us, the rest of the village will leave us alone."

He was right, but it didn't mean I liked it. "Anything else?"

"I know it isn't what you want, but it's for the best. For everyone," he replied, ignoring my question. His dark eyes skimmed over my features as if he was trying to read my thoughts.

I shivered despite the heat of the day.

My emotions were still running high, and having Griffin this close wasn't calming them. He was attractive—too attractive—and he was hard to ignore when I could smell the sweat on his skin and feel his breath on my cheek.

Especially hard since I hadn't had a boyfriend in over a year.

I took a step back.

Disappointment flicked across Griffin's features. "One more thing. You're staying here tonight. With Efra. She seems to have taken an interest in you and your education regarding her people."

"What?" All happy, horny thoughts dissipated.

"I know these people well enough to know that her opinion means a lot to the community. We need the good PR. Don't waste this opportunity." He turned on his heel, ignoring me, and strode back to the door. "I'll be back in the morning to pick up you and the kid's father."

"You can't leave me—"

The door slammed behind him.

"—here," I finished, but there was no one to listen.

"Where is Griffin going?"

Efra. I turned toward her voice. Still in her blue robes, she emerged from the same doorway she'd disappeared into earlier. I wondered what was behind the one on the right.

"Back to camp," I replied, not caring to disguise the bitterness and anger in my voice. I'd been on my own since I was eighteen, and I did not like being manipulated or told what to do.

"I asked him to stay for our evening meal. I suppose that is a no."

Coward.

"No matter," she continued as she walked past the pulpit, her robes swooshing across the floor, but barely audible above her litany. "It was but a courtesy. He is not the one with whom I wish to speak."

"He could have said something to me," I said. Why did I have to stay? And by myself?

She stopped in front of me. Now that I was vertical, I realized she was shorter than I'd thought, barely clearing five feet.

I felt like a giant even though I was barely five foot six.

"Men." She said it like a combination of a swear word and an endearment.

"Can't live with them," I muttered, and left it at that.

Efra laughed, a deep throaty sound. "We shall make the best of this. In fact, he did us both a favor. Now we can talk about that of which you do not want to speak."

Despite the hope that she was a dowser, my internal guard roared to life, banishing any emotion other than the suspicion and the accompanying fear I'd lived with my entire life. "I don't know what you mean."

"I think you do." Once again, her hand gripped mine, but this time she pulled me with her. I followed her past the pews to the bit of raised floor that served as the church altar. "Wait here," she said.

She disappeared into the doorway on the left again.

"Brace yourself!" she called.

"What?"

The energy wave that had hit me earlier rolled over me again. My breath caught in my throat as I fought to absorb the power. My muscles stiffened, fighting the onslaught.

I focused on my heartbeat, determined to remain awake, and realized that I had neither passed out nor dropped to my knees as of yet.

It seemed my body and mind were already compensating.

When my dowser talent had first emerged, it was much the same way. The first time I *felt* the earth, I was on a school field trip to the Metropolitan Museum of Art in New York, visiting the Egyptology exhibition on loan from the Egyptian Antiquities Museum in Cairo. Everything in the display was either created from gold or embellished with the yellow metal.

Perhaps it was the sheer volume of gold, or puberty playing one of its nasty little tricks. Why my talent decided to kick in at that moment, I never knew.

I'd been overwhelmed by an internal heat, and when I woke up, I was looking up from the marble floor, with my classmates surrounding me.

The teacher thought I'd had a seizure.

One of the girls started a rumor that I was pregnant.

A CAT scan and blood test said no to both scenarios.

A few days later, I was walking the grounds of my parents' estate, and when I came to the pond, I fell to my knees, the intensity of *wet* obliterating all but the most primitive of movements.

It took a year of browsing everything from simple medical journals to a few of the more colorful Internet Web sites before I figured out what I was, before my body and mind learned to manage the talent....

I refocused my thoughts back to the energy wave still washing over me, refusing to dwindle.

In. I inhaled and willed my body to relax.

Out. I exhaled through my mouth, and my legs stopped shaking.

"Are you all right?"

I focused my eyes on Efra.

"Sit." She held my arm and helped me to the floor.

Crossing my legs in a lotus position, I focused on breathing while my body finished adjusting to the new experience. It might have been five minutes or five hours, but eventually, the energy was a part of me. While it was still strong, it was no longer foreign. I opened my eyes.

Efra sat across from me. Her position mirrored mine.

In her cupped hands was a fistful of tiles. The kind used to make mosaics.

Like the one Aleta wanted to create.

"Yes," Efra said.

My breath caught. Had I said something aloud?

"Here," she offered.

Automatically, I held my hands out. She dribbled them into my open palms. They clinked together with a delicate sound as they poured like water into my hands.

My breath caught in my throat, and my battle to remain in control was lost.

"Aleta, we're so glad you're here."

"Thank you," she replied. *She'd been traveling for days, making her way to France and the uncompleted mosaic, and was stopping for the night at one of the safe houses along the way.*

Her hostess, a woman dressed in a brown, homespun robe with the hood hiding her countenance, shut the door to the hut once Aleta was inside.

Aleta surveyed her home for the night. It was simple, with a single chair for guests and a pallet on the floor for sleeping.

On the table lay a small mound of mosaic tiles.

She turned to her benefactor, one of the women who had helped find and relocate her scattered, frightened acolytes, including her beloved Cleo. "You saved my girls. It is the least I can do."

The woman flipped back her hood to reveal dark hair and even darker skin. "You would have come anyway. Eventually."

"I am not so sure."

"I am." She grinned, her teeth a bright contrast to her skin. "We have waited for someone like you. Someone who knows the old ways. An artisan. A woman of power who uses her gift in the servitude of others."

Aleta waved away the compliment, swaying on her feet.

"I apologize." The woman hurried over and escorted her to a chair. "You must be tired. Famished.

*I was simply excited to meet you." She moved to leave,
and Aleta touched her arm.*

"Please. What is your name?"

"You may call me Tamira."

*Aleta nodded and shut her eyes, wondering when
her grief would end and she'd feel the same joy that
seemed to consume the rest of the women.*

I opened my eyes, confused and a tad disoriented.
What was happening to me?

The question pounded in rhythm to my heartbeat.
I focused on the beating and fought to ignore the
voice in my head that whispered I was going crazy.

"What happened?"

Efra's question dragged me back from myself and
the fear that threatened to overwhelm me.

Grateful for the distraction, I blinked to focus my
eyes, but like the ghosts left behind from a photographer's
flash, I still saw Aleta and the mosaic tiles.

These tiles.

My hand tingled unnaturally, but I curled my
fingers around the bits of ceramic, keeping them close.

"I'm not sure," I replied, trying to sound strong, but
even I couldn't miss the shakiness in my voice.

"Tru?" Efra sounded worried, and I felt her hand
on my shoulder, giving me strength.

"Yes." I blinked again, and the ghost images finally
disappeared.

Efra now knelt in front of me, but when I focused
on her face, it wasn't her worry that caught my attention.
She stared at me like one might stare at an
animal in the zoo or an alien—a mixture of curiosity
and pity in her eyes.

It was a look I knew well. I'd seen it on my parents' faces. My best friend's. My first boyfriend's.

Anyone I'd ever confided in about my talent or who'd been present when my talent overwhelmed me.

I knew the look, and I loathed it.

She squeezed my shoulder, then skimmed her hand up to my forehead like one might do when checking to see if a child ran a fever. "Your eyes rolled back until all I saw were the whites. I thought you were having a seizure, and then you seemed to awaken."

I didn't want her sympathy, and jerked away. Her hand fell to her lap, but her expression never changed. "Nothing happened," I replied.

"Something happened," she insisted.

What was I suppose to say? That I had a vision?

I tilted my hand and let the tiles spill to the floor. "I was just...thinking," I finished, wincing at the inept attempt at deceit.

What was it about Efra that tripped my tongue? Even I didn't believe the lie.

Neither did she. Her dark eyes narrowed. "Why do you insist on dishonesty? I showed you my village's most precious treasure, and you disgrace both it and yourself by claiming to not feel a connection."

She took a long breath, and the anger morphed into displeasure.

If she had children, I could only pity them. I could barely stand up to that jolt of unabashed disappointment.

"What would you like me to say?" I asked.

"The truth."

God help me, I wanted to believe her. Wanted to believe that I could talk to her, share my burden with someone. But years of caution are not so easily dismissed. "I...I..."

I clamped my mouth shut, unable to get the words out.

Her hand snaked over to grasp mine. "I know you are frightened to tell me what happened, but I beg you to trust me."

I'd heard that plea before. From my mother. From my friends. Even my father.

All had asked for my trust, but when I gave in to the need to connect with another human being, the result was always the same.

They betrayed me.

"Why should I?"

"I can give you no concrete reason, but I can see the fear in your eyes and feel it racing through you like blood."

I tried to pull my hand away, but she tightened her grip with surprising strength. "Who hurt you? Who caused such distrust in one so young?"

Everyone. "No one."

"Again, you lie." Her grip lessened as she seemed to realize the depth of my doubt. "I have seen much in my life. Some of it quite unexplainable."

Her free hand reached down to pick up a tile. "What do feel when you touch the tiles? A tingle? A sense of familiarity?"

The hairs on the back of my neck rose.

"You are not the only person to feel this way," she continued. "There are others. Other women, to be precise."

I must have looked as shocked as I felt, because

she chuckled, and a smile curled her mouth upward. "Why are you so amazed? Did you think you were the only one?"

"Yes," I whispered, before I could think to continue my denials. I'd always been the only one. Always. Like a sighted man wandering the land of the blind.

"You are not. Not by far. In fact, you are part of a legacy greater than you can imagine. You are a Marian."

"A Marian?" I asked, confused at hearing a proper Anglo girl's name used as a noun.

"Yes," she replied, like a mother might confirm a child's innocent question. "They are the women who created the tiles and the mosaic, before it was disassembled."

Aleta's mosaic. I nodded, overwhelmed by the continuing influx of information. But there was still one question that nagged for attention. A question I had waited a lifetime to ask. Now, I was ready.

Now that it seemed I might be a part of something more. "Do all Marians feel the tiles like we do? Are they like us?" As long as I'd waited to ask the question, I still found myself unable to utter the word *dowser* aloud.

Efra hesitated, and in her dark, sympathetic eyes, I saw the answer before she replied. "Some are, but no, not all."

It couldn't be. "But *you* feel them. Like me."

"Yes. I feel the tiles, but not as you do. Not really. It is more a sense of…" She hesitated, as if searching for the words. "Pressure. It's unexplainable and almost so negligible that if I were not paying attention, I might dismiss it as the beginnings of a headache. What happens to you is different from anything I have ever seen."

Different. I hated the word. It was right up there with *unique. Special.*

Freak.

And I knew what happened to freaks. They ended up alone once people realized just how deep their differences went. I turned away, not wanting her to see me cry.

Efra touched my cheek and turned me back to face her.

"Do not despair. You are Marian, as well, so you are not alone. Not anymore."

Had I spoken aloud? Or did she just know? I wiped my cheek, wishing I could believe her.

"Being different is not a bad thing," she continued. "Hold on to your strengths. Embrace them and know that you are much more than a Marian. Stronger. Special. You are part of a legacy and did not stumble into our village by chance."

A legacy. It was the second time she'd used the phrase. I took another deep breath and tried to bring my careening emotions under control. "What legacy?" I asked, my desire to belong to something proving greater than my fear of discovery.

"I will tell you, but first, you must tell me." Her eyes bored into mine. "What are you?"

Her words washed over me. The need to belong was strong. The part of me that was weary of being alone begged to take a chance. Just one more time.

Just one.

How much could it hurt?

A lot. But I breathed deep and met Efra's steady, dark-eyed gaze, hoping for the best but prepared for the worse.

For the first time in ten years, I stepped into the unknown and took a chance that someone would accept me and what I was.

"I'm a dowser."

Chapter 4

An hour later, I knew more about a Nubian village, Efra and the supernatural than I ever thought I would. I also knew that the church was not just a place of worship, it was functional, as well.

Constructed as a large square, there were the rooms—the Sanctuary in the front and two rooms in the back. Doors connected all three, creating a circuit of sorts.

I sat with Efra in her room—the one on the right. It was small, but efficient. The bed and a mirrored dresser hugged the far wall. There was a two-burner stove to the right. A window let in sunlight.

We sat at a wooden table in the center of her bedroom with a plate of figs in front of us, for nibbling, and a ceramic pitcher filled with water. Part of me wished I could go back to my safe, hidden existence, while another part begged for more information.

The latter won and I listened in wide-eyed amazement as Efra told me about her life. She did, indeed, speak five languages, had been educated in England and the U.S., and had even spent significant time in Italy.

Despite that, she retained her love and respect for the beliefs she was raised with—beliefs that were female-centric and spanned thousands of years.

Beliefs that seemed unbelievable unless one had experienced the unusual and the inexplicable.

"The tiles protect us," Efra said.

I clutched a few bits of ceramic, reluctant to let them go.

Clucking, Efra unfolded my fingers and took one of the pieces from my palm. "They might appear common, but they are not, as you know. Their energy keeps our village safe from war, protects us from famine, but more important, keeps the well filled."

I nodded, not sure if I believed, but willing to entertain the possibility. After all, my ability to dowse was implausible, yet it was as real as the clothes I wore and the food I ate. "Have they ever been taken?"

Efra continued. "Once. Many generations ago."

"What happened to the village?"

"The mythology explains that if stolen, the tiles must be returned within seven days, or our village will not survive." She dropped the tile back into my hand and poured water into a ceramic cup, sipping the liquid like one might sip an expensive wine.

"And?" I said encouragingly. I saw she wanted to drop the subject, but I had to know more.

She set the cup down. "There was a brief battle. Much bloodshed. The tiles were returned on the tenth day."

"Did the curse come true?"

Her brows rose. "Curse? That is not the right word, but the village suffered as if cursed. The well dried up, and we were forced to move, but not before we regained that which was stolen."

"What happened to the people who took them?"

"All dead," she stated, her tone bitter and ashamed. "Men. Women. Children." She sighed, shaking her head as if the memory were hers. "None were spared. It was not a fine moment for my people."

She picked up her cup again, the topic ended.

I set the tiles down in front of me, trying to match the assorted bits together much like a modern-day puzzle. "How long have your people guarded the tiles?"

"Many generations before the church was built," Efra explained, pouring water into my cup. "The priestess who founded our village brought them with her."

"A Marian?" I asked, eager to learn more about my heritage, no matter how loose the connection.

"Yes."

"Do you know how she got them? Why she brought them here?" And was it Aleta or one of her friends? In my vision, Aleta was to build the mosaic, but it was clearly in pieces now. Either it had been finished and later destroyed, or Aleta had never completed her work.

Which was it?

I wanted to ask, but years of hiding are difficult to

let go, and I wasn't ready to reveal my visions about Aleta and the women she'd worked with to create the mosaic. Not even to Efra.

Efra ran the tip of her finger around the rim of the cup, thinking, and I wondered if she heard the hidden question that plagued me. "I do not know how she came by them or why she came here, but the responsibility to keep the tiles safe was never forgotten— not by the priestess who followed in her footsteps nor by the villagers."

I didn't ask why the devotion. I felt it myself. Plus, there was the curse as incentive for those who were unable to feel the tiles' true properties.

Setting my water aside, I picked up a blue tile. My skin prickled with electricity, and I shivered. "I've never experienced anything like these." I rubbed the tile between thumb and forefinger. The glazed surface was smooth, but beneath the common material was something not so common. The magic that Aleta spoke of. Power. A kind of strength.

I clenched the piece. If these tiles were made into a mosaic, I could only imagine the power it would wield.

We sat in companionable silence for a while—an unusual feeling for me, when the few people I'd confided in tended to run away and never return.

"What do we do now?" I asked.

"What do you mean?"

"Now that I know about this." I set the tile back with the others, a neat little pile on the table in front of me. "What do I do with this knowledge that you've given me?"

She shrugged. "You tell me."

"I'm a dowser, not a psychic. Why would I know?"

"You were meant to know," she replied, looking puzzled. "You can feel them like no other. It's obvious you are a part of our history and our future."

I sighed and ran a hand through my hair. Part of their future? Only if one counted ruining their way of life by bringing in oil rigs and people to destroy their land.

Guilt tugged at me, and my stomach clenched as I remembered the father and son I'd agreed to hire. Suddenly, it didn't seem like the best solution for a village founded by a Marian.

Unfortunately, progress, such as it was called, was also inevitable.

"You think otherwise?" Efra asked.

"Yes. No. Maybe." I groaned, unsure of what to do.

She gave me a quizzical look. "I do not understand."

"I am not helping the future of the village. The oil site is a distance away," I explained. "But if the reserve's as big as I think, the entire production will encroach on your village. Your young people will leave, and you'll lose your way of life."

Efra chuckled again. "You worry too much, and while you can read the earth, I do not think you are so good with people."

I frowned.

"We value education, Tru. We already send our young people away to school for a few years, and more, if they like. Some come back and some do not. What matters is that the ones who return want to be here. They are educated, but respect our way of life." She patted my hand. "Like me."

Heat flushed my face. Trust a Westerner to take on the job of guardian when it wasn't necessary. "Point taken."

"The question I want to ask is, what do you plan to do with the knowledge I gave you?" Efra asked.

"I don't know," I answered. "I need to learn more."

She smiled again. "So many people do not know how to admit a simple lack of knowledge." Rising, she pulled a box of matches from a pocket in her robe and made her way around the borders of the room, lighting the candles.

Until that moment, I hadn't noticed that the sun was going down.

"Others will be coming to worship," she explained. "You are welcome to join us if you like."

"No, thanks." I wasn't ready to face the rest of the village. Not yet.

"As you wish," she said.

"How about the tiles?" I scooped them up, and for a moment, I saw Aleta again. Then the present reasserted itself. "How about these?"

"Take them to the back." She pointed to the door on the left wall. "There is a container. Do not open it, but place them on the head where the third eye resides."

The space between the brows where psychic, supernatural power resides, if my memory served me correctly. It was fitting, if one believed such stuff, of course. I finished my water and rose, clutching the tiles, and went to the next room.

As soon as I crossed the threshold, I knew it was sacred. My breath caught in my throat. There was energy here. Ancient. Pure. As if the holiness that permeated the room went far beyond mere walls.

Scarcely daring to breathe, I looked around. There wasn't much. Besides the door I came through and the one that led to the Sanctuary, the room had a third door that led out back. The room was almost barren. No art graced the walls. No table was present. Only a single chair, a small rug and the container Efra told me about.

I walked over to it with the reverence with which one approached a shrine. It wasn't a container. Not really. It looked more like a sarcophagus. Five feet in length, with an image of the Madonna carved on the lid. I ran my hand along the pale, cream-colored stone. The material was like nothing I'd ever felt or seen. Oddest of all, it lacked an energy signature. No heat. No cold.

Nothing.

What did it contain? There must be something inside, hidden from even my dowser senses. A mummy, perhaps? Maybe the priestess who'd brought the tiles. Perhaps Aleta?

Reluctantly, I set the tiles on the third eye, then glanced over my shoulder. I was alone.

I pushed on the lid, but it didn't budge. I pushed harder.

"Tru—"

Efra's voice caught me off guard. I straightened, trying to wipe the guilt off my face, and hurried out of the room.

When I reentered her room, she was pulling her blue robe over her dress. Tying it closed, she took my hands in hers. "Even when we do not understand it, the universe unfolds as it should. I do not know why fate brought you to me, but I wanted to tell you that I am grateful."

Pulling me close, she kissed both my cheeks. "I will return soon. Make yourself comfortable."

She left, and I sat on her bed, the secret of the sarcophagus calling me. "Secret of the sarcophagus," I mused. "Sounds like a Nancy Drew mystery."

But laughing about it didn't dim my curiosity.

I fell backward on the bed and listened to Efra's voice drift through the semiopen door.

She spoke of trust, faith and doing what was right.

"Like not snooping where you're not supposed to," I muttered.

How ironic.

The next morning, Griffin arrived to both retrieve me from my involuntary overnight stay and continue negotiations with Efra and the elders.

Once again, I lay on a pew. Bored. "This is becoming redundant," I muttered.

"What is?" Efra asked.

I sat up. "I didn't hear you return."

She smiled. "It is time for you to go."

As bored as I had been waiting for Griffin, I found myself loath to leave. But she held out her hand, and I knew there was no choice in this matter.

"You will come back soon?" she asked, walking me to the Jeep. Griffin spotted us and revved the engine to show his impatience.

"Of course," I replied, ignoring him. I'd been patient during those annoying few hours of clandestine dialogue. Now it was his turn.

"Good. There is much to teach you. Much to discuss."

I smiled from ear to ear at the thought of spending

time with Efra. Behind me, I heard someone call her name. She looked past me and gave an almost imperceptible nod. "I must go," she said, returning the smile.

"Of course," I replied, missing her already.

Minutes later, Griffin and I barreled down the road. "Go ahead, let me have it," he said once we cleared the village's perimeter and there was no chance of anyone hearing us.

I'd been holding back my ire since he'd arrived, but between the thrill of meeting Efra and the waiting, my anger had cooled.

Not that he needed to know that. He'd kept me wondering and worried, and it was time I returned the favor. "Do you want to explain yourself? Leaving me behind like that?" I asked, my voice modulated but tighter than I planned.

"I already told you. Public relations," he replied, keeping his eyes on what passed for a road.

"No. It was punishment," I corrected, leaping on what I knew was an excuse.

His shoulders tightened, and I wondered if I'd manage to make him lose his ever-present cool. Then he relaxed. "You're right. I was angry."

"Oh," I said, my indignation and remaining anger deflating at the unvarnished truth.

Griffin continued. "But it wasn't just anger. Efra wanted you to stay—"

"And you, as well," I interrupted.

"Yeah," he agreed. "But I thought it more important you get to know her. She likes you for some reason, and if she supports you, the rest of the tribal elders are less likely to break contract with Dynocorp."

I frowned. We were having a normal, almost pleasant conversation, but somehow, it felt *off*. He focused his attention back on the road.

Then I knew what it was. He was being nice. Giving in too quickly. Not even trying to claim victory.

There was only one reason for that. He was hiding something from me.

I turned to face him, the seat belt straining against my torso. "What else?" I asked. "What are you not telling me?"

He sighed, and I knew I'd called it correctly. "Yesterday, the council meeting didn't go well. The elders wanted more than jobs for the boy and his father. They wanted you gone, and nothing I said made a difference."

"It was Efra who changed their minds?"

He nodded. "Almost, but even she wasn't quite convinced you were trustworthy or capable."

"And so you thought you'd let us cultivate our friendship?"

"Something like that," he replied.

"Did it work?" I asked. Though if it hadn't, Efra would have surely said something.

"That was what this morning's meeting was about." He took his eyes off the road for a second and glanced at me. "Thanks to Efra, you still have a job."

I shook my head in surprise and turned to look out the window. He was always so straightforward. Abrupt even. I hadn't expected him to manipulate a situation so thoroughly.

"It worked, didn't it?" he asked when I didn't reply.

I remembered the hug Efra had given me when I left, and how good it felt to have a friend I could confide in. Plus, there was the fact that I was still employed. "Yes, I guess so."

"Good," he said with a pleased smile.

I wasn't ready to return the sentiment. It had all worked out in my favor, but I didn't like being manipulated. I'd grown up in a world where everything was contrived, and my decisions were made for me.

I hadn't liked it then, and I didn't like it now.

The day was promising to be a hot one. I lowered the car window and untucked my shirt to let the morning air cool my skin. "It wasn't your call to make," I said.

"Would you have stayed?"

The wind took hold of my shirt, blowing it upward. I grabbed the hem and yanked it down, but not before I'd exposed my braless state. My cheeks heated at the unintentional flashing.

Had he seen?

"I guess we'll never know, will we?" Staring straight ahead, I finally managed to force the words past my lips.

"*I* know," he replied, his voice firm with conviction.

I glanced at him out of the corner of my eye.

His face was as red as mine felt.

Yep, he'd seen.

A minute later, when both our skin tones had returned to normal, he cleared his throat. "It was for the good of the project, Tru."

He wasn't lying. Everything he did was for the good of the project. It was what he was paid to do, and Griffin always did his job.

But running my life was not his job, and I needed him to understand that. I pushed my blowing hair out of my face. "Next time, ask," I said. "I might surprise you."

He nodded. "I'll try to remember to keep you in the loop."

I smiled at the minor victory.

A mile down the road, he broke the silence again. "What did happen with you and Efra?"

Nothing you'll ever understand. "We talked."

"About what? The project?"

"No. Stuff," I replied. "You know, *girl stuff.*"

Girl stuff. The phrase that men feared. Still smiling, I silently dared him to ask me to elaborate.

He ran a hand over his hair and focused on the road.

Another win for me.

"By the way, what did you tell the crew about my being gone for the night?" I asked, changing the subject and letting him off the hook.

"Don't worry, your authority is intact," he said. "I told them that you decided to stay to help mend relations, and I'd pick you up this morning."

I frowned, a little disappointed. "Part of me was hoping for a revolt once they discovered you'd abandoned me."

He chuckled.

"Anything else I need to know?" I asked.

Griffin took a deep breath, and the air in the small cab changed. "I called Dynocorp last night."

With that one sentence, he snatched away all my good feelings of winning an argument. I saw my career flash before my eyes. "What?"

"They needed to know about the shooting," he explained.

"What are you trying to do? Get me fired?" I blurted out, incredulous at his betrayal and the fact that I was surprised.

"What did you expect me to do? Hide it?"

I quivered with anger, unable to control myself. "It's taken care of. They didn't need to know."

"They didn't need to know that the head of their project, a project based in a foreign country, shot one of the locals?"

"It's not like I killed him."

Griffin's hands tightened on the wheel. "It doesn't matter. You know that."

"Puh-lease," I said, still unwilling to accept the fact he'd told them about the shooting.

"They're heading this project, and they write the checks."

"And you're bought so easily?" I retorted, unable to put a lock on my mental editor even if I wanted to.

"Enough!" Griffin slammed on the brakes and I jerked, the seat belt catching me across the chest.

When I looked at him, he still faced forward. His fingers gripped the steering wheel with enough force to turn his knuckles a few shades paler than his tanned skin. "I do my job," he said, his voice cold.

I swallowed, preferring hot anger to chill.

He continued, "And I don't see you burning your bank account."

I sighed. "I can't win this, can I?"

"No. This isn't your project. It's Dynocorp's."

"And you're their man," I finished.

He didn't argue, but pushed the gas pedal and continued driving.

"What are they going to do?" I asked as the camp came into view.

"There's a rep in Cairo. She's in the middle of some negotiations. When those are finished, she'll come here. Should be a few days at the most."

"She?"

"Pauline Adriano."

"Hell." I'd never met Pauline Adriano, but I'd read about her and even seen her picture in the occasional tabloid. "Why are they sending her? She's the kind of woman who wears Chanel and attends movie premieres. She'll melt out here."

"I have no idea," Griffin muttered.

I slumped in my seat. "This should be fun," I said not even trying to hide my sarcasm.

"Doubt it," he replied.

"How would I know what's taking her so long?" Griffin said. "Negotiations. Shopping. She's a socialite and a woman. You figure it out."

It had been almost two weeks since the *incident,* which was how I referred to the shooting in my mind, and Pauline Adriano still had not arrived.

Griffin and I were both antsy to get this over with.

"Can you call someone?" I asked, wiping down my tools with a dry rag. I'd been working on Abraham's—the father of the boy I shot—Jeep. When he'd arrived this morning, it had been blowing white smoke, never a good thing, and my first thought was that the head gasket had blown.

When I looked at it, I was right.

I could fix it, but it would take time to get the parts, and in the meantime, we'd have to pick him up in the morning, then drop him off after work.

I wasn't upset about the inconvenience. Quite the opposite. Dynocorp wanted me to keep away from the village, and I'd been searching for an excuse to return. Just once more. When my curiosity was satisfied and I'd seen Efra one more time, I could walk away.

Maybe.

"I called Dynocorp this morning on the satellite phone," Griffin said. "They said she should be here any day now."

Griffin's comment brought me back to the conversation. "They said that five days ago."

"I *know*."

I glanced at him out of the corner of my eye. He didn't watch me but alternated his attention between the men and the high dunes that made up the northern horizon. "Are you worried you'll lose your contract?" he asked.

I turned back to cleaning my tools. The thought of losing it was distracting, and it kept me awake nights. I didn't support just myself with work. I supported my employees and their families. "Do you think they'd have fired me by now if that was what they wanted?"

"Probably. They're more of an *immediate action* kind of company," he agreed.

"Probably?" The uncertainty wasn't comforting, and it was also what had kept me from visiting the village. As much as I wanted to touch the tiles again and let their energy run through me, I didn't want to compromise my position with Dynocorp. Not when given explicit directions to stay away.

"I wouldn't worry about it," he said. "After all, they're sending Pauline. From what I understand, they don't send her to the crucial sites. She's more of a debutante they send out when she wants to feel important, and they know there's little chance she can screw up."

I wasn't sure if I should feel insulted that my site wasn't crucial, or touched at his lame attempt to make me feel better. "Uh, thanks," I managed to say, going for the latter.

"You're welcome."

I finished wiping down my tools, placed them in the red metal toolbox and went to find Abraham—trying not to appear too excited at the prospect of driving him home.

"Tru!" Griffin's voice cut across the small complex.

That's when I heard the distant thumping sound.

A helicopter. Pauline.

Not now. No. No. No. The litany looped through my thoughts as every concern, every worry that I'd managed to push to the back of my head reared forward and demanded immediate attention, and a horrible, sinking feeling settled over me, smothering coherent thought.

What if they fired me? They'd escort me off the site and perhaps out of the country. I'd never touch the tiles again. Never talk to Efra. Never find out what was in the sarcophagus.

Dynocorp would make sure I never came back—retribution was as important as profits to their powerful board members.

I grabbed Abraham's arm and pushed him toward my Rover. "Get in."

He stumbled over to the vehicle, then hesitated, half in, half out of the passenger's side, and looked toward the helicopter.

Go. Go. Go.

I couldn't shut the voice up. "Now." I shoved him in, ran to the driver's side and cranked the engine.

Griffin knocked on my window. "What do you think you're doing?"

The helicopter hovered over the site, and sand flew through the air in response, creating a minisandstorm.

The urge to flee was overwhelming now. My heart pounded inside my chest, panic overwhelming me. Go. Go. Go.

"I'm taking Abraham back to the village," I yelled.

"Let one of the men do it." He looked at me as if I was crazy.

He was right. Leaving like this—when Pauline was arriving—would make matters worse. The smart thing to do would be to call one of the men over and let him drive Abraham.

Sand pounded the windows.

I locked the door.

Griffin and I stared at each other through the glass, his dark eyes furious. *I'm sorry,* I mouthed. I've never been known to do the smart thing, not when my gut told me to do otherwise.

I gunned the engine as the helicopter landed in a flurry of sand and noise. In my rearview mirror, I watched Pauline step out just in time to see me drive away.

Chapter 5

"Why did you wait so long to return?" Efra asked when I stepped through the doorway of the church. The inside of the structure was cool. Comforting. Incense wafted through the air, and I sniffed, inhaling the spicy scent.

The church wasn't the mansion I was raised in. It lacked the decorator touch. The expensive furniture. The maids. The gilt and glitter.

But it felt more like home than that two-story Massachusetts monstrosity ever did.

Now that I was here, I asked myself the same question. Dynocorp had probably already made their decision as to my fate, and visiting Efra, someone who wanted to see me, would not make a difference. "No good reason. Just dumb ones."

Accepting my explanation with an understanding

silence, she linked her arm through mine and escorted me through the sanctuary and back to her chamber.

Sitting at the table, I watched while she brewed tea on an ancient stove. Minutes later, she joined me, cups in hand.

I sipped the beverage and took a few minutes to bask in the unexpected joy of being with another human being who knew me for what I was and didn't run away screaming down the street.

Finally, Efra spoke. "You realize that by staying away, you have shortened the time I'll have to teach you about your legacy and what it means."

I nodded, anxious and excited about the visions, and the tiles that brought them.

"You want to touch them, don't you?" Efra asked. The fire and certainty in her eyes told me she already knew the answer.

Heat flooded my face. "Am I that transparent?"

"No, but I know their power. I feel it, as well."

I nodded again. It was one of the things that drew me to her.

Neither of us spoke, and our mutual eagerness electrified the air. As if from far away, I heard sounds of the village outside. People talking. Walking past as they performed their chores. Laughter.

"Wait here," Efra said. She left, and for a brief second, the tile energy filled the room, then quickly disappeared. Almost. When Efra returned to my side, I felt the few tiles she held in her hand. "Do you believe in destiny?" she asked, placing her free hand on my shoulder.

I looked up at her and hesitated. Destiny? "Not really," I confessed. "This is the twenty-first century, not the Middle Ages. I believe in coincidence and rational explanations. Not destiny."

Her brows rose in surprise but her dark eyes remained compassionate and warm. "Your talent is far from a rational gift. How do you explain that?"

I'd spent many years asking myself the same question. "I can't, but that doesn't mean there isn't a good reason for what I can do. A good scientific reason."

"The visions?"

She knew. There didn't seem much point in denying them. "How did you know?"

"You spoke of dreams. The mosaic. Aleta. There would be no other way for you to know these things." She pulled her chair close and sat next to me, putting the tiles on the tabletop. "Plus, I am a priestess. I have had experience with visions."

"You've had them?" I asked, eager for another connection.

She shook her head. "No. Not me. But I have seen the same disorientation in others when they wake." She toyed with the tiles. "But we must talk of other things. Such as your destiny. Much like your talent, destiny is real whether one believes in it or not."

I waited, wondering where this was going.

She placed her hand over mine. "Events are unfolding now. Unexplainable events, but part of a greater scheme, of that I am certain. *You* are part of it, whether or not you believe."

I'd heard this speech before. I believe a small, green alien living in a swamp gave a similar one to a young Jedi.

"Perhaps," I conceded.

Now her black eyes flashed with irritation. "There is no *perhaps*. You are destined for great things."

"How can you know that?"

"First lesson." Taking my hand in hers, she placed the tiles in my palm. "Have faith."

"Faith?"

"Yes, in yourself and your abilities," she replied. Sitting across from me, she appeared wiser than I could ever hope to be. "Concentrate on them, and tell me what you see."

I shut my eyes and opened my mind.

Aleta touched the partially finished mosaic, running her hands over the tiles.

Some were glossy—obviously ceramic and fired. Others were made of carved lapis, mother of pearl and even alabaster.

Others were strange. Unusual and foreign. Stone of some sort, but like none she'd even seen before. "Where is this from?" she asked, running her hand over an ivory-colored square, her voice echoing in the natural cavern that was the home of the mosaic.

Cara, a descendant of one of the first priestesses who began the Order, smiled and touched the tile, as well, taking obvious pleasure in its texture. "There is a land covered in snow and ice more than a year's travel from here. I was told that it is inhabited by a people very different from us. They hunt great creatures that live on the ice."

"Seals?"

She shook her head. "No. Bigger and with giant tusks. These are made from those tusks."

"Tusks? Perhaps it was a sea elephant," Aleta
mused.

Cara chuckled. "Perhaps."

"She traveled a year there and a year back?" The
dedication and faith it took to make such a journey
was almost unfathomable.

*"No. We sent out our seeker two generations ago.
The woman who brought the tusks was her grand-
daughter."*

When I opened my eyes, I was on the floor. Efra
sat next to me. The crux of the vision overwhelmed
my mind.

So many women sent out. Women like me.

Their blood must populate the world by now. Scattered and diluted, but there, just the same.

Efra was right.

Destiny. And not just mine. But for all the Marians.

"What happened?" a male voice asked.

At the question, I rolled.

Griffin stood in the doorway. Beside him was a
woman. I blinked, forcing my eyes to adjust.

She wore pressed designer jeans, a tan T-shirt and
polished work boots that looked appropriate for
anything other than work. Her highlighted, honey-
blond hair was pulled back into a neat ponytail, and
even in the dim lighting, I noticed that she wore lip
gloss, eye shadow and mascara.

She didn't belong here. She belonged in a
shopping mall or an exclusive day spa.

"Hello, Mrs. Adriano," I said.

She smiled. A big, ultrabright smile, with nothing
behind it. I knew the look. I'd seen my mother flash

the same emotionless grin at countless dinner parties. The kind of gathering where everyone called each other "darling" while they stabbed each other in the back.

"Please, call me Pauline."

She had a slight accent that I couldn't place, but thought was European. "Tru Palmer."

She smiled at Efra. My mentor smiled back but did not offer her hand. "Efra Binte Nur Um Fatima," she said, introducing herself.

I realized that, until now, I did not know Efra's full name.

Pauline gave a polite nod, then turned her attention back to me.

One thin brow rose, and she walked toward me, her steps as delicate as a deer's even in work boots. "Are you all right?"

I nodded, struggling to sit up, surprised that she acted as if she cared. "I...I slipped."

Griffin edged past her, offering me a hand. Still a little shaky, I took it and let him pull me to my feet.

"Ms. Palmer," Pauline said, extending her own hand.

"Please, call me Tru," I replied. And when our palms touched, I knew she was different.

Perhaps it was the tiles' influence. Or maybe the visions were changing me. Making me stronger than before. Whatever caused the change in my dowser senses, I *knew* Pauline was like me. Or rather, like Efra. Not a dowser, but still of Marian blood.

I swayed, confused and disoriented by the energies in the room. They almost vibrated with life. Then Griffin's strong arm was around my waist, steadying me. "You sure you're okay?" he asked, helping me to the chair.

"Fine. I'm fine." My hand slid toward the tiles. I knew they meant nothing to Griffin, but I still felt protective of them.

"What are those?" Pauline asked. Her slim hand touched mine as she picked up a tile.

My breath caught in my throat. Did she feel them? Actually *feel* them? "Tiles," I replied. "Just some tiles."

"They are beautiful," she said, almost breathless herself, her voice warmer than it had been earlier. She surveyed the bit of ceramic she held between a manicured forefinger and thumb. "They appear to be quite old. May I ask where you found them?"

"They are mine," Efra said tightly. "A legacy of sorts." Her eyes met Pauline's.

I glanced at my mentor and friend. Was she upset or simply protective?

I couldn't tell.

"I adore antiquities," Pauline commented. "They have an energy of sorts, do they not?"

My breath caught in my throat. "Yes," I croaked.

She smiled again, but this time it was genuine. Warm. "You understand, do you not?"

I nodded, transfixed. We were no longer sweaty grunt and debutante. We were women of the same blood. Sisters in ways that few could imagine.

I felt like a fool for stereotyping her so quickly. I had forgotten how painful it could be to be judged on something as shallow as one's clothes.

I glanced at Efra. She stared at Pauline with the same sudden realization. "They are special, but they are also fragile. I should put them away." Efra scooped up the rest of the tiles, held out her hand, clearly asking for the one Pauline held.

Pauline hesitated. "Do you know their provenance?"

My mentor shook her head. "Their origin is lost."

A lie. They were brought to the village by Efra's ancestor. Why hide the truth?

"Now please, I must put them away," Efra said.

With obvious reluctance and a small sigh of regret that I understood, Pauline handed the tile over. "Of course."

"Pauline, can you give us a moment?" Griffin asked as Efra walked to the tile room.

Pauline gave a gracious nod and stepped back into the main sanctuary.

I hated to see her leave. What I felt in her wasn't what I felt with Efra, but it was similar. Perhaps I might be wrong, but I suspected that, given time, we would become great friends.

Another friend. That was two in a month.

A heady thought. I grinned.

"Are you trying to get fired?" Griffin demanded, once we were alone.

My grin died in the full force of his anger. "No." What was I supposed to say? The truth? That I was obsessed with bits of ceramic?

"Would you care to explain why you took off like that?"

Once again, the truth would only get me in more trouble. "I have my reasons."

His jaw tightened. "Right now, you are a hair-breadth from getting tossed off this job. You want my help? You want my endorsement? You better tell me your fucking reasons."

My eyes widened. Griffin didn't swear much, and when he used the *F* word, I knew I'd pushed him close to the edge, if not over it. Unfortunately, what little patience I possessed was at an end, and I didn't care. "It's not like you'll believe me anyway," I retorted.

"Try me."

"Fine!" I bolted to my feet, knocking my chair over. "I'm a—" A scream cut me off before I could finish.

Efra.

Without hesitation, Griffin and I raced next door. The back door was open, flapping in the slight breeze.

My mentor and friend lay crumpled on the floor, blood pooling around her like a halo.

I had no idea how much time passed as I waited for Griffin to return with help. Two minutes, two hours or even two days. Time came to a screeching halt as I held Efra's head in my lap.

We hadn't known each other that long in the traditional sense, but already she was more of a mother to me than my own had been. I stroked her dark hair and waited for help to arrive, all else forgotten. My job. Pauline. Even the tiles.

Who had done this? Why? She was a holy woman, for pity's sake. "It'll be okay," I murmured, wanting to believe my words.

A woman rushed through the door, followed by two others. She said something, but I had no idea what and ignored her.

"She wants you to move."

I looked to see Griffin standing at my shoulder. "Okay." Taking care, I shifted from beneath Efra.

Griffin picked her up, her petite body dwarfed in his arms. After laying her on the bed, he stepped aside. Among the myriad pillows and blankets, she appeared even smaller and frailer.

The three women converged on Efra, muttering among themselves. One reached for a bucket of water that was next to the fireplace, and pulled a clean cloth from her pocket to sponge the wound.

The rag was deep red within seconds, and the woman sneaked a glance at me, then back to Efra, her expression unreadable.

"Your hands," Griffin whispered.

I held them up. My palms were stained red from when I'd held Efra's head in my lap.

"You might want to clean them."

I went to wipe them on my shirt and realized my clothes were just as bloody. I wiped them on my pants, leaving dark red trails down the sides of my thighs. "Do you think she'll be okay?"

Griffin said something in Arabic, and one of the women replied. "They think so."

I clung to that hope like a child clings to its mother.

A few seconds later, Efra groaned, her eyes fluttered and opened. She muttered something in Arabic and received a whispered reply.

"What are they saying?" I asked, matching the quiet tone.

"She wants to know what happened. They're saying they don't know. That she was on the floor. Hurt."

Griffin listened and translated as the low chatter continued. "They're asking if she knows who did this."

Efra shook her head. More words were exchanged

among the group. This time three pairs of eyes looked at me, and the accusation in them was as readable as if they spoke aloud and in perfect English.

Efra's own eyes widened and she sat up partway, shouting. I didn't know Arabic, but I knew she was angry.

The women turned red and fell over themselves trying to leave.

"What was that about?" I asked as the door slammed in their wake.

Griffin grinned. "They accused you of being the culprit, and Efra told them they were mistaken."

I suspected that her words were not as polite as Griffin made them sound, and was grateful I wasn't on the receiving end of her ire.

Now that the women were gone, I hurried to her bedside and knelt down.

Efra looked older. Tired. I took her hand in mine, surprised to find her grip strong.

Maybe not so old and tired. Not yet. I squeezed her hand. "I'm glad you're all right."

"I am not important," she said. "I did not want to alarm the women, but I was putting the tiles away when I was hit. Go see if they are safe."

I hesitated. I didn't need to check on the tiles. Now that I knew Efra was going to be okay, I could feel them.

Or rather, feel that they were not here, and getting farther away.

I stood anyway. I've been known to be wrong, or perhaps, in this case, I wanted to be wrong. I went back to the tile room. Standing in the doorway, I focused my attention on the container.

It would be so easy to open.

But I was no longer in the mood to satisfy my curiosity, and I had more important matters to attend to.

I walked over. The carved top was beautiful—and bare of tiles. Quickly, I scanned the floor, even lifting the small, woven rug, in case they had magically fallen beneath it when Efra was hit.

Nothing.

I left the room and returned to Efra's side. I hated being the bearer of bad news. "I'm sorry. They're gone."

Once again, her hand gripped mine. "That woman took them."

Woman?

"The one who left. Pauline Adriano."

"Pauline?" Griffin asked, even as my mind reeled. "That can't be."

I wanted to agree, but it was Efra who made the accusation, and if she said it was Pauline, then it was Pauline I needed to talk to. "Get her," I said, still unable to wrap my thoughts around the possibility that Pauline had hurt Efra and stolen the tiles.

She was a Marian.

I wanted Efra to be wrong.

"I can't," Griffin said. "She took my Jeep and volunteered to go for help. To get Pete and bring him back."

I pressed a hand against my forehead. "She's gone?" That explained the sensation of the tiles getting farther away.

"Yeah." He shook his head. "But she couldn't have done it."

"Why?"

Instead of answering, he ignored me and went to

Efra. "Did you see her?" he asked, his voice insistent but tender at the same time. "Are you sure it was Pauline?"

"No, but it was her," Efra said. "I am sure of it."

"How?"

Efra looked to me for confirmation. I closed my eyes and focused on the tiles. They were moving faster than a person on foot could travel. And more damning, they moved toward my camp. I opened my eyes and nodded. "It's her."

Griffin looked at me, his brows arched. "And you know this how?"

"I just do," I replied, wishing I could tell him of my talent but knowing that doing so would not convince him of the truth. It could also lose me my contract and possibly my freedom.

I'd already lost enough today.

Sinking into the pillows, Efra closed her eyes, weariness overtaking her. "You must get them back, Tru."

"I will," I promised. "I'll bring them back."

Griffin took my arm and pulled me from the room. "Let her rest. We'll catch up with Pauline and find out what's going on."

We walked toward my Rover, and I wondered if this was the destiny Efra had spoken of. The greater purpose.

If so, it was a crappy sort of purpose.

Whether or not I believed in destiny or curses, Efra believed. That was enough.

Chapter 6

"What do you think you're going to do?" Griffin stood outside, leaning in the open window as I started my Land Rover. "Track Pauline down?"

"Whatever it takes," I replied, idling, waiting for him to either move or get in. I tried to ignore the villagers' glances and whispers. Between the incident with the boy and the suspicions of the three women, I was sure that many of them already knew what had happened, and judged me guilty.

I wished I had time to explain, but I'd have to leave that to Efra. Even as I spoke, the tiles' energy dwindled. If I waited much longer, their energy signature would disappear, and both Pauline and the tiles would be impossible to find. Grabbing the gearshift, I resolved to drive through the village slowly.

I did not need another incident, no matter how minor.

Griffin stared down at me, his mouth pressed into a tight, angry line. "We don't even know if she took the tiles."

I struggled to control my raging emotions. I saw Efra in my head. On the ground. Hurt. Her brown eyes almost black with pain. And my sense of injustice took over, making me see red. "Are you saying Efra lied?"

"I'm saying she is old and was hit from behind. It could have been anyone."

"No," I countered, wishing it was true, but knowing that Efra was right. "The tiles are gone. Pauline's gone. I, for one, do not need to be hit over the head to put it all together. We're also wasting time." I shifted the vehicle into Reverse.

Reaching through the window, he grabbed the wheel, and I held back the urge to peel his fingers off. Around us, a few more people had stopped to watch the escalating argument.

Or they were waiting to stone me. Either way, I wanted to leave.

"She went for help. Are you going to convict her for being a Good Samaritan?"

It sounded so convincing, but then so was Efra. And there was the matter of the tiles. How could I tell Griffin that I *knew* they were being moved? "How well do you know Pauline?" I asked. "I mean, really know her?"

"Mainly hearsay," he admitted. "But I know her kind, and she isn't the type to hit someone. She might break a nail or something."

Under any other circumstance, I'd agree. Wealthy women like doe-eyed, twig-thin Pauline bought antiques, they didn't steal them.

But these were no ordinary antiques and Pauline was not an ordinary affluent woman.

As if to emphasize my thought, the energy from the tiles disappeared. Cut off.

The sudden absence felt like a punch to the gut. "Oh my God," I whispered, gripping the steering wheel for support. Out of the corner of my eye, I saw the mother of the boy I'd shot. Almost hidden by the group, she was pointing at me and whispering something to the man next to her.

This was going to get bad on many levels if we didn't leave soon.

"What's wrong?" Griffin leaned in closer, his hands still gripping the wheel.

"Nothing." I reminded myself that I needed to remain calm or I'd end up explaining things I'd best avoid. "I have to get to camp."

"Talk to me."

I glared at him. I needed to get moving before the tiles were so far away I'd never find them. "Let go or get in." I tried to pull Griffin's fingers off the wheel. He tightened his grip, not even bothering to acknowledge the fact I was trying to leave.

Part of me wanted to gun the engine and just *go*, but knowing Griffin, he'd hold on and I'd end up dragging him across the desert—with him lecturing me the entire way.

I rested my forehead against the steering wheel and took a deep breath. "I'm sorry," I said, forcing the words past my mouth and hoping they sounded more sincere than they felt. "I'm worried, and we're losing time."

His fingers relaxed. "I know," he said. "I'm

worried, too. We might think these tiles are ordinary, but Efra and her people believe they have special powers, and that's enough for me."

Relieved, I sat up. He was watching me, his eyes deeper than I thought possible. My breath caught, and for a moment, we simply stared at each other. If the circumstances weren't dire and immediate, I knew I'd kiss him and damn the consequences.

And he'd return the sentiment.

But Pauline was getting away.

I nodded to the passenger's seat. "Get in. We have to go *now*. If Pauline is the thief, we'll get the tiles. If not, then we'll prove her innocence."

Griffin pulled the door open. "Move over."

I yanked it closed again. "You wish."

With an annoyed huff, he began to walk around to the passenger's side. Through the rearview mirror, I saw him stop at the back of the Rover, hesitating. "Come on," I yelled out the window. "She's getting away."

He came around, and the Rover shifted as he got in next to me. "We need to hurry," he said, buckling himself in.

"I know."

"No, you don't." Reaching across me, he buckled me in, as well. "Look behind us."

I stuck my head out the window. On the horizon, the sky was dark, the color of an intense orange sunset. It looked almost liquid with movement.

But it was early afternoon, and the movement I saw wasn't rain. My stomach dropped as I realized what it was.

Sandstorm.

The villagers scattered. Doors slammed and windows closed. Within seconds, we were alone.

I pressed the accelerator. We raced down the road with the sandstorm roaring in behind us. We might make it back to camp before blowing sand obliterated visibility. Or we might spend the storm sitting in the Rover.

At least Pauline wouldn't be able to fly away. There was no way for a helicopter to take off with a sandstorm coming in.

The sky continued to darken, and I pressed the accelerator to the floor. As long as there was a hint the dirt road, I wasn't slowing down. The Rover fishtailed around a corner and went into a skid on the loose stones that covered the hard-packed earth.

"Turn into it," Griffin said, gripping the dash.

"I am," I exclaimed, working to keep control of the vehicle even as he spoke. Within seconds, I'd aligned the Rover and floored the accelerator again.

"You might want to slow down," he suggested as the car caught air when we topped a hill.

"Stop backseat driving," I said, glancing at the sky through the rearview. The orange cloud was getting closer. Fast. Would we make it to camp before it hit?

"I'm not. Just trying to keep us alive."

I ignored the jab at my driving skills and kept my eyes on the road. Men.

We crested another hill and the oil rig came into view, silhouetted against the sky.

And the familiar energy of the tiles touched me. The force was faint, but unmistakable. And came from the direction of my camp. Thank God.

"Turn off the road. Cut across the desert," Griffin said, half turning in the seat to watch the progression of the storm. "It'll save time."

I yanked the wheel to the right and raced across the sand.

"Are you trying to kill us?" He stomped his foot on an imaginary brake as I dodged a rock the size of a couch.

"This was your idea," I reminded him. And a good one, though I wasn't about to admit it aloud.

"Just don't get us killed."

"We won't be, unless a satellite drops out of the sky and smashes us flat."

"Sometimes you're an odd woman," Griffin said. I glanced sideways and caught him rolling his eyes.

"You have no idea," I replied, but slowed down as I went around another rock.

"Just be careful."

"I *am*."

Then the sky tumbled, pain shot through my head and I heard a scream.

It was mine.

When I opened my eyes, the sky was gone. The world looked tilted and awkward.

I took a deep breath, trying to get my bearings and inhaled sand. Pulling up the neck of my T-shirt, I covered my mouth.

I realized that the world wasn't tilted. It was the Rover. It seemed I'd hit a hole.

I groaned. I knew I'd never hear the end of it. I shifted until I faced Griffin. His eyes were closed, and his head lolled against his chest. The passenger window was cracked from impact, and when I felt his skull, I found a growing lump behind his ear.

But his chest rose and fell. He might be unconscious, but he was alive. "As long as you're breathing, I can deal with the rest," I muttered.

As much as I hated it, the tiles would have to wait. The storm was worsening. We'd have to sit it out in the Rover. I'd deal with Pauline when the world was back to normal.

Leaving Griffin buckled in so he wouldn't pitch forward into the dash, I managed to pull his shirt over his mouth.

My feet sloshed as I moved around.

Sloshed?

I squinted at the floorboards, but even though the Rover was keeping the worst of the sandstorm out, the air was thick with dust. Reaching down, I touched water, and I knew what it was without having to see it. My pulse kicked up.

Quicksand was one of those weird phenomena that, as a child, I'd associated with swamps. It wasn't until I started working in the desert that I discovered it occurred in some of the most arid places on earth.

We had to get out of the car before it sank and we drowned in sand and water.

"Griffin." I shook him. "Wake up."

He remained limp.

I patted his cheeks. Pinched his arm hard enough to leave a mark. Screamed at him.

No response.

"Hell." It would be up to me to get him out of the Rover. Moving a conscious person was difficult enough. With Griffin's height and mass, moving him would be impossible unless I had help. But by the time I returned with it, Griffin and the car would be beneath the murky water.

~ I'd have to do it myself with whatever I could find.

I crawled into the backseat, trying not to jostle the vehicle. So far, it seemed stuck. Perhaps the back end was hung up on a rock.

I wanted to keep it that way.

Eyes squeezed shut against the gritty air, I felt around the seats and through the back until I found the supply box. Opening the lid, I went by touch.

I found tools, the metal smooth and cool. Lose screws and nails. What felt like a lightbulb.

My fingertips skimmed something braided. Rough.

Rope. I breathed a sigh of relief. Rope I could use. I seized it, tossing it into the front seat. I continued to feel around and found a pair of glasses. No, goggles. Quickly, I slipped them over my head.

I blinked sand from my eyes and observed the world through yellow-tinted lenses.

Weird.

I went back to the box and found another pair. I grabbed them and hung them around my neck. Griffin might not need them now, but he would when he woke up.

There wasn't much else. Water. Compass. Shop rags. I tucked the compass in my pocket, then grabbed the rags and tied them together.

Crawling back to the front, I tied a rag around Griffin's mouth to keep the sand out, then slid the rope around his waist and tied it in a sturdy figure-eight knot. "Griffin?" I asked, praying he'd wake up.

Still out cold.

I felt the bump behind his ear. It seemed larger. I prayed I hadn't killed him.

I should have stuck to the road.

The vehicle shifted, and I squeaked at the sudden movement. It was time to get out of here. "Hang in there," I whispered in Griffin's ear.

With the free end of the rope in my hand, I crawled to the back of the Rover, braced myself and opened the hatch, letting the wind in.

Instantly, sand filled the car. I yanked my shirt back over my mouth, coughing.

Crawling out the back, I entered the storm. Between my yellow goggles and the orange of the storm, the desert seemed foreign. Alien. Otherworldly.

I stood in the howling wind and peered through the sand, searching for anything I could tie the rope to. If I could find something strong enough, I might be able to secure the Rover.

Fifteen feet away, I saw a dark shape. Fighting against the wind, I trudged to it. A Nubian dragon tree. Its spiky leaves topped the spindly branches like a crown. I knew these trees were an endangered species. They were also tall and tough. Wrapping my hands around the trunk, I touched fingertips. I frowned. The tree was smaller than I'd hoped. Too small to be useful for much of anything I worried. Unfortunately, there wasn't another tree—or much of anything at all—in sight.

It's a desert tree, I told myself. That made it strong enough. Besides, it didn't have to pull out the Rover. Just Griffin.

Looping the rope around the trunk, I held the free end and followed the line back to the sinking vehicle.

My fingers hurt from gripping the coarse braided hemp that was Griffin's lifeline. Tilting his seat back until it was horizontal, I braced my feet against the headrest and pulled on the free end, using the tree as a pulley.

Griffin slid toward me, halfway up the backrest.

Beneath us, the Rover started to sink again.

Panic roared through me. "Come on," I screamed at Griffin. Myself. The freaking car. "Come on!" Within seconds, he was in the back of the Rover.

The vehicle sank faster now. I kept pulling, fighting to keep ahead of the rising quicksand. The beating of my heart and the harshness of my breathing drowned out the sounds of the storm.

We cleared the window, and I braced my feet against the back of the car, using it for leverage one last time. I pulled Griffin free.

The Rover sank into oblivion with a giant sucking sound.

And reality set in. How was I going to drag Griffin out of the quicksand with nothing to brace against? His head fell forward. Floundering, I gripped his hair in my fist and yanked his face out of the sandy water.

Dark eyes blinked, then focused on me.

"Griffin?" I wanted to cry with relief. Instead, I pulled him to me and kissed him. Hard. Intense. A primal, joyous response at seeing him awake.

He hesitated, then his mouth pressed into mine. Just as fierce. Just as needful.

Warning bells echoed in my head, reminding me that now was not the time. I pulled away. Griffin touched his lips, as if unsure whether or not the kiss was real. "What happened?" The question barely penetrated the howl of the storm.

I assumed he meant the wreck. "We're in quicksand," I shouted, handing him the extra pair of goggles from around my neck. He slipped them on and I nodded approval. "Less talk. More action," I shouted.

The change in his appearance was immediate. My sight was limited, but I felt the sureness in his touch as his hands searched under the water, feeling the ropes. He tied my end around my waist.

"At the same time!" he yelled.

Pulling on the rope at the same time to keep the tension even, we inched our way out of the quicksand and to freedom. Once the sandy earth was firm against our backs, I breathed a sigh of relief.

But we still weren't safe.

My skin stung from the sand. It was painful but not lethal, and I prayed it didn't grow that strong.

Worse than the sand was the dropping temperature. With the sunlight blotted out, it was already cooler. If we were still out in the open without protection when night fell and the temperature dropped to freezing, we'd be dead by morning.

"We need to get to camp!" I shouted in his ear.

Looking toward what I thought was the direction of camp, I barely made out the oil rig in the deepening storm. Another fifteen minutes and it would be swallowed from sight. I pointed toward it. "Come on!"

Griffin wrapped his arm around my waist. I grabbed him in return, and we stumbled toward our haven on the horizon.

* * *

When we arrived in camp about an hour later, Griffin was on his last legs. It had been a silent trek, but I guessed his head wound was sucking the energy from him, making him unsteady.

What if he had a fracture? A concussion? Bleeding in his brain?

There were many ways to die in the desert that didn't involve dehydration. Sometimes, they involved careless, stupid driving....

Once in camp, we made our way to my tent. The full force of the storm was on us now and the sand was scouring my bare arms like a wire brush.

Unzipping the canvas door, we stumbled in and I led Griffin to my cot. "I'll get Pete."

He grabbed my arm. "I'm fine. You shouldn't go out there."

I've thought it before and I'll think it again. *Men.* "You were knocked out for at least five minutes, possibly longer. You could have a concussion."

"I said I was fine," he growled, yanking off his goggles. I glanced at his eyes in the dimming light. His pupils looked to be the same diameter, but it was hard to be sure.

"Do you want to be macho or do you want to be dead?" I asked.

"I'd be fine if you'd learn to drive," he retorted.

I stared at him, refusing to rise to the bait.

After a few seconds he waved me off. "Go ahead. Get Pete if it'll make you feel better."

Catching Pauline would make me feel better, but I couldn't tell that to Griffin.

"It will." Grabbing a large cotton scarf, I wrapped

it around my head and over my mouth. I hesitated at the flapping door and looked back to see Griffin stretched out on my bunk.

I realized it *would* make me feel better to get help. Griffin might work for Dynocorp, and he might be a well-muscled pain in the ass, but we'd worked together for months now. I wasn't about to lose him.

Besides, it *was* my fault he was hurt.

I worked my way through camp, using the rows of tents as a guide. I arrived at Pete's living quarters but didn't bother to call out, knowing he'd never hear me through the growling storm. So when I unzipped the door to his tent and stepped in, he looked startled as hell.

"What are you doing here?" he asked.

"A cheery hello to you, too," I said. Closing the flap behind me, I unwrapped my scarf.

"I thought you'd wait this out at the village."

"Something came up," I said, not telling him about the tiles. The fewer who knew, the better. As it was, I was having a difficult time keeping the truth from Griffin. "Is Pauline here?"

"No. I haven't seen her."

I'd known the answer. Felt that the tiles were not in camp. But still, I was disappointed. "Damn."

He squinted at me, then touched my cheek, and I winced. "What happened to you? You've got a nice bruise there."

"I wrecked the Rover," I explained, reminding myself why I'd come to Pete. Everything else could wait. "Griffin's hurt. I need you to check him out."

"We have Rovers to spare, but only for one of you. Sit," he said. Grabbing his medic bag, he flicked on a penlight and shone it into my eyes.

I blinked at the brightness, but Pete grabbed my chin. "Hold still."

I held. He checked.

He flicked the light off. "No concussion, but you'll be hurting later. Here." He handed me a bottle of aspirin. "Where's Griffin?"

"My tent."

His bag in hand, Pete unzipped the door. "Coming?"

"In a minute." I held up the bottle of aspirin. "I just want to sit for a minute without having to deal with Griffin and his terminal crankiness."

Pete grinned in understanding. "There's water under the table," he said, and let the flap close.

I took the aspirin. Medication was great, but what I really needed was to be armed. I searched until I found his 9 mm tucked under his pillow. I checked the clip. It was full. Quickly, I ransacked the rest of the tent. There wasn't much else I could use. An extra blanket. A knife.

What I needed was my passport and identification, but to get that, I'd have to go back to my tent. Once there, Griffin would do his best to keep me there, or demand to go with me.

I didn't need him slowing me down. Tucking my ill-gotten booty in one of Pete's backpacks, I picked up a piece of scratch paper and a pencil.

I trust you to run the show. Will call as soon as I can. Tru.

I left the note on Pete's pillow. It wasn't any kind of an excuse or explanation, but would keep him satisfied until I got to where I was going and could call him. I was betting that Pauline was driving Griffin's Jeep to Cairo, since it was the closest city with an international airport, and that was the last direction in which I'd *felt* the tiles moving.

I stood in the doorway of the tent, the canvas flapping against my leg and the storm making visibility ten feet at the best.

"This is nuts," I told myself. "A bad idea."

Thirty seconds later, I was back on the dirt road, driving out of camp and into the heart of the storm.

Chapter 7

Twenty miles from camp, I questioned my impulsive action. I hadn't felt the tiles' energy since before the wreck, my head hurt and the road was becoming obscured by drifts of sand.

The Rover lurched sideways, and I swung it back onto what I hoped was the road. I wasn't even sure of that anymore. The swirling grit covered everything, making it difficult to make out the dirt roadway.

Luckily, it was difficult but not impossible.

Impossible would occur when night fell, and that wasn't too far away. A few hours at the most.

If the Rover's air filter doesn't give out before then.

But I'd made this decision, and I wasn't about to give up yet. If Pauline reached Cairo, I might never get the tiles back.

Pauline. I wanted to find her and shake her and ask *why?*

She was like Efra. Like me. How could someone feel the energy and abuse the trust that went with it? Even I, the woman who checked the "spiritual but not religious" box on questionnaires, knew they were sacred.

Stealing the tiles was like burning a church or peeing in the holy water font.

Some things are not done.

What if it wasn't her fault? a voice in my head asked. What if she was an innocent bystander? Abducted? Hurt? Scared? And waiting for you or someone to save her?

Guilt warred with betrayal, but I knew neither would win until I found Pauline and the answers I needed.

The Rover lurched again. I took my foot off the gas pedal and fought to keep the vehicle under control. Whoever designed the roads needed to be smacked. When they canted the curves, they'd slanted them outward, making the car slide toward the edge of the road instead of inward. The whole ordeal was nerve-racking, and my jaw hurt from gritting my teeth.

A shadow loomed ahead through the sand, and I slowed down, not sure what it was. As I drew closer, I realized it was a road checkpoint.

I stopped the car. I knew these buildings and their occupants all too well. Anyone who drove in Egypt knew them, or at least, their types.

The cinder block building housed a few men whose only job was to search cars as they passed through the checkpoint. Other than that, the inhabitants played cards, sat around and, if they were lucky enough to have one, watched television. A single woman traveling on the road was bound to interest them. Not that I feared for my safety, but a woman alone was always suspicious in a primarily Muslim country.

I wondered if Pauline had bothered to go through. If so, she'd probably paid them to let her carry on without a fuss.

I didn't have that kind of money. I also didn't have my identification. That left me with two choices: bluff my way through or drive cross-country and go around.

With the former, there was good chance the guards would detain me until Griffin caught up. With the latter, I might end up food for the vultures.

I pressed the pedal to the floor and turned off-road, choosing the lesser of the two evils.

It wasn't long before I regretted my latest impulsive action. I could see only a few feet in front of me, had no idea where I was in relation to the checkpoint, and the engine was beginning to sputter. A few more miles and it would die when the air filter clogged with sand.

Plus, it was getting dark.

I slowed and came to a reluctant stop. There wasn't much point in driving any farther. Not with night coming on. I turned off the engine, wanting to preserve the air filter.

It was amazing how loud the storm was. More so now that I didn't have the sound of the engine for distraction. Rummaging in the backseat, I found the blanket I'd taken from Pete. Wrapping it around myself, I curled up as tight as I could and waited for morning.

When I opened my eyes, the sunrise was cutting through the glare of the sand-filled air. Surprised I'd managed to sleep, I stretched, working out my cramped muscles.

Outside, the storm continued, but seemed to be lessening.

Time to get moving, I thought with a sigh. I started the Rover, pressed the gas pedal—

The wheels spun, kicking up sand, but the car didn't move an inch. "Nooo." I let my head fall against the steering wheel. Then, cautiously, I unlocked the door and opened it. It moved an inch and stopped. I pushed, but it remained as immobile as the Rover.

Rolling down the window, I looked out to see what could be blocking it. Sand had covered the vehicle up past the wheel wells during the night, and with the storm still on going, it would only get worse.

I'd have to dig myself out.

Two hours later, the Rover was still buried, and I was covered with sweat and so thirsty I could barely stand it.

I crawled back through the driver's window and found the emergency water. There was a gallon left, and that wasn't much out in the desert. I drank my fill without gorging, then closed the bottle.

As long as the storm continued, I'd be stuck. In the meantime, I'd have to wait. And conserve both my water and my energy.

I wondered if Pauline was having as much trouble as I was. Closing my eyes, I opened my mind and tried to find the tiles and the woman who stole them.

Wherever they were, it wasn't close enough for me to feel them.

I opened my eyes with a sigh, wondering if the tiles were within my grasp, perhaps over the next dune, or if she had reached Cairo and safety.

There was one way to find out. I'd done it before on projects, when my mind was too busy to immediately feel the oil beneath my feet. But I'd never used it to find a human or anything as intense as the tiles she'd stolen.

In fact, I'd avoided even considering it because it opened my mind so completely, and amplified everything around me, making the experience difficult to control.

Lifting my necklace over my head, I pulled it off. The chain dangled from my hands, the amethyst swinging like a pendulum.

Reflected in the orange light, the crystal looked almost brown. I held it in my right fist. My hand trembled. I gripped the crystal tighter. I hated feeling like this. Scared. Panicked.

Excited.

"Please let me be safe," I murmured. Sending the prayer to whatever deity protected dowsers and impetuous women, I envisioned Pauline and the tiles in my mind's eye, determined to find her. I shut my eyes, focused on the crystal and opened my thoughts to the universe.

Within seconds, I *knew* everything around me.

The layer of limestone miles beneath my feet. Sandstone. Oil. A vein of copper worth millions.

I sank into the feeling. I was the earth and it was me. My bones. My blood. My skin. The rhythm of nature was the beating of my heart. The water of the Nile was blood through my veins.

I never wanted to let the sensations go.

The tiles, a whispered voice in my mind reminded me.

Indeed. I spread my thoughts outward toward the north and focused on my memory of the tiles' energy, until I found it in the form of a thread. A thin trail of pure white as bright as the sun, it trailed across the desert toward Cairo. Bingo.

Without thought or hesitation, I followed the trail like a bolt of electricity through wires. Quite suddenly, I reached the end, and once again the tiles overwhelmed me.

Aleta sat in front of the mosaic, knees to her chest, and pondered what it meant.

Almost a year ago, she'd come here. Filled with anger and sorrow from the loss of her temple and her way of life, she'd taken on the task of completing another's work—something she rarely did—hoping it would serve as a distraction.

She had not expected it to heal her.

Rising to her knees, she ran a callused hand over the blue tiles that created a swatch of the Lady's robe. Life-size, the figure was complicated with its multiple iconic imagery.

Dark-skinned, the Lady already carried a sword on her belt and a key. The sword symbolized protection for herself, her faith and the baby in her arms. The key was for leadership and the way through any closed door into the brave new world these women hoped to create.

Finally, at the Madonna's feet would be a white jar—the symbol for the impending Age of Aquarius, which the Marians were ushering in.

But what always touched Aleta was the smile that curved the Lady's mouth. "Such kindness," Aleta murmured.

"Did you speak, mistress?"

"Just to myself," she said, smiling at her new apprentice.

When Mayahuel had first arrived from a land across the water a few months ago, Aleta found her disconcerting, with her brown skin, black hair and language that none of them had ever heard.

However, Maya proved to be an apt student and a brilliant linguist. And Aleta now could not imagine working without her deft hands and keen eyes.

"Where I come from, people who muse aloud are sometimes given to the gods," Maya said, picking up a tile and holding it to the light before setting it in one of the many piles that covered the tables.

Aleta raised one blond eyebrow. "Where you come from, many people are given to the gods."

"True," Maya said with a matter-of-fact nod.

Aleta shuddered, remembering stories she had told. The live sacrifices, people skinned and their flesh worn by the priests in an obscene caricature of clothing.

Maya's people were a bloodthirsty lot, and if Aleta had her way, her apprentice would never return home.

Besides, Aleta assured herself, there was nothing for Maya to go back to in her country. Her parents were dead, and she had no siblings. Here, there was work. A purpose.

For both of them.

"Tru!"

A voice woke me, called me back from the past. Slowly, the vision faded, and I realized that my crystal had cut into my hand. I loosened my grip. It had done its job almost too well. A groan escaped my lips as I shook history off my shoulders.

"Are you all right?" the voice asked. It was deep. Masculine. And familiar. "Griffin?"

I blinked, my sight adjusting to the bright sunshine that blazed through the Rover's window.

"Who else?"

He was the last person I wanted to see. I sat up and whacked the top of my skull against something hard. "Ouch!" The pain brought focus to my eyes, and I realized that somehow, I'd managed to fall to the floorboard. I lurched back into the passenger's seat. "How did you find me?"

"GPS on the vehicle, but that's not important."

How could I have forgotten the GPS? I cradled my head in my hands. I felt as hungover as if I'd drunk a fifth of rum.

Impulse, that little voice whispered. It always gets you into trouble. Always.

I told it to shut up.

"What were you thinking, going out again in the sandstorm?" Griffin asked. "Are you trying to get yourself fired? Or killed?"

"No and no," I replied, taking a deep breath. My head started to clear, and I realized that I didn't have to shout to be heard. "Hey, the storm ended."

"An hour ago." Griffin felt my head and looked into my eyes. "You've been unconscious that long?"

"Of course not." The lie slipped past my lips, honed by years of practice in covering up my gift.

Trying to remain inconspicuous, I slid my necklace into a pocket. "I was asleep."

"I know sleep, and that wasn't it. You wouldn't wake up. I tried." Griffin frowned, feeling the glands in my neck with a sureness and professionalism that surprised me. Then he lifted my arms out in front of me. "I'm going to push down on your hands. Try to hold them as steady as you can."

He pushed down. I pushed back to keep them in midair. "I was dreaming, and what are you doing?"

"You wouldn't wake up, and I am checking your reflexes."

"Okay."

His brows shot up. "You don't sound surprised. I take it this wasn't the first time?"

I tucked my hands into my lap. "Of course not. I've had physicals before."

"That's not what I mean, and you know it." He leaned back, seemingly satisfied that I wasn't going to pass out or explode. "Have you ever had a seizure?"

"It wasn't a seizure," I said, grateful he'd come in on the tail end of my episode. From what I'd been told, they looked very much like seizures. My body jerked. My muscles were uncontrolled. After that ended, I was essentially unwakeable for anything from a few minutes to almost ten, depending on how over-whelmed my body and mind were by the experience.

"What is it then?"

"A form of deep sleep," I said, dredging up a lie I'd used before. "It's rare, I know. I go so far into REM state that my body is uncontrollable. It might look like a seizure, but it isn't."

Griffin didn't seem convinced. He ran a hand through his hair, but never took his dark eyes off me. "Tru, epilepsy isn't a big deal unless you make it one."

Hell. There was no way he was letting this go.

He continued. "Most people can control it with medication. I'm more concerned that it isn't epilepsy and there's something else going on. This is the second time you've passed out." He took my hand in his. "We need to get you to a hospital and get an MRI done."

"No."

"Tru—"

"No!" I snapped, cutting him off with my vehemence. When I'd left home at eighteen, I'd sworn I'd never get another one. Besides, it was a waste of time and money, and I had better things to do. "If you're so eager for an MRI, then you get one. You're the one who was knocked out."

"I'm fine. Pete said so."

"And that's supposed to be good enough?" I countered.

"Yes."

It wasn't and we both knew it. I also knew that getting Griffin to submit to an MRI was about as probable as me telling him I was a dowser.

However, I did not have time to argue or persuade. "The more we dither, the farther away those tiles get. I promised Efra I'd get them back, and I am *not* going to fail her. Not for you and not for some hypothetical medical condition."

Griffin's expression changed, softened for a heartbeat and then returned to its usual enigmatic, slightly angry stare. "I'll help you recover the tiles."

I realized he wasn't arguing about Pauline anymore. "You believe that Pauline took them?" I asked.

"Yeah. She wasn't at the camp. Never arrived," he replied, his expression clouded. "Now I want to know *why* she did it."

"Thank you," I said. I didn't need his help to find Pauline—once I got close enough, I'd feel the tiles. But I needed his vehicle, since it was mobile and mine wasn't going anywhere. "Let's go get her."

He held up a finger. "*After* you go to the hospital in Cairo and get checked out."

I gawked at him, dumbfounded. "Excuse me? I am not a child, and I will not—"

"Those are the terms. Accept them or I'll take you back to camp and go after her myself." He crossed his arms, his body as solid as his ultimatum.

"Fine." I needed his cooperation as much as I needed his car. Besides, I could always ditch him later. Grabbing Pete's gun, I tucked it into my pocket before Griffin could see it, then climbed out the window and followed him in his waiting Rover. He started the engine and cool air blew over me. Heaven. "Any thoughts on how we find her?" I asked as we rolled away, leaving my beat-up vehicle.

"Same way I found you." He handed me a GPS unit.

A little green dot blipped at me. It wasn't that far from Cairo. Pauline.

Another dot blipped. It was in the middle of nowhere. Me.

Seems I navigated as well as I shot a gun. With an exasperated sigh, I handed the equipment back to Griffin. "I want those tiles. Let's go."

Chapter 8

Near an upscale shopping mall on the way into the city, the GPS showed the stolen vehicle was close.

"All we have to do is wait till she comes out," I said. "It doesn't get any easier."

Griffin scowled but took the exit.

We didn't find the car. We found an ancient, rust-colored Mercedes. She'd obviously taken the magnet-mounted system off her car and abandoned it here, and now tracking Pauline was impossible. Disappointment rolled through me. "Now what?" I asked, tossing Griffin the useless GPS device.

"We go to the hospital and get you tested."

"You're still stuck on that?" I asked. The man was a pit bull. "I told you, I'm fine."

"I know what I saw." His scowl deepened.

"MRIs aren't exactly a walk-in procedure," I said, hoping to dissuade him.

"*Anything* is walk-in if you have enough money."

I sighed and let the issue go, since an MRI was preferable to the truth.

Besides, during the six-hour drive to Cairo, he'd been surprisingly accommodating and kind. We didn't share what I would call scintillating conversation, since he was avoiding anything he thought might upset me, but he tried.

If an MRI would put his mind at ease, I owed him that.

We pulled back into traffic. I'd been in Cairo a few times, and each visit, what caught my initial attention was the sound. It was a noisy city—on a par with New York. People shouted, talked and laughed, cars honked and the occasional camel bleated.

Even with the car windows rolled up, the noise was deafening.

Griffin was silent. Focused. Probably thinks I'm dying, I thought, guilt pressing like a weight on my chest. I wished I could tell him the truth about my gift. Hell, the desire to confess everything pushed against my closed teeth. I swallowed it down.

My relationship with Griffin had been much easier when I thought he was a good-looking, tattletale company man. The surprising kindness humanized him too much for comfort.

We turned a corner, and a series of large white-and-green buildings came into view—the International Medical Center. They had the best of everything. Specialists. Equipment.

I wanted to run. A sigh escaped my lips before I could stop it.

"What?"

"I hate hospitals," I said. "Nothing good ever comes from visiting one."

"That's a little extreme," Griffin chuckled.

"Perhaps."

"Here." He tossed my wallet into my lap. "In case they ask for identification."

I picked it up, realizing he must have brought it thinking I'd be stopped at the checkpoint.

He *did* think of everything.

It was an annoying habit.

We pulled into the hospital complex and I shrank into my seat. I'd had countless MRIs done, and they had yet to reveal any information about my dowsing abilities or what happened to me when visions overwhelmed me.

I knew this much: it wasn't a seizure.

After eight grueling hours and a session in an MRI machine that Griffin had bribed a doctor to authorize, Griffin knew it, as well.

He was silent as we fought our way through traffic. The lack of conversation did not bode well. I didn't need his help so much, but I didn't need him hindering me, either. "It seems like you've been to Cairo before," I commented, uncomfortable in the silence. "Where are we going?"

"You know what's happening to you, don't you?" he asked, steering through the city.

Not what I asked. I reminded myself to learn to grow comfortable in silence and leave well enough alone. "I told you already."

"Ah yes, the *extreme deep sleep* condition."

I could take the scorn and the worry over my health, but I was not in the mood for sarcasm, or contempt for keeping my secrets secret. My parents and supposed friends had provided enough of both to last the rest of my life. I refused to swallow another spoonful.

Did he thinking harassing me was going to make me open up and spill my life story into his lap?

"Believe what you want," I said, leaning back in the leather seat. "Just because some doctor hasn't heard of it doesn't mean it doesn't exist." Tired of the conversation, I closed my eyes and focused on the tiles.

Wherever they were, it wasn't close enough for me to feel them. I tried to console myself with the fact that Cairo wasn't that big in diameter. We were bound to get close to them at some point. When we did, I'd get them back.

"I looked it up," Griffin continued. "Researched while you were getting checked out. *No one* has heard of it, Tru."

I shrugged, since there was nothing else to say.

He wove the car through traffic, deeper into the city, and I maintained my silence, focusing my attention on the tiles.

For a moment, I felt…something. I straightened.

"You okay?" Once again, concern colored his voice.

"I'm fine." I settled back. Whatever it was, it was gone.

I ignored the guilt rising in my chest. I could deal with his anger, but his worry was another matter.

"I'm taking us to the Marriott on Zamalek," Griffin said, finally answering my question. "I don't know about you, but I need to sleep."

"A hotel? What if Pauline is headed for the airport?" I asked. "She's on the run with stolen property after cracking a holy woman on the head, so there isn't much point in her staying in the country any longer than necessary."

And a full day had passed since the tiles' theft. That left six for me to recover and return them.

"She won't. I've heard enough about her to know that she isn't the kind of woman who goes anywhere in public dressed in anything worth under a thousand dollars. She'll take the time to get fancied up, trust me."

He sounded somewhat revolted, which made me feel better about my sweaty, grubby clothes. But he didn't understand. She might live in the world of the rich, but these were the *tiles*. They were more important than Chanel suits and fancy shoes. If we knew why she'd taken them, I'd feel more at ease, but we didn't know. We couldn't. Until we caught up with her.

And I doubted that was going to happen in a mall. "I'm not so sure she'll shop. She—"

"I also made a few phone calls after I researched your condition," Griffin interrupted. "My sources told me that Pauline phoned for the company's private jet, which won't be here until late tomorrow. So we have between now and then to find her, figure out what she's doing, and get the tiles back."

I clutched that hope like a child clutches a rag doll, and tried to focus on the positive. With luck, I'd get the tiles by tomorrow and take them to Efra with days to spare. "Thanks," I said, meaning it.

He glanced away from the road long enough to

give me a hard stare. "Remember that when we catch up to Pauline, I do the talking."

"You?" How like a man. How like Griffin. And not a chance of that happening. I had questions to ask Pauline that he'd never understand.

"Yes. Me."

"I may be in a country where women keep quiet, but that doesn't mean I have to follow its rules. I am just as capable of getting information from her. Maybe more so."

"You're too close to this. Too emotional. We don't know the whole story."

"And you can discover that better than I can?" I asked.

"Yes."

The set to his jaw and his military-rigid posture told me this was yet another battle I'd lose if I chose to pursue it.

"Fine," I replied. Besides, I'd do what I wanted, anyway. I just wouldn't tell him.

He turned, and we crossed the bridge to Zamalek. I liked to think that Pauline was there, as well. It made some sense that she'd head toward the upscale Nile island that separated old Cairo and Giza. To her, the wealthy district would be familiar territory with its exclusive restaurants and clothing stores.

But no tile energy tickled my mind, and I knew I was wrong. I settled back into the plush leather, worrying a hangnail as I tried to figure out Pauline's next move.

"What's on your mind?"

I put my hand in my lap, my mother's voice reminding me that only little girls with no breeding and bad manners chewed their nails. "I was wondering what Pauline would do next. Do you think she'll try to sell them before she leaves?" Although I couldn't imagine her selling them. She felt their power.

Or maybe that was why she would.

Frustrated, I wanted to cradle my head in my hands.

"There are a lot of buyers around here," Griffin said.

"Maybe one of her rich friends," I commented, my thumb sneaking back to my mouth. "We could ask around."

"I already have. I made phone calls. Remember?"

"Yeah." Why did he insist on parceling out information? "What did you find?"

He glanced over at me. "You're not one for patience, are you?"

"I guess not." I kept my thoughts about his control-freak nature to myself.

"Learn it." His attention turned back to the crowded highway. "In the meantime, we'll eat, sleep and take showers."

I shifted in my grease-stained, stiff cargo pants. They hadn't been washed since who-knew-when, and it showed. A shower wouldn't hurt me, either, and since I couldn't feel the tiles, I'd have to rely on Griffin for information.

For an impatient woman like me, that was akin to torture.

The car came to a halt, waking me. I blinked. I'd been dreaming about Efra. That she wasn't recovering from her injury. I rubbed the sleep from my eyes, the anxiety of the nightmare fading as reality took over.

"Having a bad dream?" Griffin asked, unbuckling his seat belt.

"How did you know?"

"You were talking. Nothing coherent, but you didn't seem happy."

"Just a dream," I said, sure that, if I thought too much about it, I would turn around and go back to the desert.

And that wasn't in the plan. I had a job to do.

A bellman opened my door and held out a hand. I took it, but didn't miss his quick glance at my ragged nails and callused palms. "Luggage?" he asked as Griffin came around the front.

"No." He handed the bellman the keys. "Just the car."

Taking my arm in his, Griffin escorted me into the hotel.

Heads turned as we crossed the lobby, but not in an appreciative way.

We must have looked like quite the pair. Both filthy. Old sweat staining our clothes. Griffin's hair stuck up ten ways to Sunday and mine, well, it was gross. Besides being dirty blond in color, it was dirty blond in appearance.

"There is no way they're going to give us a room," I whispered out of the corner of my mouth.

He ignored me.

I watched the check-in counter, prepared for the worst. There was a flurry of activity as we drew near.

Someone went to the back and returned with another man, who walked around the desk and crossed the lobby.

We were about to be kicked out, and I gritted my teeth in response. *A lady does not cause a scene.*

Shut up, Mom.

"Let's go," I whispered. "Find some place less swanky."

"Trust me," Griffin said out of the corner of his mouth, then smiled as the man in the suit closed in on us.

Oddly enough, he in the suit smiled back, and when he reached us, he extended his arm. "Mr. Sinclair, how good to see you again."

"You, too, Xavier." Griffin shook his hand. "Your mouth is open," he whispered in my direction.

I clapped it shut.

Xavier nodded hello to me, then returned his attention to Griffin. "Your suite." He handed Griffin a card key. "Please do not hesitate to call if you need anything."

Griffin pocked the card. "Thank you."

"Of course."

We made our way to the elevator. The doors slid closed, and I turned to Griffin. "What was that about?"

"What do you mean?" he asked, but the sly smile on his face told me he knew what I was talking about.

"That. What was *that*? You have a suite?"

"Yes."

"How?"

He shrugged.

"A hint?" I begged.

He smiled. "I haven't always been a security man."

The elevator rose and I waited.

"Cenospheres," Griffin confessed, as we reached the twentieth floor.

"Cenospheres?" I asked. Small, miniscule glass bubbles that were the by-product from coal-fired power, cenospheres acted as lightweight filler—especially in the oil industry. "Oh," I said, once I made the connection between cenospheres and the fact that he worked for an oil conglomerate. "Investment?"

"Owner."

"Owner?" I leaned against the back of the elevator. If he owned a cenosphere company, he wasn't just rich, he was filthy rich.

He smiled, obviously pleased with my reaction.

We reached the thirtieth floor. "So, why security?" I asked. It seemed like an odd choice for someone who could afford to do anything he wanted.

"A couple reasons," he explained. "I have to do something productive."

I nodded. I was much the same way. I didn't ever want to become a rich party girl whose biggest problem was that the latest tabloid posted an unflattering picture of her ass.

"I know the industry."

He'd have to if he owned a cenosphere company.

"And this gives me a reason to still carry a gun even though I'm no longer in the military."

I smiled. "Yeah, guns are the fun part."

"Only if *you're* not on the other end," he said, smiling back.

I rolled my eyes. "Shoot one person by mistake…"

A chime sounded, signaling our stop.

The door slid open, and I followed Griffin down the hall, our feet silent on the Persian carpe-covered floors. His suite was at the end of the hall. He unlocked the door and stood aside, letting me enter first. "Son of a bitch," I swore under my breath, not caring that ladies didn't swear.

It wasn't a suite. It was an apartment.

"Your mouth is open again," he chuckled.

"With good reason." Desert-inspired jewel tones decorated the living room. Gold. Bronze. Dark green. Rich and decadent. I trailed my hand along the arm of the couch.

Silk.

I walked through the living room, being careful not to let my dusty, sweaty clothes touch anything.

"I'm very good at what I do," he said.

"I guess," I replied, not sure if he was talking cenospheres or security.

I pushed open a carved hardwood door, and the bedroom spread out before me.

Opulent. That was the first word that came to my mind and the only way to describe it. What caught my attention was the bed.

A mahogany sleigh style, it was big enough for Griffin, a few close friends and me. A deep blue comforter spread out like a calm ocean, and I wanted to do nothing more than climb beneath it and sleep.

But first, a shower. I opened a door and found a walk-in closet filled with clothes. It didn't just *look* like an apartment. It *was* an apartment. "You live here?"

"Sometimes."

"Sometimes? What does that mean?"

He shrugged. "You tell me yours, and I'll tell you mine."

My secrets? I flashed him a weak, sarcastic smile. "I'm not that easy," I sniffed, slamming the closet door and heading toward what I hoped was the master bath.

I walked in and wanted to cry.

A Jacuzzi tub occupied the middle of the white-and-blue-tiled room. In the corner, a shower with multiple showerheads taunted me with the promise of hot water and cleanliness. "Oh. My. God."

"Do you want to go first?" Griffin stood behind me, his hands pressed against my shoulders.

At his touch, the same heat, the same need that I'd felt when I kissed him in the quicksand, roared to life.

Did he feel it, too?

He stilled and his breath grew ragged, answering my question.

I swallowed, the heat in my core radiating outward. I was sure if I leaned into him, he wouldn't protest, but would turn me around and continue where we'd left off.

"Do you want to go first?" he asked again, his breath hot against my skin. I knew he wasn't talking about the shower.

Focus, I reminded myself. He doesn't know what you are. He's a company man.

He is *not* the one.

I stepped away, leaving the delicious heat behind, and though it was a conscious decision, I couldn't face him. If I did, I'd kiss him and damn the consequences.

I ducked my head and scooted past him. "Thanks, but I better not," I replied, trying to breathe. "Once I get in there, I plan to stay awhile."

"Fair enough," he said, regret tingeing his voice.

I ran for the door.

"Tru?"

I stopped in the doorway, halfway out, and prayed he wouldn't ask me to stay. If he did, I would, and I was sure we both knew it.

"Order up some food from room service. Whatever you want and anything for me as long as there's cheesecake for dessert. I'll be out in a few."

"Thanks," I replied, disappointed and relieved at the same time. I shut the door, and in a few seconds, truly horrible singing accompanied the sound of running water.

I picked up the phone, wishing I was with him.

I took a long shower after we ate—both activities helped calm my raging hormones—and settled my naked self between the thousand-thread-count sheets with a sigh, physically content even if my mind was racing.

Griffin slept on the couch. I wondered if he was comfortable, but I didn't wonder long.

Physical won out, and I was asleep in minutes.

So when the phone blared, I rolled over and yanked a pillow over my head. I was almost back to sleep when Griffin knocked on the bedroom door. He didn't wait for me to answer, but came in.

I sat up, gathering the covers around me, fully aware of my nudity. "What?"

He wore boxers and seemed unconcerned with his own state of dress.

Or mine.

"That was one of my contacts. He has some information for us, but we'll need to go to him to get it."

From the businesslike way he spoke, it seemed his hormones were under control, as well. I nodded, but didn't rise.

Griffin went to the closet and pulled out a tan skirt and a white, long-sleeved shirt. "Here." He tossed them to me. "It might be a bit big, but you can belt it."

I gathered the tan cotton skirt in my hands. It was soft as butter. "Yours?" I mocked.

"Hardly. A friend's."

A friend? I bet. Obviously, I was not the first woman to stay here. I ran my hands over the skirt, wondering what its owner had worn when she left.

Ten minutes later, with my backpack slung over my shoulder, I was once again crossing the lobby with Griffin. This time no one bothered to give us a second glance.

I still needed to call Pete, but it could wait until we returned and I had news to report.

"Where are we going?" I asked as a taxi pulled up.

"Khan al-Khalili."

I'd heard of it. One of the oldest markets in the world, where you could buy anything from gold to rugs to weapons. "I've always wanted to go."

"You haven't been?" he asked, incredulous.

"No. I mean to, but it never happens." He opened the door, and I got in the taxi. Hidden by the untucked shirt, the 9 mm I'd shoved into the waistband of the skirt dug into my back.

I hadn't told Griffin I was bringing it, and knew that if I were caught with it, I'd be in serious legal trouble. I also knew the odds of capture were low. Most women did not carry weapons here. Didn't even think of it.

I was the last person they'd suspect.

Griffin slid in next to me and shut the door.

"In fact, I'm not sure I've seen much of anything other than the airport," I finished.

"How can you fly into Cairo and not go anywhere?"

I shrugged, annoyed at his tone and angry with myself for feeling like I needed to defend my decisions. "I get busy."

When we arrived, the market was everything I'd heard it would be.

People drowned the streets, tourists and locals alike. Vendors called to them, offering the best, the newest, the oldest, whatever it was that they thought would catch someone's attention.

Taking my arm in his, Griffin led me through the crowd. "Do not smile at the men," he whispered.

Out of the corner of my eye, I noticed a man in black pants and a light gray shirt watching us with interest. Probably a slave trader, my imagination whispered. After all, this market had everything.

"I'm not dumb," I replied, glancing away before the man saw me looking at him. I knew that *any* smile or sign of interest meant that I was a woman of loose morals.

"I'm sure you're not. Just don't forget yourself."

We worked our way north through the market, passing tourist trinket shops and produce stands, and ended up in an area that focused on gold and jewelry.

"Here." Griffin pulled me into a shop with necklaces in the window display. A salesperson approached us, then stopped when Griffin faced him.

"In the back," he said, before turning away to attach himself to a tourist entering the door.

We hurried through a curtain. The back of the store was well-lit. It seemed that "deals" were no longer made in dark alleys and dingy, smoke-filled rooms. A man wearing a white sports shirt and tan slacks sat at a desk, writing. Beardless, he looked like a Westerner with his Elvis hairstyle.

His face broke out in a grin as we approached. *"Ás salaam alaikum."*

Though I didn't speak Arabic, I recognized the standard greeting *Peace be upon you.*

"Wa alaikum es salaam," Griffin replied. *And upon you be peace.*

The man smiled and pointed to the chairs. We sat. "Griffin. I am pleased that you received my message."

"Yes. Thank you, Kamal, for responding so quickly. Your dedication to your work is much appreciated and admired."

Kamal waved him off and gave me a perfunctory nod of acknowledgment. "Would you care for chai?"

"Please," Griffin said.

I spent the next ten minutes listening to Griffin and Kamal exchange information. I sipped my sweet, hot tea as each man tried to gain information from the other without giving anything away.

Both were masters of the art of saying something but saying nothing, so I breathed a sigh of relief when it was time to discuss business.

"Here is the weapon you requested." Kamal pulled a 9 mm and a box of shells from a desk drawer. Griffin tucked the gun into a pants pocket and the shells into another.

Kamal crossed his hands, resting them on the desk. "Now about the matter of Mrs. Adriano."

I leaned forward, eager for information.

He glanced at me, then away. "First, while I do not like to speak of payment between friends..."

Griffin stopped him with an upraised hand. "Say no more. Your services are invaluable and deserve compensation. I will have the money wired to your account this afternoon."

Kamal gave a nod of agreement.

I sat back, more surprised than I should have been. They must have done business before. Most businessmen would not agree to such a transaction without money changing hands.

He slid an envelope to Griffin.

Griffin opened it, and his eyes widened. "She's at the Marriott?"

Our hotel? "That can't be right," I said, before I could think to stop the words.

"Why not?" Griffin asked.

What was I going to say? "Um, wouldn't we know?"

Or more likely, wouldn't *I* know. If she was at our hotel, then she did not have the tiles with her. The realization made me want to cry.

"How?" Griffin asked, interrupting my thoughts.

"Intuition?" This was true, in a way.

Kamal laughed. "Women."

I glared at him, but Griffin chuckled, as well.

Men.

"And, my friend, I have some worrisome news for you," Kamal said, after their laughter died.

Griffin pulled out his wallet, but Kamal waved him off. "Please, this is between friends."

More like he doesn't want to lose a good client, I thought.

Kamal leaned forward, his thick brows knitting in worry. "Mrs. Adriano is aware that *people*—"

He looked pointedly in my direction, and I knew that by people he meant me.

"—will be looking for her, and she has hired men to stop *people* from finding her."

Griffin frowned. "Stop as in *dissuade?*"

"Dissuade if possible, but if these *people* will not be dissuaded, then a more permanent solution will be found."

Griffin's face darkened even as mine drained of blood. I suppose I should not have been so surprised. She'd hurt Efra. Sending someone else to hurt me wasn't that much of a reach.

"Thank you, Kamal." Griffin rose. "You are a good friend."

"Thank you and be safe."

Our business at an end, I followed Griffin outside.

"Hell." I said. "I didn't think she'd go that far."

"I have to admit, I didn't think so, either," Griffin muttered. "Let's get back to the hotel and get this taken care of before anyone has a chance to find you."

"Good plan."

Taking my hand in his, he wove it through his arm. "Stay close."

We worked our way through the throngs, and my anger at Pauline simmered down to a low boil as we walked and no threat emerged. Besides, I had bigger things to worry about, and the sooner we got back to our hotel the sooner I could start knocking on doors.

I had to find those tiles.

Suddenly, the hairs on the back of my neck rose. I stopped in front of a shop and checked out the reflection of the crowd behind me.

And spotted the man in black I'd seen earlier. The one I pegged as a slave trader. Hell.

Taking Griffin's hand and leaning against him like we were a couple, I pointed at a white vase with maroon stripes circling both the base and the lip. "We're being followed," I said, trying to look unaware and innocent.

"I know," Griffin replied, going along with my act and kissing the top of my head.

"The man in black."

For a microsecond, he stiffened. "I was talking about the man in the tan jacket and aviator sunglasses."

Again I used the window as a mirror. Griffin's tail stood across the street, looking a little too interested in a vase displayed in the shop opposite ours. "The one with his back to us?"

"That's him."

"Then we have more than one."

"So it seems."

Oh hell. "Suggestions? You know more about this city than I do."

"We're going to make our way east and out of the market. If we get separated, we'll meet up in an hour."

"Where? Back to the hotel?"

He shook his head. "They'll be waiting there. Trust me. Head for the City of the Dead."

Chapter 9

Unfortunately, I had no idea how to get to the City of the Dead, but now wasn't the time to delve into my lack of knowledge.

Besides, unlike a man, I would ask directions if needed.

"They know we know," I whispered as we worked our way through the crowds, trying to appear nonchalant. Behind us, Black and Tan kept closer than I liked.

I wondered if there were others—better, less obtrusive tails that we'd missed. I was sure Griffin wondered the same thing.

"Perhaps," he said.

The hairs on the back of my neck refused to lie flat. "Any doubt is going to disappear when we clear the crowds and make a run for it."

He nodded in agreement. "So, let's lose them before we leave the market." Grabbing my hand, he pulled me into an alley crammed with people. "This way."

We wove through the throng. Noise, heat and the smell of sweat overwhelmed me. The squeeze of bodies threatened to separate us, but Griffin's fingers tightened, almost crushing mine in his determination to keep me close.

Despite the oppressive heat, a chill ran down my back. Our tails still followed us. I *knew* it. I refused to look back, knowing that if I did, I'd tip them off and we'd lose our advantage.

The wall of people ended, and Griffin and I emerged in an open square.

"I feel like I'm in an Indiana Jones movie," I said, dodging the foot traffic and ducking to keep a tamed monkey from grabbing my hair.

"Yeah? Just don't end up kidnapped in a giant wicker basket."

"I'm not planning on it," I replied, taking comfort in the hidden weapon in my waistband.

"And don't draw your gun."

Hell. "You know?" I thought I'd hid it well.

"It's my job to know. I work in security. I can tell when someone carries a gun."

"How?" I asked, curious despite our increasingly precarious predicament.

"The walk. I've seen yours enough to know when something changes. You're right hip is heavier than normal, making you drag your foot just a tad."

Jostled by the bodies around me, I was unsure if I should be flattered or annoyed that he watched my ass on a regular basis.

Griffin stopped, letting go of me. I heard a cry and turned to see him gripping a kid's wrist in one hand and my weapon in the other. "And don't get it stolen," he said, unzipping my backpack and dropping it in. "There are pickpockets all over the place. You've got to be more careful."

He gave the juvenile delinquent a shake and said something in Arabic before he let him go. The urchin didn't look upset. He smirked at us and disappeared into the crowd.

I glanced over my shoulder, watching the kid scoot through the crowd—

And caught Black's eye.

He held my gaze, and then his attention flickered to my backpack. He knew. He met my eyes again, and our cover was blown.

I grabbed Griffin's arm to get his attention. "If there was any doubt about us before..." I nodded at Black, who was pushing his way through the crowd toward us.

"There isn't now," Griffin finished.

Tan came up on the left, flanking us.

"Run," Griffin said.

I didn't need to be told twice, and we shoved past people, knocking a few down, as we headed for an exit at the opposite end of the square.

But getting through the sea of people in the market verged on the impossible, and progress was slow. I expected to feel Black's hand on my shoulder at any moment, pulling me back.

Finally, Griffin and I broke free of the crowd and stumbled into the street. I didn't recognize any of the buildings, and I hoped he knew where he was going because I was lost.

"This way." His hand still gripping mine, Griffin pulled me down the sidewalk. We ran, our steps in unison as we sprinted away from our pursuers.

After six blocks, my lungs began to burn. I was fast, but my legs weren't as long as Griffin's, and it was becoming an effort to match his pace.

He didn't appear to notice as he hauled me around a corner. The street opened up into a complex of mosques.

I wasn't sure if the open space was a godsend or a disaster.

We could make better time through here—if my legs didn't collapse under me and if the men chasing us didn't catch us. But it also made us easier targets.

Something whistled past my ear, disturbing my hair. I never heard the shot. Silencers, I realized. These guys were professionals.

"They're shooting at us." My voice trembled with anger and adrenaline, and it took a supreme effort not to return the shot.

But I know my limitations. I'm good at some things, like hand-to-hand, but accuracy with a gun isn't one of them.

Griffin increased his pace.

I pushed myself harder, forcing my legs to keep up, but I didn't know how much longer I'd last. I glanced at the mosques. It was tempting to run into one. But entering a mosque with my head uncovered would be inviting more trouble than either of us wanted.

The pavement in front of us exploded as another bullet missed.

"We need to split up," I panted. "Better chance."

"Over there," Griffin said, leading me into the

mosque complex. We started to slow, not wanting to attract attention. "Meet me at the Tomb of Qaitbay in the City of the Dead. Be careful." He peeled away, going in the opposite direction.

I looked over my shoulder. Neither Black nor Tan were visible.

But they would be any second. I headed toward the nearest mosque, going around the back, then toward another building.

Undoubtedly, my pursuers would find me at some point, but the simple maneuver might buy me a few seconds. I leaned against the wall to catch my breath and think.

Why was Pauline going to these lengths to stop me? Did she know something about the tiles that I didn't?

The destiny Efra had talked of came to mind, and I wished I knew what it was.

Shouts and chatter coming from the front of the mosque caught my attention.

My pursuers, no doubt.

My first instinct was to duck into one of the doorways and take a chance that they wouldn't find me. But that kind of luck only happened in movies.

Then when they did find me, I'd have to shoot them, and while I'd be safe from them, it was quite possible I'd spend the rest of my life in an Egyptian prison.

Not an option.

Pushing myself away from the wall, I ran as silently as possible, following the side of the building, heading back toward the street and, hopefully, something that was familiar.

When it was safe, I'd find the City of the Dead. I'd heard of it before. An ancient graveyard, it now housed the poor of Cairo. Unfortunately, I had no idea where it was.

I was beginning to regret not sightseeing in Cairo.

There was a crowd of tourists ahead. Possible salvation. Slowing to a walk, and hoping I didn't appear as sweaty as I felt, I tucked my gun back into the waistband of my skirt, and worked my way into the crowd, trying to blend.

"I think they're brilliant," a feminine voice with a British accent commented. A short blond woman pointed at the mosque I'd just come from.

There were accompanying agreements, all in English, some accented and some not.

They stopped as a guide gave a verbal history of the complex. I kept within the group. Out of the corner of my eye, I saw Black walking toward us.

It required every ounce of willpower not to look at him. I took a nonchalant step forward, using the bulk of the crowd to hide myself.

I am invisible. I chanted the phrase in my head, willing it to be true.

He skirted the group, scanning for me.

My luck ran out. Our eyes met. His anger and frustration was palpable. A smug woman would have smiled. A scared woman would have shrunk.

I did neither. I raised my hand.

"Yes?" the guide asked.

All heads turned to me. "Is it true that if you go into a mosque without your head covered they'll beat you? Maybe even kill you?"

"There are protocols and traditions...."

I tuned out the guide as he explained what was acceptable and what was not. No one asked who I was. No one pointed a finger to me as an intruder.

I was now an accepted part of the group.

Ten minutes later, we boarded a bus. I took a window seat in the back. With no cabs in sight, I watched Black fume as we pulled away from the curb.

I had no idea where the bus was going, and it didn't matter. For now, I was safe.

I hoped Griffin could say the same.

Ten minutes later the bus stopped at another mosque. I ditched the group and grabbed a taxi to take me to the City of the Dead and the Tomb of Qaitbay. I prayed that I'd find Griffin once I arrived.

If he was hurt or captured, Pauline would pay.

I sighed and watched cars whiz by. This mystery was getting stranger by the hour, and there was only one person who could shed light on it—Pauline.

When we found her, I definitely had some questions for the pampered nuisance who was also my sister-of-a-sort.

The taxi slowed and pulled into the graveyard.

Built along the base of the Moqattan hills, the four-mile-long graveyard also served as housing for approximately fifty thousand Egyptians who had neither the money nor means to build better homes.

Instead of living in the street, they moved into the mausoleums. And though their occupation was illegal, it was also tolerated.

I looked at the taxi meter. The cabbie was charging me twice what he should, but I didn't have time to argue. "Qaitbay?" I asked.

He pointed down a street toward what I hoped was the tomb. I handed him a wad of bills and got out. Walking up the street, I tried not to stand out. For a cemetery, this was a busy place. Laundry lines hung between gravestones. Through an open door, I saw a family eating their evening meal, using the top of a stone sarcophagus as a table.

I had no appetite, for the entire *city* reeked of garbage, but these people had no choice. If they didn't live here, they'd be living on the streets with no shelter.

Even as my heart ached for them, I found myself avoiding their curious eyes and walking faster, wondering if I'd end up in an attempted mugging before I found Griffin.

It seemed like forever, but was probably less than a mile when I found what I hoped was the mosque that housed the Tomb of Qaitbay.

The building was a work of art. Inlaid with wood and gold, the main turret towered over the City of the Dead, an island of reverence and beauty in a sea of despair. "Please be it," I muttered, walking faster.

I rounded the front.

Standing there, with his back to me and one foot tapping with impatience, was Griffin.

"Griffin!"

He turned and then walked to meet me. "What took you so long?"

I ran to him, so grateful that he was safe that I threw my arms around his neck.

He hesitated. "You're causing a scene," he murmured against my neck, his mouth firm and hot on my skin.

"Let them watch," I replied, not caring that my display was completely inappropriate in Muslim society.

As if reading my mind, he wrapped his arms around me and pulled me close, lifting me off my feet. His mouth came down on mine.

The kiss was perfect. I parted my lips, wanting more, and was rewarded with a low, rumbling groan and a husky, "Damn it, Tru."

He didn't fight me off, and the world went away as I sank into the kiss. Nothing mattered but Griffin and the heat that rose in my body.

Finally, he set me on my feet and pulled my head to his chest, his hands in my hair. "I was worried about you, too."

I looked up into his dark eyes. If we were anywhere else, I'd do more than kiss him. Instead, I grinned. "I never said I was worried," I teased.

He chuckled. I took a deep breath, releasing my tension as I exhaled. Play was over, and it was time to get down to business.

"Did you have much trouble getting away?" I asked. Our hands slid together as we walked back the way I'd come.

"A little. A thump on the jaw as he came around a corner stopped him cold."

"Nice," I replied, a little envious of Griffin's strength.

"How about you?" His thumb stroked my skin, and I shivered at the unexpected, pleasant familiarity.

"I infiltrated a tour group and used them as cover. There wasn't much he could do but let me go or cause a scene."

"Nice, yourself."

My mind raced, searching for our next move. "Do you think we should go back to the hotel and try to find Pauline?" I asked.

"I'd like to, but I suspect that whoever was chasing us today will be waiting there for us." He looked around. "As much as I hate to say it, we might be safer staying here for the night."

"Here? In the City of the Dead?" I stopped in the street, facing him. "Where?" I gestured around. "There isn't exactly a Holiday Inn here, and I can't imagine the locals being too thrilled with putting us up."

"Yeah, you're right," he said. We started walking again. "I know a place. It's not the Marriott, or even a Holiday Inn, but no one will look for us there. Tomorrow, we can catch Pauline at the airport and get some answers."

We continued in silence until we cleared the City of the Dead and found a taxi. Griffin gave the driver directions, and we stopped in a poorer section of Cairo. The adobe house Griffin led me to was small, but if he said it was safe, that worked for me. "Do you know these people?" I asked, as he knocked on a heavy wooden door that was partially covered with peeling red paint.

"Kind of. They rent rooms."

The door opened, revealing a short, brown-skinned man dressed in a traditional white *galabia*. There was no smiling. No familiar conversation. Griffin said something in Arabic. Our host replied with a scowl. Griffin countered with something that sounded like it might be rude, and the man waved us in. Griffin handed him money, then tugged me up a set of creaky wooden stairs to the second floor.

The room was simple. A double mattress on the floor with a small trash can next to it. A chair. No dresser. No mirror. Nothing that would indicate this room was anything more than a place to sleep. "The bathroom is down the hall. If you have to go, now would be a good time," Griffin said. "Otherwise, you can use that." He pointed to what I assumed was a chamber pot.

"I'm fine." And if I had to go later, I'd hold it.

After wedging the back of the chair under the doorknob, he shuttered the windows to hold in the warmth from the impending chill of the night.

Bending down, I pulled back the embroidered bedspread to reveal white cotton sheets. "Thank God," I said.

"What?"

"They're clean."

Judging from his expression, I'd just stuck my entire foot in my mouth all the way to the knee. "They're poor. Not slobs."

I flushed, my cheeks burning. "I'm sorry. I didn't mean to imply they were unclean."

"S'okay," he said, smiling at my discomfort. "I'd think the same thing if I hadn't stayed here before. It doesn't help that Sayyid is as pissy as they come." Griffin pulled off the bedspread. "I'll take the floor."

Surprised and pleased with his gallantry, I stared at him. I wanted him, and not just for his body heat. "The bed is big enough for two," I offered before I could second-guess myself.

He met my gaze, looked at the bed and then

returned to me. We knew that if we shared the bed, we'd share more than just the blankets.

"Are you sure?" he asked, a thousand questions behind the single sentence.

I nodded, never more sure of anything or anyone. "Positive."

"Okay then." He spread the blanket back over the bed and held his hand out. I took it, and he pulled me close. "You know we won't get much sleep." His other hand stroked me from hair to hip, and I shivered.

"I'm counting on it," I replied, rising to my toes and touching his lips with mine.

His mouth was both sure and soft, and neither of us was in a hurry.

He nibbled my neck, and I was barely aware of movement as he lowered me to the bed, until his weight was on me. He slid his hands up my arms, twining his fingers with mine and pressing both my hands into the pillows. "We're going to be a little limited," he said, biting my neck and making my breath catch in my throat. "I don't have any condoms."

"I thought you were prepared for everything," I teased.

"Not for this." He leaned up, pressing our hands deeper into the pillows and looking into my eyes. "Not for you."

I smiled. "It's okay. I have some in my wallet."

His brows shot up. "You have got to be kidding."

"A woman should take charge of her sexuality." I took a playful nip at his chin and missed. "And so I do. As long as you don't mind chocolate-flavored condoms."

He looked at me as if I'd broken some social taboo.

"They sounded fun," I said in my defense. "Besides, if you brought your own instead of making me do all the work, they'd be more normal."

"Point taken." He pushed a strand of hair away from my face. "You are quite the surprise, Tru Palmer."

"So are you, Griffin Sinclair." I tried to bite him again, and this time succeeded in capturing his ear.

An hour later, the sun had gone down, and the only light in the room was the moonlight that made it through the shutters. I knew one thing for certain— Griffin had more control than any other man I'd ever been with. He'd touched me. Fondled me. Kissed me. Licked me.

I was so close to the brink of orgasm I had to either climax or kill him. "Damn it," I whispered as he put his head between my legs, teasing my thighs. "Do something."

The reply was a chuckle, and the mattress shifted as he scooted up until we were chest to chest. "Where are those condoms?"

"Here." I grabbed my wallet from my backpack, pulled one out and handed it to Griffin.

He chuckled again, a dark, dangerous sound. "Back in a minute," he whispered in my ear.

The mattress shifted again as he licked his way down my body, his tongue and teeth taking detours to torture my nipples and, I was sure, leave his mark on my hip.

Finally, his head was between my thighs again, his breath hot against my skin.

And nothing.

I nudged him with my foot. "What are you waiting for? An engraved invitation?"

He chuckled again and bit me.

I kicked and was rewarded with an, "Ow, damn it!"

"Then quit teasing me," I said.

He did as I asked. His tongue licked me, and I tightened. I was close now, and all I wanted was release.

"Griffin," I pleaded. "Please, don't stop. Don't stop."

He pressed his fingers into me, pushing me over the edge.

I had the sense of mind to grab a pillow and hold it over my face as my climax washed over me, and then I was oblivious, lost in sensation and arching against his mouth while he held my hips, refusing to let me relax.

It seemed to last forever and not long enough.

Then he was leaning over me, flinging the pillow aside. Lifting my legs, he plunged inside of me, sending me over the edge again and then joining me in a few thrusts, groaning into my neck.

Finally, the room was silent except for our breathing.

"Oh my God," I giggled, euphoria rushing through me. Were we insane? Part of me wanted to think so, but it had felt so good. So right.

He rolled over and off me, foil rustling as he disposed of the condom. "What's so funny?"

I shook my head. "We just had sex."

"Not just sex," he said, pulling me into him, one arm over my waist. "Great sex."

"Oh yeah." Being wedged against Griffin's chest

was like lying next to my own personal heater, but I didn't care, and snuggled closer. He threw his leg over me, pinning me down and holding me close.

His fingers skimmed my flesh, caressing me with a familiarity that I found comforting and as intimate as what had happened just a few minutes ago. When he reached my necklace, he rolled it in his fingers. "Do you ever take this off?"

I shrugged in answer, but the truth was, no. I never took it off.

"It's pretty." His voice was slow, and I knew he was going to sleep.

Such a man.

When I opened my eyes again, the sun was shining through the shutters and someone was trying to break down our door.

Chapter 10

"Move!" Griffin rolled away from me and to his feet, offering me his hand at the same time. I took it, flying up as he jerked me free from the covers.

The door rattled. I barely noticed, yet saw everything from the hinges shaking to a waft of dust falling from the lintel above.

It was an adrenaline-fueled moment that left me both detached and so involved that I was drowning in detail.

"Tru!" Griffin's shout kicked me back into reality, and I grabbed my clothes from the floor. Yanking on my skirt, I stuffed my bra in my backpack, pulled my shirt over my head and grabbed my gun.

Griffin was already dressed.

"Out the window?" I asked, sliding my sneakers on while I tried to ignore the fact that my heart was crashing against the wall of my chest.

He gave a curt nod.

Once again, the door rattled as a body slammed against it. It wasn't going to last much longer. I was surprised it hadn't already been yanked off the hinges.

Another hit. The chair slid, and the door opened a few inches. Someone yelled something in Arabic. Griffin yelled back.

I hated not knowing what they said.

I looked out the half-open window. Below us, Black stood next to a dark red Capri parked at the curb.

I pulled myself back into the room before he could glance up and see me.

"They brought friends," I said, weapon at the ready.

"Damn it."

"Exactly."

He yelled something else in Arabic.

"What's going on?" I asked, watching the chair slide another quarter inch.

"I asked why they were chasing us."

"And?"

"We're wanted for questioning."

Questioning? "Are they cops?" My heart beat harder, and I pressed a hand against my chest to hold it in. This was getting more and more complicated.

What was going on and how was Pauline involved? Did she own the police force?

That was a scary thought.

Maybe she isn't involved, I assured myself. Maybe they wanted us for a reason I wasn't aware of. Maybe this was coincidence.

Maybe I believed in fairies and flying pigs.

"Don't know. Don't care," Griffin snapped. "How's our friend outside?"

Black looked alert but so far, hadn't looked up yet. "Bored but ready."

The voice in the hall shouted something else, and Griffin's eyes widened. "Time to go."

"How? We're surrounded."

Behind Griffin, a small black object rolled through the crack in the door and into the middle of the floor. A white gas began filling the room. Instinctively, I backed away, but I was already against the wall.

Griffin followed my gaze until he spotted the gas grenade. When he turned back, his expression was blank. He was next to me in less than a beat. Another beat and he'd surveyed the sidewalk outside.

He threw the window open.

Black looked up, and before he had time to raise his weapon, Griffin shot him in a final, third beat.

I wanted to throw up and high-five Griffin at the same time. I did neither. He grabbed my arm and shoved me to the open window. "Hang on with your hands and drop. I'll cover you."

I coughed in the smoke, and my eyes started to tear. There wasn't time to argue that I didn't want special treatment or that I didn't need him to tell me how to climb out of a window.

Dropping my backpack to the sidewalk, I followed it, and in seconds, was safe outside. At my feet, Black moaned, rolling on the cement, his blood staining the concrete.

I picked up his gun, pocketing it. "Hold still." I grabbed him, looking at the wound. Griffin had shot him in the shoulder.

"He'll live." Griffin said behind me.

I hadn't heard him land.

Quickly, he rummaged through the groaning man's pockets until he found the car keys.

"Let's go."

The sidewalk exploded, and we dived for the car as bullets struck the concrete around us.

Griffin took the wheel, and the vehicle roared to life. With tires screeching like the special effects in a bad B movie, we raced away, crouching as bullets shattered the car windows.

When the bullets stopped, I raised my head. Warm wind blew through the broken windows. Frankly, the constant rush of adrenaline was starting to wear on me. "What was that about?" I said, my voice more shrill than I liked.

Griffin glanced at the rearview mirror, the road, and then me. "I have a few ideas."

I picked tempered glass fragments from my hair. "Want to share?"

He shook his head. "You first. I'm sure you have some ideas of your own."

As much as I hated to put the blame on Pauline, I didn't see how I could *not* implicate her. "I think this has everything to do with Pauline."

He didn't argue.

I continued. "I'm sure she has the tiles, but I don't understand why she took them. And why send men after us? That seems a little extreme."

"Money," he offered.

"Not unless she's in trouble and doesn't want the family to know," I replied.

"Status?" he suggested.

I shrugged, at a loss as to what to believe.

I tossed a small handful of glass to the floorboard. This would all be so much easier if I could in confide in Griffin. Tell him the connection between myself and Pauline.

Picking more glass from my hair, I watched the side mirror, but didn't see a tail.

"Call me crazy, but I don't care what her reasons are," Griffin said, breaking the silence and catching my attention. "I don't expect my employer to hire people to shoot me."

I realized then that he wasn't angry. He was disappointed. "I don't think that's too much to ask," I replied, wishing I could do more or say more. After a moment I added, "Where are we going?"

"The airport to have a chat with Pauline."

"Airport?"

He turned onto a four-lane highway. "The private plane. She's on her way to Paris. Her flight leaves at five."

Right. That gave us more than enough time. I threw another handful of glass to the floor. "Sounds good," I said, both eager and anxious to find out what was going on. Pulling my bra out of my backpack, I finished dressing in the car.

He drove into long-term parking. "Leave the weapons here," he said, parking away from other vehicles and killing the engine.

I rolled my eyes. "Why do you keep assuming I don't know what to do?"

His faced reddened. "It's not you. I know what *I'll* do in a given situation," he explained. "I'm trained. I don't know your reactions yet or what you know or how you'll respond."

"You seemed to know them last night," I interrupted, changing the topic to stop his out-of-character babbling.

He laughed, relaxing. "That was good, wasn't it?" He ran his free hand through his hair, managing a boyish cuteness that I hadn't thought possible.

"Oh yeah," I said, remembering how comfortable I'd been with him. "But your morning-after technique leaves a lot to be desired. Most women don't have to ask to hold the bullets with breakfast."

He chuckled. "I'll work on that next time."

"Already planning a next time?" I teased.

He pulled me close. "Oh yeah," he whispered, echoing my earlier sentiment before kissing my mouth.

His lips were firm and familiar, and I could spend hours kissing him, but there wasn't time for that. We pulled away at the same time. "Let's go find Pauline," he said, shoving his gun under the front seat.

I did the same with mine.

I wove my arm through his as we walked into the airport, my stomach doing summersaults. It wasn't the fear of capture that made me nauseous. It was the airport itself.

I hate to fly. I do it, but generally require Valium to get me into the seat. Better living through chemistry, I thought, reminding myself that I was not getting on a plane.

We were here to catch Pauline. Not board.

The butterflies in my stomach tried to exit through my mouth anyway, and I swallowed hard, hoping that I looked more relaxed than I felt.

"We have to buy tickets to get through security," Griffin said out of the side of his mouth as he led me to a counter. "Don't worry. I'll take care of it."

He smiled at the bored-looking ticket agent. "Two for Paris. The afternoon flight. First class."

"IDs?" the agent asked, not batting an eye.

I dug in my backpack, retrieving my identification and praying that the woman behind the counter didn't see my hands shaking. If the police were chasing us, there was bound to be some kind of bulletin at the airport.

Griffin appeared normal and calm. Not as if we were possible fugitives looking for a millionaire thief. I envied his ability to distance himself. We handed over our IDs, and I tensed, waiting for an alarm. Armed men.

Something.

But nothing happened.

"Luggage?" the ticket agent asked, her brown eyes widening when she finally looked at us. I couldn't blame her for her shock. With our uncombed hair, sweaty skin and wrinkled clothes, we looked more like street people. Not the kind of individuals who bought first-class airline tickets.

At least I'm wearing a bra, I mused, trying to transform my semihysterical grin into something less suspicious. I settled for coughing into my hand.

"Not today." Griffin slid his arm around my waist. "I'm taking my girl on a shopping spree."

The agent handed us our papers. "Have a good flight."

We walked away, tickets in hand.

"You okay?" Griffin whispered. "You looked a little pale back there."

"I'm fine." And I was, until I saw the security checkpoint.

"Be calm," Griffin said. "We're going shopping. Remember that." He squeezed my hand and laughed as if I'd said something funny.

I giggled in response, but shut my mouth when it edged toward hysteria.

We're shopping. Two people going shopping. I chanted the words like a prayer in my head.

We went through the metal detector without a hitch. Once again, I breathed a sigh of relief. Perhaps events were turning in our favor.

I was putting my shoes back on when something hard jammed into my side.

Flinching, I tried to pull away, but a firm hand grabbed my elbow. "Please come with us, Ms. Palmer. Quietly. We have a few questions."

I looked down. The something hard wedged into my flesh was the barrel of a gun.

So much for *our favor.*

It wasn't unlike a cop movie. The security room was small and stale, with a table and a few hard-back, wooden chairs. Fluorescent lighting flickered overhead, making my eyes hurt. The mandatory glass-and-chrome wall clock remained mute and unmoving—stuck at 8:00 a.m.

They'd taken Griffin to another room without giving us a chance to talk to each other.

Not that I needed to speak with him. I knew Griffin. He'd never admit to anything. Not that there was anything to admit to. We'd been shot at and had defended ourselves.

But I didn't plan to admit even that much.

What really pissed me off was the fact that Pauline was leaving, and Efra's village was running out of time.

"Damn it," I whispered, crossing my arms over my chest.

As if on queue, the door opened and Tan walked into the room. I tried not to look surprised. "Hello, Ms. Palmer."

"Hello. I want a lawyer."

He shook his head as if disappointed with my typical American request.

Bite me. It was all he was going to get.

Sitting down opposite me, he slid a folder across the table. "Open it."

I glared at him, but uncrossed my arms and flipped it open. On top of a small stack of papers was an eight-by-ten of myself and Griffin, running down the street. "So?"

"Keep looking."

I flipped through the photos. Me in the group of tourists. Griffin running. That must be after we split up.

Then nothing until the final one of us driving the stolen car down the street.

I breathed a sigh of relief and closed the folder. If this was all they had, we were safe. Not one of the photos showed us shooting at anyone. "I don't get it. Why are you holding me and my friend?"

He pulled the file back. "Gertrude Palmer."

Inside, I cringed at hearing my given name.

"You are from a good family," Tan said, looking as cool and calm as Griffin. "The best education.

THE EDITOR'S "THANK YOU" FREE GIFTS INCLUDE:

▶ Two NEW Kimani Romance™ Novels
▶ Two exciting surprise gifts

YES! I have placed my Editor's "thank you" Free Gifts seal in the space provided at right. Please send me 2 FREE books, and my 2 FREE Mystery Gifts. I understand that I am under no obligation to purchase anything further, as explained on the back of this card.

PLACE
FREE GIFTS
SEAL
HERE

168 XDL EF2H   368 XDL EF2T

FIRST NAME	LAST NAME

ADDRESS

APT.#	CITY

STATE/PROV.	ZIP/POSTAL CODE

Thank You!

(KR-SA-11/06)

The Reader Service — Here's How It Works:

Privileges. Servants. Why have you turned to a life of crime? Drugs?"

I leaned back, refusing to react. "What do you mean?"

"You assaulted a citizen." He went to the bottom of the pile. "An Efra Binte Nur Um Fatima."

He hesitated, waiting for a response to the accusation.

I wanted to scream at the obvious lie and ask him how he knew about Efra, but I took a deep breath and refused to accommodate him either way.

After a few seconds, he grunted and continued. "You are accused of striking her. Possibly killing her."

I refused to let his accusation scare me. She wasn't dead. I would know if she were. But he knew that we were friends, and there was no point in denying it.

Give him just enough. No more. "She was fine when I left her."

"You know her, then?" Tan asked.

I nodded. "She's a friend. You say she was assaulted. Will she be okay?"

"For now." He closed the folder and lit a cigarette. "Tell me what happened."

"There's nothing to tell," I said. There was no way I was telling him anything. Not about Pauline. The tiles.

Anything.

"I hear otherwise," he said, blowing smoke in my face.

I coughed. "What have you heard?"

He frowned. "I ask the questions. Not you. Now, tell me what you know."

I told him the same thing. Again and again.

I think it was midafternoon or later when I glared at the broken clock. I'd denied knowing anything a hundred times and in a hundred different ways.

"One more time," Tan said, lighting another cigarette in an endless chain of them. I coughed in the smoky air. "Tell me where you were when your *friend* Efra was assaulted."

I rested my head on the table. "No. I'm done." I tried to look at Tan's wristwatch and failed. Though I didn't know the time, it had to be close to Pauline's departure. If she left, the location of the stolen tiles went with her.

"We are not done," Tan said.

"Then tell me about Pauline," I said.

I peeked up at Tan over my forearm. For a fleeting moment, his eyes widened in surprise. I hadn't brought Pauline up until now, not sure of the consequences and not wanting to incriminate myself further in case she hadn't bought the police, and this investigation was legitimate.

Now, I wanted to stop her, and if it took handing her over to the police, so be it.

"Why do you want to know about Mrs. Adriano?"

"She's the one who assaulted Efra," I said.

His surprise was genuine, and I wanted to kick myself for not speaking sooner. Perhaps he was on the level. "My cell phone's in my backpack," I said. "Call my assistant. He'll take the phone to Efra. You can get the truth from her."

Tam's mouth thinned, and he stubbed the cigarette out on the table.

"I'll be back," he said, rising to leave the room. The lock on the door clicked.

I pulled the file back and opened it again, flipping through the pictures. Some weren't too bad. There was one of us hand-in-hand that would be a great candid shot if I didn't look scared as hell. Griffin looked confident and sexy. Bastard.

Tan came back and tossed me my backpack. "You are free to go."

"Griffin?"

Tan lit another cigarette. "He is waiting for you."

I edged by him and walked down the hall, glad to be free. Opening the door, I found myself next to the airport baggage claim. Griffin waited, arms crossed.

I ran to him, and he opened his arms. "You okay?" he asked, pulling me close.

I breathed him in, the butterflies finally disappearing. He cupped my cheek, checking for injuries. "They didn't hurt you?"

"Not unless you count asking the same question repeatedly as torture," I said. "How about you?"

"The guy lived, so it's all good."

I'd been so wrapped up in Pauline I hadn't even thought about that. "But you still shot him. How did you get away with that?"

"The same way anyone around here does. Money talks."

I huffed in frustration, and for the first time in a long time, I regretted that I'd severed ties with my wealthy parents.

Griffin pulled me to his side, wrapped his arm around my waist and led me toward the exit. "I told them where the car was, so we'll be taking a taxi back to the hotel."

His suite? "How about Pauline? We need to catch her before she gets on the plane."

"No can do," Griffin said, nodding toward a clock over the exit.

It read eighteen hundred hours. My heart sank.

She'd left over an hour ago.

And I had only four days left to retrieve the tiles.

Chapter 11

We boarded a plane for Paris the next morning. I wasn't sure what bothered me more—flying or losing Pauline's trail. I took the window seat and stared at the tarmac, wishing I was standing on it instead of sitting in a first-class seat, fighting the urge to panic and run screaming out the door.

"Are you okay?" Griffin asked, buckling himself in.

"I'm fine. Why?" I flashed him a smile over my shoulder, trying to look sincere. It must have been too forced. Too bright. He frowned in response. I turned back to the window. It was easier to count the bags being loaded into our plane than face Griffin's concern. I wasn't used to him caring, and though I enjoyed his attention, it was still a bit disconcerting.

"You don't like to fly, do you?"

I shook my head.

"Phobic?"

I shook my head again. "If it was a phobia, I wouldn't even be on the plane," I replied, wishing he'd shut up.

"You're pale as a sheet."

"Just leave—" I bit off the retort, reminding myself that it wasn't Griffin's fault I was scared. "It's more like a healthy respect," I finished in as calm a voice as I could manage.

It was a short flight. A few hours at most.

I could stand anything for a few hours.

"Do you want a drink? Something to relax you?"

"No thanks." I shut my eyes, wishing my anxiety could be cured that easily. That a rum and Coke would fix everything.

But the reality was that nothing would ever make me like flying, because for me, flying was like being blind.

When the plane reached approximately twenty thousand feet, I lost contact with the earth beneath me. All contact.

I shuddered, knowing what was going to happen.

"Tru?"

"What?" I squeaked, peering at him through half-closed lashes.

He slid his hand on top of mine and squeezed my fingers. "We don't have to fly. There are other modes of transportation."

I smiled, genuinely this time, grateful for the kindness. And found myself wanting to tell him why I hated to fly. What I was.

For a long moment, we stared at each other,

expectation in the air. The urge to blurt the truth grew stronger, but undercurrents of confusion and uncertainty stopped me.

I wasn't sure how he fit into my life anymore. Certainly not as a coworker.

Lover? Boyfriend? Friend with benefits?

Our growing, changing relationship was confusing.

But I knew one thing. I wanted him to know *me*. Not Tru the businesswoman or Tru the tracker-of-lost-tiles.

But *me*. Tru, the dowser.

Confession is good for the soul, my mother's voice whispered.

It was. Until you ended up in a sanitarium—put there by those who you thought loved you best.

I squashed the urge to declare my abilities. "I'll be fine once we take off."

He kissed my knuckles. "You sure?"

"Yeah. Besides, the trail is getting colder. This is the fastest way to get there."

"Okay." He accepted my answer without argument.

The engines of the plane whined, revving up to speed. I gripped the armrest with one hand and Griffin with the other.

"Sure about that drink? Or I could just knock you out," he teased.

"Stop trying to make me laugh," I said, my fear dissipating a little. "I can't be scared when you make me laugh."

"That's the point." He squeezed my hand again. "When we get airborne, I'll wow you with some great knock-knock jokes."

"Thanks." I snorted in amusement, unable to stop myself.

"You're welcome."

The plane started to taxi, and I mentally held on to the earth beneath us. Normally, I don't even notice the connection, but that doesn't mean it isn't there. It's like one of the five senses. They're all so integrated that I never think of them.

Until one is taken away.

The plane gained speed, and I shut my eyes, keeping my breath steady and even.

Liftoff.

My breath hitched in my throat. Griffin's thumb stroked my skin, and I exhaled. My connection to the earth grew weaker as we rose into the sky. I clutched my crystal necklace in my fist and intensified the connection, aware that Griffin was probably watching, and no longer caring if he did.

I concentrated, opening my mind.

There. My senses touched the ground. Rock. Water.

The earth. As comfortable as a blanket, and as necessary to me as breathing.

But not even my necklace could maintain the connection when faced with the force of man and his machines.

We rose higher, and at twenty thousand feet, the earth disappeared from my senses, and I was crippled.

When we began descent, relief washed through me, and by the time we landed, my sixth sense had returned, making me giddy. Chatty. Drunk.

An unfortunate side effect that was a combination

of extreme relief and saturation of my dowser talent by my reconnection to the earth.

Worse, I knew what I was doing, and why, but couldn't seem to stop myself.

"You sure you weren't sneaking drinks in the restroom?" Griffin asked as we walked through the terminal, pulling wheeled overnight bags stuffed with clothes from his Cairo apartment.

"I didn't leave the seat, you know that." I laughed, reminding myself not to skip with delight. "I'm just glad to be on the ground. Don't you love it?"

"The ground?"

"The ground. The trees." Shut up!

My mouth kept going. "The water. Everything." Shut up!

I clamped my jaw tight.

"I swear you're drunk." He took my elbow and steered me toward a door and the waiting taxis. Putting our bags in the trunk of one, he gave directions to the driver.

In French.

"Is there a language you don't speak?" I asked, wishing I was more surprised at his additional skill. "I only speak one. I'd like to speak more but never found the time. Spanish—"

"Tru." He placed a finger on my lips as the taxi left the terminal. "Please."

I took a deep breath, realizing I was talking at breakneck speed, and reminded myself to get a grip.

"Where are we going?" I asked, concentrating on slowing my voice. My stomach growled, and I remembered I hadn't eaten since last night. "I'm starving."

"The Sheraton."

"Do you have an apartment at this one, too?" I asked.

I took another breath…and the world fell into order in my head with the force of a hurricane. I was suddenly sober.

Finally.

"No, and what's with the necklace?" He nodded toward me. "You haven't let go since we left Cairo."

"Oh." I realized I was toying with the crystal, and let my hand drop.

He lifted the gem from my shirt, running his fingers over the edges. "Pretty. A gift?"

"No," I said, glad my senses had cleared. Drunken Tru would have yanked it from his hand. "I found it."

He let go and leaned back as the taxi buzzed toward the city. He didn't ask more questions, and I didn't offer an explanation.

What was I going to say? That when I was thirteen, I was walking on my parents' estate, and there it was?

I say there it was, but in actuality, it was a foot below the ground. I dug it up. My unique connection to the earth telling me it was special.

"What comes after the hotel?" I asked. Last night, after a day of interrogation and the loss of missing Pauline, neither of us had felt like talking, and had gone to bed, lost in our own thoughts. Tired, frustrated and cross, I hadn't even bothered to call Pete. Speaking to him in that state of mind would cause more trouble instead of setting his mind at ease.

"Same as before. I'll use my contacts to see if we can find Pauline."

"That's good, because I have nothing," I replied,

gazing out the window. Much like Cairo, I'd only seen the airport and the highways in Paris. I kept meaning to tour the city, but so far, that was another promise I'd yet to fulfill. "How and when do we talk to them?"

"*Him.* And there is no *we.* I'll talk to him."

I understood his need to protect me, but now wasn't the time. "This is my fight as much as it is yours. Probably more so."

"That's why I don't want you involved. You'll get too emotional, and in these circumstances that's not useful."

I fumed but held my anger in check, paying attention to his comment on my emotions. "I held my own during the interrogation."

"I know, but this is more difficult. This takes finesse, not bravado."

"I can be discreet."

"I'm sure you can." He sighed, running a hand through his hair. "I am not going to argue about this. Or discuss it. Or negotiate. You're not going. That's it."

"At least tell me who it is."

"Pauline's husband. Joshua Adriano."

For a heartbeat, I couldn't speak, but I know I stared at Griffin as if he was crazy. "You've got to be kidding."

"I never kid about these matters."

"Why talk to him?"

"Rumor has it they're estranged. If it's as bad as I hope, he might be useful. If not, I'll keep the topic on work. That's where the finesse comes in. You can't tip your hand by blurting out what you want."

"I don't blurt."

"You would."

"You don't know me well enough to say that."

"I think I do."

His gaze swept over me, and heat flushed my face. "Sex is different."

"I know you want to go, but please, trust me on this. I had better do this. Alone." He squeezed my thigh. "Promise me you'll stay away."

Lips pressed tight, I crossed my arms and my fingers at the same time and nodded in agreement. "Fine. You pay for the hotel, and I want a separate room."

"Okay," he agreed.

Disappointment colored his voice, and I regretted my words. Perhaps he had a point. Maybe I was too emotional. I'd have to work on that.

And what better place to start than by talking to Joshua Adriano?

I uncrossed my fingers.

"Tru? Where the hell are you?"

I held the phone away from my ear. I'd known Pete was going to be angry, but I didn't think he'd yell. Pete never yelled. He must be seriously pissed. "We're in Paris," I replied, holding the receiver away again.

"Paris!"

From the intensity of his shout, I was glad I had given my ear some distance. "Yeah," I replied after a moment. "Griffin and I arrived just awhile ago."

"He found you then." Pete sounded calmer, and I breathed a sigh of relief. When he got angry, it was intense. It was also short-lived.

"Yes," I answered, then got to the more important issues. "Is everything okay at the site?"

"No oil yet," he replied, his voice all business now that he knew I was alive and well and in France.

"And the locals?"

"Abraham is doing well. A smart guy, really, and a great cook."

That was a relief. I kicked off my shoes, undressing. "How about Efra?"

"I went to check on her yesterday, just to keep relations going. She's still weak, but I think she'll be okay."

Thank goodness. If I lost her, I didn't know what I'd do. "Good. Can you tell her that I'll be back as soon as I can?"

"Sure," Pete said. He hesitated. "Any ETA on when you're coming back? A Dyno guy called this morning asking for you."

Hell. "No," I replied. "If they call again, make an excuse. I'll be back as soon as I can. Till then, just take care of things."

"Will do, and Tru?"

"Yes."

"Be careful."

With the phone cradled between my neck and shoulder as I took off my skirt, I smiled. He was such a dad, sometimes. "I will."

Hanging up, I stripped, put on fresh underclothes and a black skirt, turned on the shower and waited for the knock I knew would come.

I didn't have long to wait. *Griffin.*

The shower running in the background, I left my shirt off and pulled my long skirt up, tucking it around my waist, before I slipped the hotel's plush terry robe over the ensemble.

I swung the door open. He wore black slacks, a crisp silver-colored shirt and black silk tie. He'd flung a long, black wool coat over his broad shoulders. He looked marvelous, but I steeled myself. "What?" I barked, louder than I intended.

"I'm leaving. When I get back, we'll talk about how to proceed."

I glared at him and slammed the door. Watching him through the peephole, I saw disappointment flicker over his features, then disappear beneath his usual controlled expression, right before he walked away. "Still the soldier," I muttered, hating what I was doing but knowing there wasn't another way.

If he had any inkling that I'd follow, he'd call the meeting off.

My ear pressed against the wooden door, I listened for the elevator. I heard the familiar chime, the slide of doors and silence. Griffin was on his way, and time was of the essence.

Quickly, I slipped on a black blouse and flats, grabbed a scarf and cashmere sweater, and ran out the door to the emergency exit stairs. I ran down the three flights, taking two stairs at a time in an effort to beat the elevator. At the bottom, I cracked open the door. Griffin was walking across the lobby, his back to me as he left the building. Good enough.

Slipping on the sweater and scarf, I counted to twenty and followed him out the door.

Even though it was midday, and despite the festive holiday decorations that adorned the building, Paris in winter was anything but pleasant. The streets and sidewalks were slushy from a surprise snow that was beginning to melt. What with both the car and foot traffic, the snow had turned an unpleasant brownish-white and made walking treacherous.

A cold breeze rounded the corner of the building, and I pulled my sweater close, wishing I'd brought a coat. Shivering, I scanned the area for my quarry.

Luckily, due to the cold weather, there were few tourists about, and even with Griffin a city block away, I could make him out through the scant crowds. He turned a corner, and I hurried, not wanting to lose him.

I took a right onto a street lined with restaurants and boutiques.

There was no sign of him.

"Damn." He must have gone into one of the restaurants, but the question was, which?

I glanced at the array of storefronts. If he was meeting Joshua Adriano, it wasn't going to be in a quaint café, but something nicer. I'd need to blend in or at least be wearing something Griffin didn't recognize.

Slipping into one of the boutiques, I bought a camel-colored coat and matching hat and gloves in what was probably one of the fastest shopping trips ever.

Wearing them out of the store, I walked down the street, looking in windows out of the corner of my eye.

My breath caught when I spotted Griffin sitting inside Le Carrefour. He was shaking a man's hand.

Joshua Adriano. I'd spoken with him over the phone, but we'd never met. He looked as good as his voice. Tall. Slim. Dark hair. Wearing an expensive, charcoal-gray suit that was not purchased off the rack but had the distinct fit of a tailored ensemble.

They sat in a booth. Griffin's back was to the door, and I thanked God for small favors.

With my coat collar pulled up, and hiding my face, I continued past them, crossed the street, wandered up the opposite side, then crossed back to the restaurant, this time entering. Thirty seconds later, I was sitting near them sipping espresso, out of view but within earshot.

"No. She should be fine," Griffin said.

Who?

"It will be a public relations nightmare if she is not," Joshua replied. "Perhaps I should send a physician."

It had to be Efra they were talking about.

"Whatever you think is best," Griffin said.

"Do we have any leads on the perpetrator?"

"A few," Griffin told him. "Tru Palmer thinks your wife had something to do with it."

I perked up and took a small sip of coffee.

"Pauline?"

"Yes."

Joshua chuckled.

"That was my reaction. She seems too…" Griffin hesitated. "Too frail."

"Frail?" Joshua repeated. "Do not let her petite stature fool you. Pauline is anything but frail."

Anything but frail. Spoken with a forcefulness that didn't indicate she was the love of his life, but the exact opposite. I hoped Griffin caught his tone and would pursue the topic.

"So she could have?"

Whatever Joshua's response, it was nonverbal.

"Anyway, the project is progressing nicely. Tru might be young, but she knows her business."

I beamed at the kudos, but fumed at Griffin's lack of pursuit. That was as far as he was going to push Joshua?

I rolled my eyes. Griffin was acting like the typical male. They never spoke. Never dug. Didn't want to appear as if they cared or wanted to impinge on someone's privacy.

I didn't have that qualm.

Rising, I went into the lobby, took off my coat and hat, and then went right to their table. "So sorry I'm late, gentlemen." Both looked up at the same time. Joshua's eyes widened in surprise, but he recovered, rose to his feet and extended a hand. "Ms. Palmer?"

"Yes," I replied, smiling. "Mr. Adriano, how nice to finally meet you in person."

He was even better looking close up. Olive skin. Great teeth. Glossy hair. His grip was firm and warm.

Then I faced Griffin.

He remained seated and looked anything but pleased. He glared at me. "Hello, Tru."

I smiled, trying to ignore the undercurrent that said we'd be talking about *this* later. "Scoot over," I muttered, sliding in next to him. "So, what did I miss?"

"Very little," Joshua said, and signaled a waiter. He came over, giving me a strange look when I ordered another espresso, but didn't say anything.

"We were discussing your friend Efra," Joshua continued. "I am going to send a physician to attend to her."

"Thank you," I said, meaning it more than I thought possible. Pete was a gifted medic, but his resources were limited.

"Griffin tells me that you think my wife had something to do with her accident."

I choked on my coffee. "You're to the point, aren't you?"

"When someone in my family is accused of assault, yes."

"I am not accusing her, Mr. Adriano," I assured him, grateful for my skill at lying. "But I think she knows more than she's letting on."

Griffin kicked me under the table. I ignored him and leaned toward Joshua, radiating concern and sincerity. "I don't know if you've spoken with her since she came to the site, but she left in a rush. I'm not so worried that she's the perpetrator, but that someone is forcing her to act against her will. She might even have been kidnapped."

Joshua chuckled again, clearly humoring my overactive imagination.

Sucker.

"To relieve your mind, I can tell you that I spoke to Pauline this morning. She is in our Paris office, reporting to my father on your operation. Tomorrow, she is attending a funeral, where I plan to meet her."

"Oh." I leaned back, puzzled. One minute she was hitting elderly women. The next, she went to the office and attended funerals. She had to be the most confusing woman on the face of the planet. Morbidly curious as to whose funeral she planned to go to, I asked, "A friend?"

A pained expression crossed Joshua's face, and I felt less like a chipper interrogator and more like a crass boor. "I'm sorry." I paid unusual attention to my half-empty cup. "It's none of my business."

"It is all right."

It wasn't.

"It is for Scarlet Rubashka. She was a well-known photographer and a...friend of my brother's. You might have heard of her?"

"No. I'm sorry."

A brief silence settled over the table, but Joshua broke it with the professional forthrightness that came with good breeding. "Tell me, Ms. Palmer, how is the operation going? Griffin and I were discussing it, but I would like your perspective."

We spent the next thirty minutes discussing business. Boring, but easy and comfortable, allowing my mind to process the information.

Joshua didn't shout it from the rooftops, but it was obvious that the rumors were true. He and Pauline were estranged, and he had no idea what was going on in regard to the tiles.

When our impromptu meeting broke up, Joshua seemed pleased with my handling of the oil site and my people. Griffin seemed equally satisfied, but I saw quiet anger in his eyes.

As soon as Joshua walked out the door, Griffin turned on me. "What are you doing here?"

"I followed you."

"I know," he said, exasperated.

I didn't care. "I was listening. You weren't asking the right questions."

"Did it occur to you that I already knew most of

what you were asking? That I've already spoken to my informants?"

"You have more informants?" I asked, feeling like a fool, but recovering my righteous anger in a heartbeat. "Is there a country where you don't have informants?"

"Yes, and no, I don't think so."

"Well, why didn't you tell me? If you didn't withhold information I'd leave you alone."

"You slammed the door in my face."

"Oh," I said, remembering my actions. I hated it when he was right. This time, my anger was not recoverable, and foolishness took up the space it otherwise occupied. "If you already knew, why did you meet Joshua?"

"I'd already made the appointment. I also wanted to know if he knew what Pauline was doing."

"Did you figure it out?" I asked, curious if we'd read Joshua the same way.

"I knew before you sat your pretty butt down and interfered." His hands clenched into fists. "He doesn't have a clue."

Neither do you, I thought.

Chapter 12

Scarlet Rubashka's funeral was easy to find, as news of it was on the front page of all the newspapers. The photographer's violent death had caused a major ripple in the artistic community.

The service started at nine in the morning.

The church was a huge stone structure, with a stained glass window depicting the Virgin Mary over the door.

The Madonna. I didn't know if the icon's presence was coincidence or wishful thinking on my part. After all, most Christian churches had a Madonna somewhere, whether it was a window, statue or tapestry.

Still, this one glowed as the morning sun filtered through it. I took that as a good sign.

Griffin and I sat in a back corner, where we'd be less obvious. A few people turned, but didn't seem too interested in our arrival.

At the front of the church, flowers surrounded an elevated casket. Roses. Daisies. Lilies. A veritable garden of color.

I noticed that the casket lid was closed, and I breathed a sigh of relief. I never understood open-casket funerals. The person was gone. What was the point in saying goodbye to a shell or taking one last morbid glimpse?

It was a gruesome custom and one I avoided.

"I can't believe I let you talk me into this," Griffin whispered, dragging my attention away from the icon of death.

I glanced at him with an appreciative eye. If it weren't a funeral, I'd say that he looked exceedingly handsome in his dark suit, but under the circumstances, getting turned on seemed a little sacrilegious. "Tell Joshua that we're being polite. Paying our respects to his friend."

"He's not an idiot. He'll know you're after Pauline."

"Probably, but the ability to be ill-mannered in public was bred out of him. He'll allow us to stay rather than cause a scene." Raised in wealth myself, I knew how Joshua's kind behaved.

Griffin was what my mother called *nouveaux riche*. New money. He wore the right thing. Owned the right apartment. Spent money without flaunting it.

But there was an air about him that came with being a working man. A soldier. An attitude that those born to wealth never possessed.

It was what I liked about him.

"Just don't cause one."

"Who, me?"

"Yes. You." He shifted in his seat as the service began.

I relaxed. He didn't believe me for a minute, but it wasn't as if I'd intended him to.

Standing behind the pulpit with tall, white candles flanking her on either side, a woman dressed in a minister's robe spoke about Scarlet. Her life. What she meant to those around her. Typical funeral dialogue by someone who didn't seem to have known the dearly departed.

But these were not *typical* attendees. Not all of them. I could only see their backs, but a number of them drew me like magnets. I opened my thoughts, my mind, and let sensation trickle in. A familiar energy made my breath catch in my throat.

Marians. There were Marians in this crowd. Women like me. Efra. And Pauline.

I wondered if they knew it. Could they feel each other like I felt them? Was that why they were all here? Had Scarlet been one of them, as well?

"Quit squirming," Griffin whispered. "You're going to call attention to us." His eyes dropped down, focusing on my chest.

I realized I was toying with my crystal pendant. Again.

The rest of the Marians and their agendas, if they had any, could wait. With only two days left to recover the tiles, my mission took precedence. I let go of the pendant and scanned the crowd for Pauline. Unfortunately, with so many of the women wearing black clothes and black hats, and emanating Marian energy, it was difficult to pick her out.

I tried to find Joshua instead, knowing that propriety would dictate he sit with Pauline, but I couldn't find him, either.

I huffed in frustration, which garnered a scathing glance from Griffin and a mouthed, *Stop it.*

I settled, trying not to fidget, and reminded myself that when they rose to leave, I'd corner her.

The sermon droned on, but I didn't hear it and instead watched the crowd. Women sniffed into handkerchiefs. Men slumped. One woman, her silver-blond hair pulled back into a neat chignon, leaned her head on her partner's shoulder. He put his arm around her, pulling her close.

The grief and sense of loss were almost tangible. Unbearable. I squeezed my eyes shut, wondering if I'd made a mistake in coming.

The church. The weeping. The vast sea of wealthy attendees. It reminded me of my grandmother's funeral. I was seventeen when she died. We'd always had a special bond. A connection.

Suddenly, I recognized what the connection was— Marian blood.

Had she known? I wondered.

I blinked back unexpected tears, missing her all over again. More than my grandmother, she'd been my champion. My friend. And before I met Efra, she was the only person who accepted me as I was and believed in my dowser gift.

Losing her broke my heart.

A week to the day after I said goodbye to her, my parents sent me to the sanitarium to "cure" me.

I hadn't been to a funeral since. Not even my mother's.

"You okay?" Griffin whispered, taking my hand.

"Fine. Why?"

"You look like you're either going to cry or beat the hell out of someone."

"Maybe both," I said, managing a smile, and focusing on anything besides the casket.

He looked at me, seeing the unease beneath the glib answer.

"I hate funerals," I said.

"I know. Me, too." He put his arm around me.

I sighed and leaned into him and endured.

Finally, the minister asked if anyone wanted to speak. There was some whispering, and the woman who'd had her head on her companion's shoulder rose from the pew and made her way to the front of the group.

She was pregnant. *Very* pregnant. Tears had washed away her makeup, but she was beautiful and elegant in a simple navy-blue dress sans any of the bows or frills that tend to accompany maternity clothes. Despite her hiccups from crying, she glowed as she spoke about Scarlet, her clear voice resonating through the church.

It seemed the deceased was loved, respected and more important than she probably ever realized.

It made me think of Efra, and I wondered how she was. If something happened to her... I shook off the black mood that was gathering around me. Pete had said she was fine.

Still, I worried.

I sighed, wishing I could walk out and leave my dark thoughts behind. I hated death. Loathed funerals. Didn't like reminders that our time on this earth was transitory.

Another woman stood, heading toward the back of

the church, and the pregnant woman's words faded in my ears as I realized who walked down the aisle.

Pauline.

"Griffin," I whispered.

"I see her."

She passed us, her black dress the epitome of class, her eyes downcast as she hurried out. She didn't notice us. I whispered a silent thank-you to whatever entity brought good luck. "I'll be back," I whispered to Griffin, untangling myself from his arm.

"Tru—"

I was already edging out of the pew. I followed Pauline down the hall, hanging back and walking with silent feet. She went into the ladies' room, and I hurried forward, catching the door before it closed.

I pushed hard and entered, slamming it shut.

"Excuse me—" She stopped midsentence as soon as she realized whom she was addressing.

"Hello, Pauline." I locked the door behind me and leaned against it. "We need to talk."

For a heartbeat, she stared at me, her eyes wide in shock. Her mouth opened and closed, but no sound emerged.

"I think the words you're searching for are 'what a pleasant surprise'," I said, wanting to shake her for betraying me. "Those are the appropriate things to say, aren't they? Under the circumstances, of course."

"Um, yes," she replied. "I was going to use the ladies' room, if we can talk later?" Her glance shifted to the doorknob.

I'd come too far and been through too much to let her escape now. "Cross your legs. I'm not leaving until I get some answers."

"Concerning what?"

Now *I* stared, dumbfounded. "About what? How about you bashing Efra over the head and taking the tiles."

She blushed, the wave of color starting with her cheeks and continuing across her face and down her neck. "I did not have a choice. I did not want to. I am sorry."

"I'm not the one who deserves an apology," I said.

"You are right."

I wanted to like Pauline. Wanted to give her the benefit of the doubt, but the easy agreement wasn't enough. I realized nothing she said or did was enough compensation for hurting someone I admired and cared for. I quelled the niggling of anger that threatened to grow as I remembered Efra lying on the floor with blood pooling around her. "Tell me why."

She looked away as if considering my demand, then nodded in agreement. Taking a handkerchief from her pocketbook, she ran water over it, then wiped at her face.

Makeup came off, revealing a bruised cheek and eyebrow.

My anger faded. "No," I whispered.

She pushed up her sleeves. Bruises circled her wrist like a bracelet. "There are more on my ribs and along my back," she said, her voice choked. "Would you like me to strip so you can see?"

"No. That's not necessary." I swallowed my shame and tried to remain focused on my mission. Get the truth. Get the tiles. Get back to Egypt. "Showing me you've been beaten doesn't explain why you hit Efra and took the tiles. You almost killed her."

"I have never hit anyone before. I swung the vase, but did not mean to hit her so hard," Pauline confessed, pulling her sleeves down and hiding the evidence of her abuse.

"Why?"

She looked up. Her eyes glittered with tears. "Because he would have killed me if I did not do as he asked."

"Who?"

"My husband."

"Joshua?" The elegant, charismatic man whom I'd had coffee with yesterday?

She nodded.

My hand clamped over my mouth in horror. I didn't want to believe it, but it would not be the first time an Italian suit was a pretty facade for a wife beater, or a wealthy man who hit his wife, and I doubted it would be the last. "Do you know what he wants with them?" I asked, angry that I'd thought him innocent and Pauline guilty. If I'd known yesterday what I knew now, I'd have demanded the tiles and screw good manners.

"No, but he does not have them, I can promise you that." Her voice peaked with desperation, and she grabbed my hand, begging me to believe her. "He hit me this morning because I refused to tell him where I hid them. I did not realize what they were before I took them. Not really. Once I did, I could not give them to him."

Relief washed over me. I clenched her hand. "Where are they?"

A knock on the door startled us. We both jumped. "In a minute," I called. "Where are they?"

Her eyes widened. "You are hurting me."

I realized I was squeezing her fingers, and loosened my grip. "Sorry. Please," I said, feeling like a bully for hurting her.

Bully or no, I had to get the tiles. "Where are the tiles, Pauline?"

Another knock and a disembodied voice spoke. "I hate to be a pain in the ass, but I'm pregnant, and this is the only bathroom in the church."

Hell. The blonde.

"Meet me after the funeral. I am staying at Hotel Meurice," Pauline said. Grabbing a compact from her purse, she swiped the puff over her face, barely masking the bruise on her cheek.

The blonde pounded on the door, and I nodded in agreement, then swung it wide. She was shifting from one foot to the other. "Sorry," I said. "Girl talk."

She flashed us an impatient smile, then pushed past us as we left.

The door slammed shut.

If my goal was to piss people off, I was batting a thousand. Pauline touched my arm. "Tonight."

Grabbing a long, black wool coat from a hook, she left. As the church door closed, I saw her hail a cab, looking waiflike and frail as the snow fell around her.

Behind me, the service had ended and people milled about talking in quiet murmurs. Griffin leaned against a wall, waiting for me, his gaze following Pauline's exit.

"Well?" he asked when I reached him.

"We're meeting her at Hotel Meurice tonight, and she'll hand the tiles over."

"She admitted taking them?" His brows arched in surprise.

"It wasn't as if she could hide the fact."

He nodded.

I continued. "Joshua made her do it, and after seeing the bruises on her face, I believe it. I don't know why he wants them, and right now, I don't care. I want them back, and Pauline taken care of."

Griffin gave me a quizzical look. "You're saying Joshua hit Pauline?"

"Yes."

"To get the tiles?"

"Yes," I replied through gritted teeth, impatient with having to repeat myself. "Is that so hard to believe?"

He looked at me as if I was simple. "You realize that neither Joshua nor Pauline *knew* about the tiles until she arrived at the village? I'm not saying he didn't hurt her, but if he did, it wasn't to coerce her into taking the tiles."

I stared at Griffin in angry shock. I'd been so eager to believe her that I'd ignored the obvious. So in need of friendship that I'd believed her. So overwhelmed with her appearance that all else had faded.

Including my logic.

The realization that I'd been duped washed over me.

For a few minutes, we watched the crowd, and I tried to come to grips with my own stupidity.

"It was an easy mistake to make," Griffin said, his voice low. "I'm sure seeing her beaten up threw you off. I'd have done the same."

"No. You wouldn't have." I didn't want his pity.

"Probably not," he admitted. "But you can't beat yourself up over it."

I stiffened. "Trying to be funny?"

He thought about his word choice, and his ears turned red at the tips. "Sorry."

I looked away, furious with myself. "No. Don't be. I'm not mad at you. I just don't like feeling like a fool."

He pulled me close. "We all make mistakes," he whispered. "The trick is to learn from them and not make them again."

I did not plan on a repeat of Pauline duping me. Now that I knew she was a world-class liar, I was going to find her, and there was no way she'd get away again.

The best place to start would be with her friends— these other Marians. I put my arm around Griffin's waist and squeezed. "Let's see if anyone here can help," I said.

"It's worth a shot," he replied.

I surveyed the crowd. It was an eclectic mix of businesspeople in dark suits and artsy types who wore anything from hot pink to lime-green.

With the exception of Preggers, the Marian women all wore black and were bunched together with what I assumed were their husbands or boyfriends.

"We should mix a bit," Griffin suggested.

"I'll be over there," I said, pointing to the women who resonated Marian energy.

Griffin didn't argue, but pushed away from the wall and went in the opposite direction.

Forcing a smile to my lips and repressing my anger, I walked over. "Hello," I said.

They turned, and a wave of energy washed over me. Familiar and welcome despite my anger. Could they feel it?

Preggers's eyes widened for a split second. Maybe. That, or she was surprised at a stranger interrupting their obviously private conversation.

"I'm so sorry about your loss." I focused on Preggers. "You gave a beautiful talk."

"Thank you." Her eyes watered, and she wiped at them with the back of her hand. "I'm sorry. I seem to be nothing but a bundle of emotions these days."

"It's okay," I sympathized. Next to her, a dark man I recognized as the one she'd leaned against earlier pulled her close and murmured something in her ear.

They had matching wedding bands. A flash of unexpected envy shot through me.

She smiled and nodded. "Thanks. I hate funerals. Hate saying goodbye."

Envy disappeared, replaced with matching emotion. "Letting someone go when you're not ready…" I trailed off. There were no words for that kind of anguish.

She nodded in agreement.

"And you are?" a French accented voice interrupted.

I faced another blonde with what I assumed was her husband or escort of some sort. She looked as unmoving as stone and about as soft despite her slim figure. I smiled, but her ice queen facade didn't melt one iota. "Tru Palmer."

"Catrina Dauvergne." She didn't offer her hand, and neither did I.

"And Rhys Pritchard," the man next to her said.

I'm not short, but I had to tilt my head to look up at him. He held out his hand, and I noticed there wasn't a ring as I clasped it.

"I'm Ana, and this is my husband, Robert," Preggers said. "That's Eve and Nick."

The other couple—she in a black knit dress and he in a black suit with black shirt—nodded hello and looked at me with a hint of suspicion in their eyes.

For a minute, the energy around Eve fluctuated so heavily that I felt it, making me stumble.

Rhys caught my arm, steadying me. "Thanks," I murmured, wondering if Eve knew what she was doing. I'd have to find out, when I had more time.

And once I knew whether I could trust these women.

"You're welcome," he said. Stepping away from me, Catrina took his arm, pressing against him. It seemed the ice queen had a weak spot. It was good to see she wasn't stone.

One thing I noticed, which hadn't occurred to me before, was that only the women emanated the Marian energy. I wondered if our gift or abilities were limited to our gender.

Another question that would have to wait.

"You know Pauline?" Ana asked, referring to the episode in the bathroom.

"Yes. You could say that," I replied. "I work for an oil conglomerate, and she's one of the board members."

"You work for the Adrianos?" Catrina asked.

She didn't attempt to hide the fact that she didn't like the Adriano family, and from the chill that settled over the group, neither did anyone else.

Interesting. Possibly useful.

"I work for myself," I corrected her. "My company was hired by Dynocorp. The Adrianos are on the board, but so are a number of people from other companies."

The women looked at me curiously.

"How do you all know Pauline?" I asked, breaking the icy silence.

They glanced at each other as if silently working out a story. Amateurs.

"We work together sometimes," Ana offered.

Work? Ha! They were Marians, and though they didn't acknowledge the connection, I was sure they were aware of it. Coincidence went only so far.

But they didn't know I knew. That was my one advantage, and I wasn't above using it.

I had to get the tiles back, and right now these women were my only connection to Pauline. "I'd hoped you could help me. Pauline left so fast that I didn't have time to get her phone number, and we're supposed to get together for a meeting. Do any of you know how to contact her?"

It was a plausible lie. A good one, and I delivered it with my usual skill.

Despite that, I saw the suspicion in their gazes.

"No. We do not," Catrina replied.

"Then maybe you could give her a message," I said.

Before Catrina could say either yea or nay, the front door opened, letting a cloud of snow in with the cold air.

We all turned. Joshua and two men entered.

When I turned back, Robert was hustling Ana past me toward the side door. The rest were following.

This left my question unanswered. I wanted to scream in frustration.

A light touch on my shoulders caught my attention, and Griffin took my arm, looping it through his. "Find out anything useful?"

"A little. They know her, but I'm not sure how well. I think they might have told me more but when those three entered—" I nodded toward Joshua and the two other men "—they took off."

"Want to go found out why?" he asked.

I grinned. "Let's."

Griffin escorted me across the room to the three newcomers. Joshua smiled when he saw me. "Ms. Palmer." He took off his gloves and shook my hand. His knuckles were smooth. Unmarred.

Not the hands of a wife beater.

He shook Griffin's hand. "I'd like you both to meet my brother, Caleb." A handsome man, his dark eyes glittered with unshed tears. He nodded before pushing past us toward the front of the church and Scarlet's casket.

The older man frowned at him, then turned back to us. He radiated an old-world graciousness.

"Duke Simon Adriano," he said. He took my hand in his. His skin was warm. The hands of an executive. Smooth, uncallused and unmarred.

Except for his knuckles. Which were bruised.

Chapter 13

"What do you suggest we do?" I asked. We'd made idle chitchat with Joshua and Simon for as long as politeness required, leaving as soon as we could without appearing either rude or suspicious.

Griffin didn't take his eyes off the road. Driving in Paris was always a little risky, but when snow was added to the mix, getting behind the wheel took professional driving skills—or insanity.

I couldn't say for sure which category we fell under.

"To find Pauline?"

"Yes," I replied, frustrated at letting her slip away.

"I'll make a few inquiries. What about the women you spoke with. Do you think they might help?"

"Possibly," I said. They were like me, but were they helping Pauline or were they oblivious to her duplicity? I thought the latter but couldn't take a chance. Not with time running out.

"But I can't imagine them offering up the information." I toyed with my necklace, searching for options. I'd used the crystal to amplify the tiles and find them, but I'd never used my powers to hone in on a person. Then again, I'd never met a group of women emanating such unique energy until I met the Marians.

Could I use my necklace to locate Pauline?

It was worth a try. The only other option was to have Griffin talk to his contacts. While we'd catch up with Pauline at some point, it could be days.

I only had two left.

I pictured Efra's village well drying up. Plague. Famine. Another sandstorm. It's a myth, I told myself. A local legend to keep the tiles safe.

Then why rush, a voice whispered in my head.

I knew why.

The myth was real, even though I might prefer otherwise.

I doodled on the window with a fingertip, drawing circle within circle. The problem was Griffin. Until I grew adept at manipulating and sensing the energies, it was going to be difficult to gauge how far I could immerse myself before I was catapulted into another vision.

I didn't want another incident like in the Rover, when searching for Pauline had sent me a vision of Aleta instead. If that happened when Griffin was present, he'd rush me to the hospital again.

There was only one option. I hoped he'd agree to what I was about to ask, but I steeled myself for a possible fight. "Griffin?"

"Yes." He switched lanes as we came upon a roundabout.

"I need you to do me a favor."

He glanced over at me, then back at the road. "What?"

"Take me to the hotel. Give me a few minutes alone in my room, and I think I can direct you to Pauline."

He glanced at me again and his eyebrows arched upward. "Excuse me?"

"Just a few minutes. That's all I need."

"I don't get it."

"You're not supposed to."

"Okay." He drew the word out, processing what I was *not* telling him. "Are you going to tell me what you plan to do?"

I wanted to. In fact, the urge to confess was almost constant now. I ran a hand over my hair, smoothing it and taking a long look at the man beside me.

He was a good man. Strong. Tender when needed.

He'd never believe me.

He was too grounded in reality, and to convince him would take longer than a few minutes or even a few hours. It would take time. Trust. And possibly a demonstration.

I thought I had his trust. The other two weren't possible. Not until I returned the tiles to Efra.

Then I'd tell him. Show him my gift.

If he was the man I hoped he was, he'd believe.

A sense of calm settled over me. I'd tell him the truth. Soon. I drew a heart on the window, then wiped it away.

"I can't tell you. Not yet," I replied. "You'll have to trust me."

He pulled in at the front of our hotel. The valet came around, and Griffin held up his hand to indicate that we needed a minute. "I'll trust you, for now. Later, if you're right and can locate Pauline, you'll have to tell me how."

"Okay."

His brows furrowed in puzzlement. "That's the deal."

"I know. I just agreed to it."

"A little too easily."

He still didn't look convinced. I laughed but didn't want to tell him about my decision. I took his hand in mine. "Deal. Let's go."

When we got to my room, my giddiness at my decision had faded. Griffin went into the living area of the suite while I went to the bedroom. "Do you need anything?" he asked as I stood in the doorway.

"Nope. Just a little undisturbed time."

"Thirty minutes."

I'd have to be careful. It might take five minutes. Or fifty. "It could take longer."

"Make sure it doesn't, or I'm coming in."

I opened my mouth to argue, but the determined expression on his face told me I'd lose. "Fine. Thirty minutes max," I agreed.

Shutting the French door that separated me from Griffin, I took off my shoes. Tossing the pillows to the floor, I pulled the bedspread back, turned off the bedside lamp and lay down. Taking off my necklace, I placed my fingers over my abdomen, with the crystal beneath.

I shut my eyes and opened my mind a fraction. No white lines to show me the way, but I sensed the energies close by. I widened the gap.

Immediately, the energies washed over me, dragging me down like the ocean's strongest undertow.

I closed my mind and opened my eyes with a gasp. "Damn it."

I'd have to be more careful. These energies were strange. Strong. Different from anything I'd ever worked with. Complicated. The more I touched them, it seemed like the less I knew.

I shut my eyes again. This time, I squeaked my mind open in stages. There it was. Marian energy. Carefully, I followed the white thread through the city, bright light touching me like a living entity.

It ended at a person. A woman. *A Marian.* I touched her. It wasn't Pauline.

It had two energies.

Ana and the baby, I realized. The energies were separate but intertwined in a way that defined the mother-child bond more than science realized.

How beautiful.

Intrigued, I went deeper, being careful to keep myself disconnected as I felt mother and child.

The baby was a girl and like us.

The temptation to stay was powerful. I'd never experienced anything so pure and deep.

But that was neither the point nor purpose of my search, and my time grew short. I gave mother and child a mental kiss before I departed and cast about for Pauline. Another thread emerged from the dark. I followed it.

Once again, I zoomed through the city. Past people with no idea of what was going on in their world. Their energies weak and uninteresting.

This time, the thread ended with a single energy. One I recognized.

Hello, Pauline.

I opened my eyes and sat up, exuberant. I did it. Used the new energy without letting it overwhelm me.

Giddy at my success, I put my necklace back on. I knew the general area where Pauline was hiding, but I'd still need the crystal for more accurate directions. Swinging my feet over the edge of the bed, I stretched, glancing at the clock out of the corner of my eye. Ten minutes. It would have been shorter if I hadn't found Ana first. I pressed my stomach with the flat of my hand, remembering how it felt to be pregnant, even when it wasn't me.

Ana was blessed, and so was the baby.

When I opened the French door back into the sitting room of the suite, I realized I was grinning like an idiot, and I didn't give a damn. "Ready to go bag a thief?"

His feet propped on a coffee table, Griffin looked up from his magazine. "You know where she is?"

"Of course."

He raised a brow in question, but called for the car. We both changed into jeans, sweaters, boots, grabbed our coats and in a few minutes were on our way. Toying with my necklace, I focused on Pauline. Now that I knew where she was, it was much easier to keep a hold on her.

To Griffin's credit, he followed my directions without hesitation, but I saw the questions in his eyes.

Was I right about Pauline, and if I was…how?

When we reached her locale, I told him to park across the street. She was staying at the Hotel Raphael.

Griffin killed the engine. "Now what?" he asked, unbuckling his seat belt and turning to me.

"Now, we wait."

"No confrontation?"

I shook my head. "I want to find out what she's up to, don't you?"

"Yeah, I do," he acknowledged. "I have a feeling it's a lot bigger than a simple theft."

"Is that why you've helped me?" I asked, curious.

He rubbed his chin, thinking. "I was wondering when you were going to ask me that."

"I'd have asked earlier, but we've been too busy."

"Guns. Sex. Lies. It's been like living in an action-adventure movie."

"Yeah," I agreed. "And you're avoiding the question. Why are you doing this?"

His back against the door, he shrugged. "Lots of reasons. You need help being the main one."

"Oh, the whole damsel in distress scenario?" I asked, a little pleased and a little disappointed.

"At first, yes."

"And then?"

"Guns. Sex. Lies."

I laughed. Who was this man? I propped my leg on the seat. "Why haven't you asked me how I found Pauline? We had a deal."

"I'm not sure you have done it," he replied. "I don't see her as of yet."

"Yet you came anyway?"

"Either way, we're no worse off." He shifted closer. "If you're right, you'll tell me how. If you're wrong, I'll know you're delusional," he joked.

Despite his teasing tone, I flinched.

"Tru? I was kidding."

"I know," I said, trying to mean it. But what if it was true? Just a little bit.

Concern colored his expression. "I don't think you do."

He reached out, cupping my cheek in his palm. "No matter what—right or wrong—I will do whatever I can to keep you from harm. To keep you safe."

It was a stereotypical male comment, but it turned my insides to jam. "Promise?"

"Absolutely."

I believed him.

His hand traced a path from my cheek to the back of my head, and he pulled me to him.

How had he come to mean so much to me in such a short amount of time? "I'll keep you safe, too," I whispered against his mouth.

"Promise?"

"Absolutely."

His kiss was tender, testing. More like a first kiss than that of someone I'd already slept with. I traced his upper lip with my tongue, then kissed his neck.

He groaned, and his hand skimmed down my side and to the small of my back.

"We should keep an eye on the hotel," I said, biting his ear.

"We should."

With mutual resignation, we separated. Me on my side. Griffin on his.

I shivered in the growing cold. "Come here," he said.

When my back was to him, he pulled me into his arms. "Now we can watch for Pauline and keep warm."

"You have some great ideas," I said, snuggling closer.

Eight hours and two pee breaks later, she emerged.

I woke up to snow-covered peaks, quiet valleys and a wooden sign that welcomed me to the tiny village of Lys, France,

Ahead of us, I spotted Pauline's black Mercedes in front of a market, but there was no Pauline. She had to be inside.

"Hey, sleepyhead," Griffin said. Driving past her car and pulling around to the back of the store, he parked and cut the engine. It was a prime location where we could watch the road, but unobtrusive enough that Pauline wouldn't notice us unless she was intentionally looking for the car. "Get enough rest?"

"Yes." I stretched, wondering if this was her destination or just a break. I hoped the former. The thought of tailing someone was exciting. The actual execution was rather dull.

"Are you okay?" I asked. "I can take over the driving if she leaves." He had to be tired. I'd slept on and off as we followed her through the early morning hours, but he'd remained awake to drive.

"I'm good," he replied.

"Typical man," I said through another yawn. "Wanting to be in control of the vehicle."

"Sometimes, yes," he replied with a chuckle. "There's no quicksand out here, but there are some serious drop-offs."

I stuck out my tongue, rubbed my eyes and

watched the road. "You think this is her stop?" I asked after a few minutes of waiting.

"I sure hope so."

"Bored?"

"No. Just ready for some answers."

You and me both. A few seconds later, Pauline's car drove past.

Instead of turning on the engine and following, Griffin opened his door.

I grabbed his arm. "What are you doing? Aren't you going to follow her?"

"Not yet. This road goes on for a while with very few intersections. We can give her a little leeway."

I hesitated. He had a point. Kind of.

He continued, "This place doesn't even have a gas station, so I'm betting she stopped for a reason. I'd like to find out if she said anything to the shopkeeper that might tell us where she was going. What she was doing."

I let go of his arm and joined him in the dirt that served as a parking lot. Shutting my car door, I didn't bother to lock it. "Think he'll tell you anything?"

"No, but I'm betting he'll tell *you* what we need to know." Meeting me at the front of the car as I came around, Griffin put his arm around my waist. "Smile big and act blond."

"You have got to be kidding," I said. I wasn't sure if I should be insulted at the label or pleased that he thought I was that good an actress.

"Nope." He squeezed me close as we walked to the front of the building. Built from local stone and looking as if it had withstood a hundred years of winter storms, it was still functional and charming. "Keep the story simple," Griffin said. "Tell him that we were following her and lost her when we stopped to take pictures."

"I know how to tell a story," I said.

"I'm figuring that out," he replied, opening the door to the store and escorting me in.

Ignoring his teasing, I removed myself from Griffin's embrace and went to the counter, where a gray-haired man was reading a magazine. As weathered as the building that surrounded him, he didn't look up at my approach.

"Good afternoon," I said with a smile and a small hair toss. "Do you speak English?"

He set the magazine down. "*Bonjour, mademoiselle*. I speak a little."

I widened my smile. "I am looking for a friend. We—" I waved toward Griffin who perused canned goods "—were following her car and lost her when we stopped to take pictures. She is tall. Thin. Big brown eyes. Drives a Mercedes."

Suspicion flickered in his eyes. I tilted my head to the right a notch and tried to appear vapid. "I'd appreciate any help you can give. We are meeting friends, and I don't have directions. I feel like a fool. I shouldn't have stopped, but the mountains were so beautiful." I worried my bottom lip with my teeth and looked as innocent as possible.

His suspicion faded as quickly as it had arrived. "She is down the road, going to the Dauvergne farmhouse."

"That's it!" I exclaimed, clapping my hands. "She mentioned the farmhouse. Could you give me directions?" I reached over and rested my hand on top of his. "It would be a help."

"Of course," he said, patting my hand.

A few minutes later, we left with a small hand-drawn map, plus a bottle of Château L'Astre Grande Signature Rouge.

A mile down the road, I felt a familiar twinge. *Tiles.*

I held my excitement in check. More energies became apparent as we grew closer. The women were present, as well.

We reached a lightning-split rowan tree and a crumbled well that were landmarks for the turn to the farm. "I'd rather not announce our presence until we know what's going on," I said, fighting to keep my voice calm. Soon, I'd have the answers I needed.

"We'll stop here and walk in." Griffin pulled over to the side of the rutted, unpaved, one-lane road.

I opened my door, anxious and overwhelmed with the feeling that soon *everything* would change.

"Tru?"

"Yes?" Halfway out the door, I hesitated.

"Call it gut instinct, but I have an uneasy feeling about this."

I wasn't surprised. He was astute enough to know that there was something different about what we were doing, and to Griffin's suspicious nature, different meant trouble. "It'll be fine," I assured him.

He frowned. "One thing I've learned over the years is to listen to my gut."

That he couldn't let his suspicions go was also not a surprise. I gave a quick nod. "Same here, but my gut is telling me that I have to find out what Pauline is up to. It's important."

He didn't look convinced. "I don't disagree, but something feels wrong."

I couldn't wait any longer. Destiny wasn't calling, it was screaming for me to hurry the hell up. "You can wait here if you want," I said, biting back unexpected frustration. "I'm going."

I slammed the door closed and faced the gathering afternoon wind as I walked in the right direction. Behind me, another car door slammed. "My gut might tell me this is a mistake, but you are not walking into it without me," Griffin said, reaching my side.

"Thanks," I said, relieved. I slipped my gloved hand into his as we trudged down the lane. When the farmhouse came into sight, we stepped off the road and worked our way across the barren, snowy field. Two stories and constructed of stone, the farmhouse hailed back to an earlier time. It was a sure bet that heating it was both difficult and expensive, but it was the type of home that memories were built on.

We walked slower, keeping low and trying to remain as invisible as two people walking in the snow could manage.

"Careful." Griffin pulled me to a halt when we reached the sparse band of trees that bordered the house.

"What?"

"Look." He crouched down and pointed at the bark.

A few inches above knee height, a tiny red dot glowed like a bull's-eye. "It's a laser. A modern trip wire," he explained, rising and taking a closer look at the trees that surrounded us. "There's only one, so far. Step over it, and don't break it."

"I'm getting the impression this a lot more than a simple farmhouse," I said as we picked our way closer.

"Much more," Griffin agreed.

We passed over three more electrical trip wires as we drew closer, each one more complex.

I spotted the fourth set within twenty feet of the farmhouse. "Well?" I asked. It was going to be a problem. No fewer than four dots appeared on the trees, and from their configuration, it was a safe bet the laser beams were intersecting.

Carefully, we circled what we could of the house, but there seemed to be a solid fence of light. There was no way through short of burrowing under the ground or growing wings.

"I don't have the equipment to get past this," Griffin said. "At least not with me. We have two choices. We announce ourselves or leave."

I frowned at the options. I wasn't ready to announce myself to the Marians until I knew their agenda, and I wasn't leaving. "There has to be a way past. If we could just listen…"

He shook his head.

Efra's charge for me to get the tiles back weighed on me.

There was a third option. Something I'd never tried before. Never considered until I met these women. Never thought about until I touched Ana's baby.

When I had, I had felt its innocence. Sensed its purity.

Could I do the same with these women? Find out

their intentions? It would be harder, since they were adults and inherently closed off, but it was worth a try.

I'd have to go deeper than ever, and at the same time, not so deep that I vaulted into vision land.

I sat down in the snow.

"What are you doing?" Griffin asked. "Staging a sit-in?"

I gazed up at him, knowing that after all was said and done, I'd have to explain myself sooner rather than later. I shuddered at the thought, but couldn't let that stop me. "Just watch over me and, no matter what, please don't panic. Just wait for me to wake up."

"What do you mean, wake up?"

Unzipping my coat, I pulled my crystal free and gripped it between my fingers.

"What are you doing?" His voice rose.

I took a deep breath. "This." Shutting my eyes, I cracked my mind open.

Even that was too much, I realized. The women were too many and the tiles too close. And combined, they were exponentially stronger.

Raw energy surged forward and widened the gap in my mind before I could close it, and blackness overwhelmed me.

Chapter 14

Aleta stood in front of the mosaic. Behind her, the cavern was silent with the depth of quiet that could only come from being housed in the heart of the earth.

She breathed deep of the cool air. She loved this place. To many, it might seem odd and somewhat sacrilegious to create such a beautiful work of art in the depths of a cave.

Mosaics belong in basilicas, they'd argue. Libraries. Public buildings. In the villas of the great patricians.

And they would be right—except this once.

Aleta ran a wrinkled hand over the cream-colored tiles that made up the face of the Madonna. This mosaic was different. Even uncompleted, it gave off an energy. An aura of power that increased with each additional tile.

It was exactly where it needed to be.

She sighed, wondering if she'd be alive to see it finished and feel the energy gain full strength. She'd been working on it for over twenty years, and there were still many bare patches. Regions that would remain unfilled until the couriers returned.

"Mistress?"

Aleta jumped. She had been so wrapped up in the mosaic, she had not heard her daughter-of-the-heart enter. "Yes, Maya."

"She is ready."

Doba. The girl had arrived yesterday from a far-off land, bringing tiles. They had not received a courier in over a year, so had greeted her arrival with great celebration.

"Bring her in," Aleta said. The mosaic pulled her attention again.

Minutes later, there was a shuffling. A cough. Aleta turned.

Doba knelt before her. Smiling, Aleta pulled the girl to her feet. "Daughter. Do not kneel before me. We are equals. Bound by the purpose and design."

Doba gave a nod, her shiny black hair falling to hide her face. Aleta pushed it back behind her ear. While Doba did not understand all her words, surely she understood the meaning behind them.

Doba gave her a shy smile and held out her hands. In them were seven tiles. Made of rainbow obsidian, they reflected the lantern light.

Aleta held out her hand, and carefully, Doba lay them in her open palm.

"Magnificent," Aleta murmured, awed by their beauty. Carefully, she put bonding material on the back of the tiles and fitted them, one at a time, into

place, filling the last blank spot that was the hilt of the Madonna's sword. A wash of energy flowed through the room, almost knocking Aleta to her knees.

"Mistress?" Maya steadied her. "Are you all right?"

Aleta patted her protégée's hand. "I am fine," she said, but once again, she could only wonder what kind of power the mosaic would wield when completed.

And whether she would be alive to finish her life's work.

I woke slowly. The vision of Aleta and the growing energy that came from the Madonna mosaic was the most powerful I'd felt to date. And that energy… I shivered at the intensity. It was stronger than I'd imagined, which made it even more imperative that I retrieve the tiles and return them to Efra.

But just my tiles. Not the rest that were in this house. And there were piles of them. Their energy tweaked the edges of my psyche.

I realized that my talent was growing. Amplifying and becoming more sensitive to nuance with each vision.

I wasn't a dowser anymore. I was more. Much more.

Who would have thought?

"Medevac…" The word caught my attention as the vision faded. I realized I was not outside. Quite the contrary. I was warm, and I lay on something that was, most certainly, not snow.

"She knew this was going to happen." Griffin's voice broke through the final dregs of the vision. I was back. "How could she know?"

I opened my eyes, both annoyed that he'd not done

as I asked, and a little flattered at the worry. "Because it's not the first time," I replied.

All heads in the room swiveled in my direction.

"I thought I lost you," Griffin said, dropping to his knees beside me, taking my hand in his and capturing my attention.

I kissed his knuckles. "You really don't listen, do you? I told you not to panic."

"Not panic? How can I not panic when someone has a seizure on command?"

"It wasn't a seizure."

"What was it?" someone asked.

I looked up to see Eve-from-the-funeral standing over us, and realized I was inside the farmhouse. Though sparsely furnished and in need of some repairs, it was as I'd imagined. Warm. Lived in. One day, given time and money, it would be spectacular. A place to host the holidays with friends and family.

"No lies," Griffin said. His gaze bored into me, and I realized how worried he must have been to bring me here and ask for help from the people we were spying on. People who might be helping Pauline.

"Okay," I agreed. He deserved the truth, and a part of me knew that if I lied, he'd know it and I'd lose him. And losing him was scarier than the thought of losing the tiles.

My gazed shifted around the room, spotting the tall man from the funeral, Rhys. "This would be easier without an audience."

No one moved. Instead, they waited. Expectant.

I shrugged. So be it. I tuned out the rest of the room. The rest of the world. They didn't matter. Only Griffin, and my need for him to believe me, were important. I knew I'd have to start at the beginning. "Griffin, I haven't been exactly straight with you."

His right brow rose. "Oh really?"

"Yes, really," I replied, ignoring his sarcasm. "There are things about me you don't know. Abilities I've hidden." I wondered how to put the long story into a few simple sentences. "Do you know what a dowser is?"

"No."

"It's someone who uses a stick to search for water," Eve offered.

"Exactly." I nodded gratefully. "Like in the movies. Someone uses a forked stick, and it points to the ground when there's water there. People used to hire them to tell them where to dig wells."

"Okay," Griffin said, looking even more convinced I needed to go to the hospital. "Are you saying you're a dowser, and that's what causes these blackouts?"

"Yes and no. I am a dowser of a sort. But I don't dowse just for water. I dowse for oil."

His other brow shot up. I continued. "I also dowse for gold. Copper. Hell, diamonds if I wanted."

"Really?" Griffin asked.

"Really."

For a heartbeat, four sets of eyes stared at me in curiosity, combined with either awe or sheer disbelief.

But only Griffin's opinion mattered. I gripped his hand, waiting. Would he believe me or would he abandon me? Please, be the man I need you to be.

As if hearing my silent plea, he cupped my cheek. "I'm going to need proof."

My heart dropped.

"But it's not the most outrageous thing I've ever heard." His acceptance was in the smile he gave me.

I grinned back, overwhelmed. He believed. Kind of.

"Women," he muttered. Shaking his head, he wiped a thumb under my eye. When he pulled it away, it was wet.

I hadn't realized I was crying.

"A dowser," Eve said, killing the tender moment. "While that's all very interesting, it doesn't explain the blackouts."

"They're caused by the mosaic tiles you have here."

Eyes widened. It was probably a mistake to show my hand, but seeing the shocked expressions made it worth it.

"What do you mean, mosaic tiles?" Rhys replied.

He was a horrible liar.

I ran a hand through my hair. This was more complicated that I'd thought. "Everything has an energy. As trite as it sounds, everything is connected by that energy. The tiles give off a significant feeling. Hot. Bright." I searched for words, but found few to describe how the tiles felt inside my head.

I continued, "Anyway, the blackouts normally happen just once, when I *touch* a new substance for the first time, but the tiles are unique. Different from anything I've ever encountered. Their energy overwhelms me if I'm not careful, and I black out."

I glanced around the room and delivered the *coup de grâce* to my audience. "And that horde in the basement about did me in."

Jaws dropped.

"Horde of what?" a familiar French-accented voice asked.

I turned to see Catrina standing at the bottom of the stairs.

"Tiles," I replied. "From the enormous amount, I assume you're planning to reconstruct the mosaic?"

She blinked in surprise.

"Pauline—how is she?" I asked before the woman could catch a mental breath and gain control of the situation. She seemed like the kind who demanded control when she could.

Her glance skated from me to Rhys and then back. "What—"

"Don't bother," Eve interrupted, looking resigned. "She knows…everything worth knowing."

Catrina's eyes narrowed. "Pauline is recovering," she replied. Arms crossed over her chest like a shield, she managed to look even more unfriendly than she had at the funeral.

"Griffin and I need to talk to her," I said.

"That is not a good idea," Catrina replied. "She needs rest. Not a chitchat with you."

I held my tongue before I said something that got Griffin and me tossed out the door. "She has something of ours," I explained as politely as I could. "We want it back."

"What?" Catrina asked.

"*Our* tiles," Griffin said.

I looked at him in surprise. It wasn't like him to lay *his* cards out on the table so abruptly. My revelation must have disturbed him more than I thought. As to whether his admission would help or hinder us, I prayed it was the former.

Not that I could complain. After all, I'd tipped our hand, too.

The mood in the room grew decidedly chilly. Whatever this group's agenda was, it didn't involve giving the tiles back to me.

"*Your* tiles?" Catrina snapped.

"Yes," I said, all semblance of courteousness gone in an instant. "*Our* tiles."

"Why should we give them to you?" she asked. She was abrupt, but I admired her frankness.

No one said a word, and I sensed that they wouldn't until I offered more in the way of an explanation. "They weren't hers to give," I explained. "I plan to return them to their rightful place."

"This is their rightful place," Eve stated. Her eyes took me in. "You are a Marian, as well, aren't you?"

I nodded. So they *could* sense other Marians. Or, Eve could.

"Marian?" Griffin whispered.

"I'll tell you later," I replied.

Eve continued, "As a Marian, you know the tiles belong here. With the others."

"Perhaps," I conceded, "but that wasn't her decision to make, and it isn't yours."

Once again, silence took over. I refused to give in to the pressure. This time, it was their turn.

"What would you have us do?" Eve asked.

"Honestly? Give them back."

"That is not an option," Catrina declared.

Rhys drew a breath, as if to comment, and Catrina sliced a glance in his direction. His eyes narrowed, and I suspected that he might be willing to compromise if it ever came to that.

Catrina focused her attention back to me. Everything about her, from her stance to the set of her jaw, told me she was ready for a fight.

And I felt ready to give her one. They had the tiles. That wasn't in question. If I could figure out where they were, maybe I could take them with Griffin's help.

Toying with my crystal, I concentrated on the cellar. Tile energy filled my head. Stone. Ceramic. Ivory and bone.

All with the Marian energy but different.

None carried the familiar signature that was indicative of Efra's tiles. Not even a shadow remained to show that they might have been present.

I scanned the entire house to be sure, but the tiles I'd come so far to find were nowhere to be found.

Disappointment crashed through me. We'd come all this way, and now, nothing.

I faced the women, hating to be the bearer of bad news, but hoping this knowledge might convince them to let me talk to Pauline.

"I don't think my tiles are going to be an issue anymore," I said.

"Why is that?" Catrina asked, her brow arched in displeasure.

"I don't know what you think you have or what Pauline gave you, but I can tell you this much. They aren't my tiles. They're fakes."

Chapter 15

"What do you mean, they're fakes?" Catrina asked.

I met her angry stare with a steady gaze. I could understand her rage. No one liked to think they'd been made a fool, but that didn't change my answer. "Just that. Whatever Pauline gave you, they were not my tiles. They were either counterfeit or a different set."

"Then you can go away now," she said, her mouth pressed thin. She made a shooing motion with her hand. *"Adieu."*

It was Eve who focused on the bigger picture. "Can you prove what you say?"

"Probably not, since it's my word against hers," I answered, wishing I had a better reply. "But give me a handful of tiles, both the ones she brought and the real ones, and I can tell you which is which."

Catrina looked to Eve, her expression questioning.

"Let her try," Eve said.

Catrina turned on her heel and went back into the kitchen. She emerged a few minutes later. I felt nothing emanating from her other than her personal energy, and already knew the answer to their question.

Still, I figured I might as well give them a bit of a show.

I held out my hands, and Catrina dropped the tiles into my cupped palms. They looked like my tiles. Same blue coloring that reminded me of the desert sky. Same shape.

And fakes. All of them.

"Well?" she asked, green eyes questioning. "Which are real?"

I dropped them to the wooden floor and brought my foot down on them, crushing as many as I could in one motion.

With a cry, Catrina dropped to her knees, her mouth open in horror. "What have you done?"

"Nothing. They're all fakes. Cheap imitations."

She looked up at me, broken tiles in her hands, her face a mask of anguish. Rhys stepped forward to put a hand on her shoulder—perhaps as much to restrain her as to comfort her. "Are you so sure?"

"Yes," I said, feeling horrible for putting her through this but knowing it was the best way. Besides, I was past subtleties. "Are you so sure they were real?"

Catrina looked at the pieces in her hands, and her eyes glittered.

"Well?"

She shook her head, but there was a hesitation. A glance. She *knew*. I didn't know how, but she did. "Catrina, quit being a pain in my ass," I said.

She dropped the bits to the floor. "I believe her," she muttered, obviously not pleased with the revelation.

I breathed a sigh of relief. "I'm more surprised that none of you knew." I looked at Eve. Despite her heavy mental shielding, I sensed she was as gifted as I was in many ways. "Especially you."

Her cheeks flushed. "Pauline just arrived. None of us really had time to verify her story. And besides, why would we think she brought us fake tiles? What's the point?"

"I think I know why," Catrina said. We all turned to her. "To convince us to bring her to this farmhouse, and more important, to what's in it."

The rest of the tiles.

Catrina's eyes raged. "I cannot believe we fell for her lies."

"We wanted to believe," Rhys added. "She was hurt. Beaten. We did not want to accuse her of lying."

I nodded in understanding. "You erred on the side of good. I get that. But she's a liar and a thief and you would do well to keep an eye on her."

"She told us Joshua hit her," Rhys offered. "*Some* women—" he glanced at Catrina as if to assure her he did not think she was one of them "—can do foolish things out of love and fear. Maybe he's the one we should speak with. Find out the truth."

"Joshua's not the one who hit her," Griffin said.

"Are you protecting Joshua Adriano?" Catrina demanded.

Griffin's face turned stony at her accusation, and he stared at her as if unsure what to say. I imagined it wasn't pleasant, but a heartbeat later, he replied, "I do *not* protect men who hit women."

"He's right," I said, backing him up. "Joshua didn't do it. When we met him at the funeral, his hands were unmarked, and you can't hit someone that hard and not bruise your knuckles."

She looked uncertain whether to believe us, but then gave a nod.

My stomach unclenched at her acceptance. It wasn't much, but it was a start, and it felt good to know that not everyone in the room was against us. I hadn't had to prove myself this much since I told my parents I was a dowser.

"Then who did it?" Eve asked.

"His father. Simon."

A gasp of surprise went through the room, but when they looked at each other, it was with realization and not disbelief.

They hadn't suspected him, but they weren't surprised. Still, I felt I knew a bit more than they did.

Hubris, my mother's voice warned. *No one likes a braggart.*

The voice in my head made me want to roll my eyes, but I held off, since it had a point. Now was not the time to crow. Besides, I needed them to trust me enough to give me free rein so I could interrogate Pauline. "I'll admit," I said. "Why she accused her husband and not the real perpetrator leads to some interesting theories, but that's all they are, theories. At least until we talk to Pauline."

"And you shall do that," Catrina said, as if offering

an ultimatum. "It is time for the truth. Let us talk to her and see what is the truth and what is the lie."

Finally. Rising from the couch, I stumbled, shaky now that I was on my feet.

Griffin caught my arm and steadied me. "Why didn't you tell me about this dowser thing before?" he muttered as we followed Catrina and Rhys, with Eve bringing up the rear.

I squeezed his hand. "Because I didn't want to see that look on your face."

"Which look?"

"The one I usually get. The look that says I need to be locked up and given medication or shock treatment. Granted, you don't have *that* look, but I see an inkling of disbelief."

He frowned. "Tru, it's not that I don't want—"

I put my finger against his mouth. "I know you want to believe, and that means more to me than you'll ever know. You will believe soon enough. I promise you that."

"I will?" he asked, his lips moving against my fingertip.

"You will," I replied. "Trust me."

We reached the top of the stairs. Eve's husband, Nick, sat on a four-legged stool outside the door, his large frame cramped even though it was a sizable hallway.

I had to admit I was relieved to see they had a guard outside Pauline's door. They might have placed it for her protection and mental comfort, but it suited my purpose of keeping her confined.

Nick rose when he saw Griffin and me within the small group walking toward him. "What's going on?"

"We need to talk to Pauline," I said. "Alone."

"I don't think that's a good idea," he replied.

"I agree," Catrina stated. "You may talk to her, but we will be present. We have questions, as well."

The others murmured agreement.

I groaned in frustration. "I need time alone with her. I've already told you what she was, and showed you that the tiles were fake. What more do you want?"

"But other than that, your stories and your big, stomping feet, we really know very little about you," Catrina said.

"And I don't know much about you," I countered, realizing the depth of that small truth. "Please," I begged. "Pauline and I have a bond of sorts. She'll talk to me. I know it. I can find out where she hid the real tiles."

Eve sighed and looked as if she might waver. I pressed my point home. "We've got to trust each other sometime. Otherwise, we'll never find the tiles."

"What happens if she confesses?" Catrina asked. "You have already said you do not plan to give the tiles to us."

I shrugged. "I don't know. I guess we'll have to cross that bridge when we come to it. But we have to find them first."

They did not look convinced.

"You can listen in," I offered. "This is an old house. How thick can the walls be?"

"Thicker than one would think," Catrina said.

"Then leave the door cracked open," Griffin suggested. "If you're all in there, we're limited in what we can say to her. If it's just us, we have a little more leeway, and we might need that. There's a lot more to Pauline than any of us thought."

They glanced at each other, silently deciding what to do.

"You have ten minutes," Catrina said. "We will even close the door, but do not think that we cannot hear you."

"Thank you," I said sincerely. They seemed to be good people who meant well.

I hated to be the one to keep them from completing the mosaic, but I'd made a promise, and I planned to keep it.

Griffin shut the door after we entered the room. It was small and sparsely furnished. White walls and a slanted ceiling with exposed beams. Wood floors. The furniture was old but in good condition.

Pauline lay on the bed with her eyes closed.

Griffin stepped forward.

I held up a finger to indicate that he should give me a minute.

Keeping my footfalls as silent as possible, I went to the bed. I don't know if it was the lack of makeup or that her wounds had blossomed, but she appeared more bruised than when I last saw her. Her right eye was purple and swollen, and the bruises on her arms were in the shape of fingers.

"Pauline," I whispered. "Wake up. We need to talk to you."

She grumbled in her sleep.

I smoothed her hair away from her face. I'd trusted her.

And she'd betrayed me. I wanted to shake her awake and demand answers, but I held my temper.

"Pauline," I said again, using a singsong voice.

Her eyelids fluttered and her brown eyes locked on to mine.

She screamed.

Between her hysterics and the group rushing in, it was almost ten minutes before Griffin and I were alone with Pauline again. She sat on the bed, head bent. She had an undeniable beauty even when she cried and was horribly bruised. Her nose didn't get snotty and her pink cheeks added to the overall effect of a wronged fairy princess.

I didn't believe it for an instant. I wanted the truth from her and would settle for nothing less, even if I had to pull it from her bit by bit. "Tell me what is going on," I demanded. "Why did you lie to me?"

"I do not understand," she said, hands twisting at her skirt.

I took a step forward, but a firm hand pulled me back. "Take it easy on her. She's had a rough time," Griffin cautioned.

"You've *got* to be kidding." I whirled to tell him to wise up, that she was scamming us, but as soon as I saw his expression, I hesitated.

He *didn't* believe her. He was using the classic good-cop-bad-cop ploy. Acting as if he was on her side in order to throw her off.

He winked at me, confirming the charade.

I blew him a silent kiss, then turned back to Pauline. She still sat there, sniffling into a handkerchief. "Enough," I said, yanking the linen square from her hand and tossing it to the floor, playing bad cop for all I was worth. "Now tell me why you did it."

She looked up at me with red-rimmed eyes. "I know what I did was wrong," she said, her voice raw. "But I did not know what else to do." She looked past me to Griffin, pleading with her big eyes for him to save her.

Nice try. "You could have told us the truth," I sneered.

"I was afraid. If he found out I had access to tiles and left them behind, he'd never have forgiven me."

Simon. "Are those bruises even real?" I questioned. Taking her chin in hand, I rubbed my shirtsleeve over the bruise on her cheek. She flinched, and when I looked, the cloth was free of makeup.

They were real. A pang of regret sliced through me, but I ignored it. I'd seen what she did with compassion. I glared at her, furious with her for being a liar and with myself for caring. "You've lied to me from the moment we met. Hurt people. Stolen items that don't belong to you." I jabbed my finger into her sternum, almost knocking her over. "Why should I believe you now?"

"She's hurt," Griffin said.

She smiled at him, grateful for the intervention.

I fought the urge to roll my eyes. I felt like I was in a bad soap opera. "Fine." I reined my bad-cop persona in a notch.

"Let's get down to why we're all here today." I grabbed a wooden chair, straddling it and leaning against the back. "Where are the tiles, Pauline? You know, the ones you beat an old lady to steal," I said, taking one last stab.

"They are here," she replied, brown eyes meeting

mine and looking as sincere as a saint's. "I gave them to Catrina. Ask her."

"I did." I took a deep breath, readying myself to deliver the blow of truth. "They're fakes. You know it. I know it."

For a split second, her eyes narrowed. Then she ducked her head and gave a little sniff. "They cannot be."

"They can and they are."

She shed another tear and looked past me to Griffin.

"Maybe we should come back later," he said. "Give her time to think and rest."

She smiled at him as if he was her knight in shining armor.

Knight, my fanny. "Maybe I should force the information out of her," I said, thinking that Griffin was taking his good-cop act a little too far. "Or call her *boyfriend*. He seems adept at slapping her around. Maybe he can beat it out of her."

I couldn't see Pauline's face, but heard a sharp intake of breath, and her neck flushed pink.

I grinned at her unexpected disclosure. I'd hit a patch of truth, and I knew just where it led, though the thought made me sick.

But not so sick that I wouldn't use it. I tilted her chin up, forcing her to look at me. "Does your husband know you're sleeping with his father?"

Her eyes widened, but what I saw wasn't outrage at the accusation. It was sheer, unadulterated panic. I felt it. Knew it.

And would follow it to the end.

"I do not know what you are speaking of," she said. "I am no adulteress."

"Yes, you are," I said, wishing she'd admit the truth for a change, and wondering if that was beyond her capabilities. "Your *lover* gave you those bruises. Griffin and I saw the evidence on his hands."

She blushed deeper.

"The question is," I continued, "was it done in anger or as a ploy to gain sympathy? To gain access to this house and these people?"

She jerked away, and when her eyes met mine, all pretenses were gone. I was seeing the true Pauline. Calculating. Ruthless. Cold.

And to think I once envisioned us as friends.

I felt like a fool.

"Do you know what those tiles do?" she asked. "What these women plan?"

"Yes."

For a brief moment, she regarded me. "Are you quite sure?"

I sighed, becoming more annoyed with the drama. "Yes, I am. But you seem to be missing the point. I don't care about you, your abusive boyfriend or what *your* intentions are. I don't care what *their* intentions are. All I want are the tiles you stole. As to the rest of them, you can duke it out with Catrina if you want."

And Catrina would win. I wasn't sure I liked the uncompromising Marian, but I respected her.

Pauline's lips pressed tight, and once again, she looked past me to Griffin.

I shifted, blocking her view. "Don't bother. He's not going to save you."

Her eyes glittered. "Out of curiosity, how did you know they were fakes when the others missed it?"

"The same way you did. I felt their energy."

Her skin went white as parchment. "What do you mean?" she asked, her voice panicked.

"You felt them. Their energy," I insisted.

"I did not!"

"You did," I said, watching her face twist in defiance. "Don't deny it. You're like me. We're descended from women who created the mosaic."

"I am *not* one of *them*," Pauline shouted.

"Of course you are," I replied.

"I am not!" She jumped to her feet, eyes blazing. "Simon would never—" She bit the sentence off, hesitated and sat back down.

"Simon would never what?" Griffin pressed.

"Allow it?" I prompted, fishing for information.

She looked away.

"Believe it?" Griffin asked.

She remained mute.

"Trust you?" I suggested.

For a brief second, she stiffened. *Bingo.*

It seemed I was on a roll. "He doesn't know, does he? Doesn't know what you are."

She whirled to face me. "You do not know anything!"

I rose and stepped into her personal space until I was so close we were almost touching. "Give me back the tiles, or I'll tell him, Pauline. I'll tell him all those important little details that you neglected to mention. Your lies. Your screwups. *Your heritage.* And I'll find the tiles, anyway. I found you. Don't think I can't find them, as well. It'll just take me longer, and I don't like wasting my time."

Her face grew red again, but it wasn't with false sorrow or embarrassment. It was pure rage.

For a moment, I thought she might spit on me.

"Let's give her time to think it over." Griffin took my elbow and pulled me away from her and out of the room.

I took one last glimpse as he shut the door. Pauline stared at me, her hands clenched.

"Remind me never to get on your bad side," he said once he closed the door. "You have a mean streak."

"No, I don't," I huffed. "I was bad cop."

"No, he's right," Nick said with an appreciative smile.

I smiled back. "Where is everyone?"

"Ana and Robert pulled in a few minutes ago. They're helping them unload the car. And Ana," he finished with a grin.

We nodded and went downstairs. "I'm sorry we're late," I heard Ana say as we came down the steps. "I just can't sit still for long."

"I think she took twenty bathroom breaks," Robert's voice teased.

"I'm pregnant," she said, her voice indignant and laughing. "You have a small child kicking *your* bladder and see how well *you* do."

We entered the crowded living room to find Ana and her belly were the center of attention. "Tru?" Ana said, her eyes catching mine.

Robert pulled her close, every ounce the protector to his pregnant bride. "What are you doing here?"

"She followed Pauline," Eve explained. "Long

story short, we were wrong to trust Pauline. The tiles she gave us were fakes."

"Are you sure? All those bruises..." Ana shuddered.

"Yes. We listened in at the door while these two—" she motioned toward Griffin and me "—interrogated her. It gets worse. She's working with Simon."

"Merde," Ana whispered.

A loud thud sounded from upstairs. We all looked up toward the noise. "Get the fire extinguishers," Nick shouted from the top of the stairs. "There's smoke, and she's barricaded the door!"

Chapter 16

I didn't have time to feel like an idiot for leaving Pauline alone and, apparently, with the ability to make a fire. Was she trying to kill herself?

Doubtful.

More than likely, she was trying to distract us so she could escape and get to Simon, the tiles, or both before I did.

Oh hell.

I ran for the front door in time to see her Mercedes roar up the lane toward the main road. My first thought was to follow her, but there were more pressing problems—like saving the farmhouse before it burned to the ground.

I went back in the house, running into Ana and Robert as he hustled his pregnant wife out the front door.

Squeezing past them, I took the stairs two at a time. The door to Pauline's room hung on its hinges. People and ever-thickening smoke filled the hallway. I looked through the open doorway. The bed was on fire, flames licking the wall behind it.

"Back off!" Nick shouted. He and Griffin charged into the room, shirts pulled over their faces and fire extinguishers in hand.

I heard them coughing and the sound of the extinguishers as they worked to put out the blaze.

Rhys pushed past us hauling two large kettles and a quart-size cooking pot. "Come on," he shouted, organizing a bucket brigade from the bathroom to the door.

With Catrina filling buckets, we formed a line and joined in. This is insane, I thought as I handed a bucket down the line to Rhys. We should be calling a fire department. Professionals.

Even I didn't want to tackle a structure fire.

Someone thrust a kettle of water into my hand. She must be using the tub, I thought, a little light-headed as my mind tried to make sense of what was happening.

Caught up in moving water, I lost track of time. Five seconds or five minutes later, Griffin emerged from the smoky bedroom. His hair was singed and there was a demarcation line between sooty and unsooty skin from where he'd held his T-shirt over his mouth. "It's out," he declared, letting the extinguisher drop to the floor.

"Open the windows," Catrina said, coughing. "Before we all suffocate."

While everyone else took a room, opening doors

and windows, venting the smoke, I returned to the bedroom to see if Pauline had left any clues. I knew she was headed for Simon and the tiles, but I wanted to make sure I hadn't missed anything.

My heart skipped a beat when I saw the damage. The room was salvageable but would need work. She'd set fire to the mattress, but also the opposite wall, using a length of fabric as fuel. I poked at it with my foot.

"I think it was the rug," a voice said.

I turned to see Robert enter. He gave me a reserved wave and began sorting through the damaged materials, piling them in the middle of the floor for easier hauling.

I should have stayed with her, I thought, watching the mound grow. I should have made her tell me everything.

I couldn't stand the guilt anymore. "When I catch her," I muttered, walking away from the damage, "I'll set *her* on fire."

"Not if I get to her first," Catrina said, watching from the hallway with Rhys at her side.

I nodded in appreciation of her need for retribution, realizing this was *her* house. *Her* bedroom.

Her family.

Much like Efra was mine.

And they could have been killed.

"We will meet you all downstairs after we assess the damage," Catrina said, her voice determined and unwavering. She's tough, I thought. I glanced down to see her holding Rhys's hand as if it were a life preserver.

But not as tough as she'd like to think.

"We should call the local fire marshal," Eve said, coming up the stairs with a black bag in hand.

I hadn't known she was a doctor.

Her gaze went back to Catrina as if she expected her to argue. "Let the professionals take care of that. I want to check everyone out. We all breathed a lot of smoke."

Catrina frowned, but before she could answer, Rhys cut in. "She's right," he said. "I can replace the house, but I can't replace you."

She softened and nodded.

Not nearly as tough as she thinks, I decided, as I left the three alone and went downstairs. Griffin was in the kitchen with Nick, cleaning up in the sink.

I went outside to find Ana, wanting to talk to her, see what I could find out about this group of women. Perhaps it was the pregnancy or the fact that I'd touched her and the baby, but she *felt* more open than the others.

I found her on the porch.

"Is everyone okay?" she asked, one hand on her stomach.

"Yeah," I replied. "Robert is assessing damage to the room, and Eve is checking everyone out to make sure no one was hurt from the smoke."

"Good," she said, the worry lines around her mouth fading.

We stood for a few moments in awkward silence. "You know Pauline got away," I commented, wondering how she'd react to the bad news.

"I know, but you tracked her here. You can find her again," Ana said.

My sigh morphed into a cough, and Ana gave my hand a pat. "Let's take a walk. The fresh air will do you good."

I followed her toward the orchard, my mind racing.

I'd find Pauline again, and that act would redeem me, to a point. I remembered my conversation with Catrina and Eve—that we all wanted the tiles but would cross that bridge when we came to it.

The metaphorical bridge was in front of me, as big as the Golden Gate, and I was no longer sure that I wanted to cross it.

Maybe it was because of the shared heritage or the bonding while trying to save the farmhouse, but I liked these women. I didn't want to have to choose between them and Efra. I sighed again. This time, sans coughing.

"You okay?" Ana asked.

"Yes," I lied.

"It wasn't your fault," she said after a few minutes.

I stopped and stared at her. "Actually, it was." I'd tracked Pauline here, wanting not just the tiles, but answers. *Reasons.* I think a part of me hoped that a closure of sorts would assuage my guilt for letting Pauline steal the tiles in the first place.

But answers hadn't helped. Quite the opposite. They only brought more questions and responsibilities I couldn't commit to. And on top of that, my great search had almost killed people and the villain had escaped.

I was most definitely at fault to some degree.

Ana shook her head. "I'd argue, but I don't think you're in the mood to listen." Smiling, she wove her arm through mine. "Let's get back to the house. I need to pee. Again."

I laughed, grateful for the distraction. Perhaps my mind would sort through this mess if given a rest.

"So, have you picked out a name for her yet?" I asked as we walked, following our footprints.

"What do you mean, *her?*" Ana asked.

I didn't care if she knew I was a dowser. If the others hadn't told her yet, they would.

I was more worried what she'd do if she found out that I'd used my skill to touch her unborn baby, even inadvertently. She might be fine with my actions. Or she might bitch slap me into tomorrow. While she was tender and sweet when it came to handling Robert, I suspected she was on a par with a tigress when it came to protecting her child. "Just making conversation," I finally replied, hoping my hesitation didn't appear as obvious to her as it did to me.

"No. You said it like you knew," Ana countered with surprising steel in her voice. Her arm tightened on mine.

Well, I had some answers. She knew what I was, and my hesitation was obvious. Hell. I stopped and turned on my best wide-eyed innocent, please-believe-me persona. "Ana, I was just talking. Nothing more. Nothing less."

Her eyes narrowed. "Really?"

"Yes, really. What is this? Some kind of interrogation?"

"I can do that," she said, and started walking again, pulling me along.

That didn't sound good. "What do you do? For a living, I mean."

She grinned at me, but it wasn't a friendly grin. It was more like the kind a shark gives right before it bites your head off. "I worked for Interpol."

"Oh." Oh crap.

"*Now* do you want to tell me how you know my baby's a girl?" she asked.

"No," I replied, telling her I had been lying but not why in the single word.

"Perhaps later."

Perhaps? I glanced at her. Now who was the liar?

I didn't say anything, but knew that Griffin and I would have to leave soon. Ana was able to see right through me, and if she asked the right questions, they might hold me here until they found Pauline and the stolen tiles.

And despite my trepidation and my growing admiration of these women, I had a promise to keep.

Giving up the tiles was not an option.

When we got back to the farmhouse, the local fire marshal and fire brigade were already inside, having seen the smoke.

By the time they left, the sun was already setting. I met Griffin on the porch. "You okay?" I asked, leaning my head on his shoulder.

He put his arm around me. "Yeah. Eve said I was a moron, but that I'd live to be stupid another day."

I snickered.

For a few minutes, we watched the sunset in surprisingly comfortable silence. "You want to tell me more about this dowsing ability?" he asked.

I worried my lower lip, anxious that the inevitable would come despite his assurances. That this was the part where he'd tell me I was on the wrong side of crazy and it might be best if we went our separate ways. "Would it matter?"

"Maybe. Maybe not." He sighed. "It's a little farfetched, don't you think?"

"Yeah. I guess a demo would help."

He shifted to face me. "I've thought about that, and the answer is no."

"No? I don't understand."

"I don't want you to do whatever it is you do if it means you have a seizure, or blackout, or whatever you want to call it."

For a heartbeat, annoyance blossomed, but then I realized what was happening. He was scared for me.

I touched his cheek, surprised and pleased at his unexpected emotion. "It doesn't hurt me, and what you saw wasn't normal. Like I told you before, it has to do with the tiles. Otherwise, the only time I experience anything close to that is when I find a new material that I've never felt before. And even then it has to be a large amount."

"So if you were in a gold mine what would happen?"

I smiled, pleased he was trying to understand. "Nothing." I hesitated, trying to think how to explain what happened. "I've been around gold a long time. My brain knows the signature. When I find something new, like the tiles, it's as if my brain can't process the information fast enough and I black out. After I wake up, it never happens again. At least not with that material."

"But it keeps happening with the tiles, doesn't it? That's why you went into the bedroom in the hotel."

I shrugged again. "Their energy signature is a lot more complicated than anything else I've dealt with." If he was having trouble with *this* aspect of my talent, there was no way I was going to tell him about the visions. Not yet.

"And you use this—" he touched my necklace "—to focus on that energy."

"It's how I found Pauline before, and how I'll do it again."

Concern changed to stiff disagreement. "I already said that wasn't an option."

"Be reasonable," I said. "It's the best chance we have."

And the only option, since I had only a day to find them and get back to Egypt. One day before the curse kicks in.

He scrubbed his face with his palms. "You say it doesn't hurt you, but I'm not so sure."

I tried not to roll my eyes, and reminded myself that it was worry that made him cautious, not disbelief. "I was checked out. You read the report."

"I don't care what it says. I saw you. Twice. Once in the Jeep and then in the snow." He slid his hand to the back of my neck, pulling me closer. "You fell backward into the snow, and I thought you were dying. You say it doesn't hurt you, but for those who have to watch you shake and shudder and refuse to wake up, it looks like torture."

"I'm sorry," I said, wrapping my arms around him. For a moment, we held each other. "I didn't mean to put you through that," I whispered in his ear.

"Then you understand why you can't do this to find Pauline?"

Leaning back, I shook my head. "Not unless you can come up with something better."

"I'll use my resources."

"Informants will take too long."

"I'm the head of security for Dynocorp. I have a tech team at my disposal."

"And they'll help you track down a member of the

Adriano family?" I asked, unable to keep the doubt out of my voice.

"Not all, but I do have a friend who might," he replied.

From his tone and the way he glanced away, I knew we weren't talking about a boys' club where information was given because of shared gender. Quite the opposite. "What's her name?" I asked. "This saint who will help us?"

He sighed. "Leslie."

A twinge of jealousy rocked me. I tried to ignore it. We'd shared one amazing night, I reminded myself. That didn't mean we were exclusive. "I hope you didn't piss her off when you stopped dating," I said, trying to sound more flippant than I felt. "Otherwise, she'll never help."

"Uh. No. It was mutual," he replied.

Perhaps it was the reflection of the setting sun, but I think he blushed.

By the time the sun set and my adrenaline rush faded, all I wanted to do was lie down and sleep, but rest wasn't an option. We had to catch up with Pauline before she got to the real tiles and moved them to where I might never find them again.

Out in the driveway, Griffin was on his cell phone. His laughter carried on the evening air, needling me as another unexpected rush of jealousy tried to take hold.

She's just a friend, I reminded myself. A friend who can help us find Pauline.

I clenched and unclenched my fingers, wishing the rest of me believed that. He flipped the phone closed and came back up the drive. "Where is everyone?"

"Catrina and Rhys are making dinner. I'm not sure about everyone else." In fact, thinking about it, I realized I hadn't seen them in quite a while.

"Good." He pulled me close.

"What are you doing?" I asked, confused.

He nuzzled my neck. "Do you want these people along with you when you find Pauline?" he whispered.

I did, and more than I cared to admit. I'd just met these women, but they were already closer to me than I thought possible. But if they were with me when I recovered the tiles, they would take them, and I had a promise to keep that did not involve rebuilding the mosaic.

"No," I whispered back, sliding my hands under his jacket and up his back.

"I didn't think so."

I caught movement out of the corner of my eye. Shadowed by the rest of the curtain and the darkened room, someone watched us. "We have an audience."

"Good."

"Good? How does making out with an audience help us slip away?" I bit his ear and was rewarded with a groan as he grabbed my hips and pulled me close. His erection pressed against me, and I grinned.

The curtain swung shut. "They're gone," I said.

"That's how," he replied. His mouth traced a path up my neck, stopping at my lips. "Once we're sure they'll stay gone, we'll leave."

"You call that a plan?" I asked.

"No. I call this a plan," he whispered, claiming my mouth with his. I opened to him, and slowly, his tongue teased mine. Tasted me. Made me crazy as heat built inside my body.

Finally, I turned my head away. Much more and I wouldn't be able to think straight, much less make an escape. "Tell me how this getaway is going to work," I said, my voice breathier than I'd intended.

He kissed my throat. "I have a knife in my pocket…."

"And I thought you were just happy to see me,"

"Brat," he said, biting my neck.

I groaned.

He continued. "I'll puncture their car tires, and we'll get away. Simple as that."

"Simple?" I said, sinking into him. "How do we get them to leave us alone for that long?"

His hands slid around my waist and moved under my shirt to cup my breast. "We'll give them a show. Trust me, at some point they'll get embarrassed and leave us be."

My heart beat hard, and my shivering was not due to the cool air. "What kind of show? X-rated? At this rate, we're going to end up naked on Catrina's front porch."

"No, we're not. We're going to move it to the hood of my car," he whispered.

"Excellent," I said. "If it were summer." A metal hood in winter was not my idea of a good time.

"You'll deal," he said, laughing as he pulled me down the porch. "And I'll keep you warm, don't worry."

I gave the appropriate giggle and followed. The cars were parked next to each other, like ducks in a row. Thanks, guys, I thought as we walked past them.

We reached our vehicle, and I found myself lifted onto the hood. I hissed as the cold penetrated my jeans. Sitting on the edge, I pressed my knees against Griffin's hips and pulled him close.

His hands went back under my shirt and unhooked my bra. "Isn't that a little more than a show?" I whispered.

"Just watch the windows and make sure they see us," he replied. "When we're sure they'll leave us alone, we'll slice tires and go."

One of his hands slid between my legs, making me sit up. "They there?" he asked.

"I can't focus on the house if you're feeling me up," I hissed.

"Sorry."

He didn't sound sorry, but he moved his hand around to my back.

I watched for signs of spying. Nothing. A few minutes later, I was ready to yank off my jeans, and to hell with pretending, when Ana opened the front door, flooding the lawn with light. "Do you two need a room?" she called out, laughter in her voice.

"We're fine," I replied. "Be there in a minute."

Seconds later, we were alone in the dark.

"Now?" I asked.

"Thirty seconds. Let's make sure," Griffin replied.

I ticked off the seconds until he pushed up my shirt and took a nipple into his mouth. Then I lost count and pulled him closer. "God, yes," I hissed.

He stopped. Though I couldn't see him in the darkness, I felt the change in attitude. Damn. It was time to make our escape.

He pressed the keys into my hand. "Keep an eye out."

Easing the car door open, I took the driver's side, ready to start the engine.

In the dark, Griffin knifed the others' tires. It seemed to take forever. I watched the house, but it remained unchanged. Silent. No alarms sounded, no outside lights came on.

No one charged out to stop us.

Quietly, the deed finished, Griffin took the passenger seat.

"I should drive," he said, closing the door.

"Why?"

"Again. Quicksand."

"That was days ago."

"And I still have the head wound," he sighed.

I ignored him, started the car and backed out. I had the car oriented when the front door opened.

"Go!" Griffin shouted.

I flicked on the headlights and floored the pedal at the same time, racing up the rocky lane.

In the rearview mirror, I saw Catrina and Eve give chase, then stop. Ana watched from the porch.

I forced myself to focus on the road, but I wanted to cry. These women were like me. We might have been more than Marians and sisters. We might have been friends.

Instead, I was leaving them behind and by this time tomorrow, I'd have the tiles. Tiles they would never own. Never use.

I turned onto the main road and realized they were right to suspect me. Right to wonder about my motives. I was more like Pauline than I cared to admit.

Just more convincing.

Chapter 17

This time, I drove and Griffin slept. Left alone with my thoughts and my conscience, I flipped through different scenarios, wondering if there was any way this fiasco might have been prevented.

From losing the tiles to Pauline, and all the way to knifing the car tires, we'd faced one disaster after another.

At three in the morning, when the stars were still out and I'd just entered Paris, I concluded that there was no good answer, and self-torture wasn't getting me anywhere.

Griffin didn't stir as I wove through the streets to the Sheraton, since we'd never checked out.

I pulled up in front of the hotel and glared over at Griffin. Even asleep, he looked like a professional soldier, his jaw set and one hand curled closed. I killed the engine.

He sat straight up, eyes wide open.

"Griffin?"

He barely hesitated as he took in the surroundings. "You made nice time."

I had to admire the fact that he could go from zero to fully functioning in seconds, and without coffee. "Yeah. It was probably best that you slept through it," I said, handing the keys to the bellman.

We dragged ourselves through the lobby and to the room. I didn't want to think another thought until I showered, slept and had a big room-service breakfast.

"I'll call Leslie," Griffin said when we reached the room. "See what we have on Pauline."

"You might want to wait until she's awake."

"Oh, she is," he assured me. "Once she locks on to a project, she keeps at it until it's finished."

I bet. "Get me a location and I'll do the rest," I promised as I shut the bathroom door, my jealousy dying and hopes rising with the heat of the shower.

When I emerged thirty minutes later, I felt both human and encouraged.

All those good feelings dissolved when I saw Griffin's expression.

He wasn't pleased. In fact, he looked discouraged. I didn't want to ask what had happened, but a perverted part of me needed confirmation. "Leslie didn't come through, did she?" I sat on the bed, one towel wrapped turban-style around my hair, and another wrapped around my body.

"Somewhat. She found the car and sent someone over to check it out. It looks like it's been abandoned."

"Not a surprise. Getting away seems to be what

Pauline does best." I rested my head in my hands. "How are we going to find her?"

"It's going to take time."

"Time we don't have," I replied. As it was, the chance of me getting back to Efra before the day ended was nonexistent. Perhaps if I found the tiles and hired a private jet, and a helicopter met me...

But first I had to find Pauline. I fell back on the bed, overwhelmed with the impossible task before me.

I wanted a break. Was that too much to ask?

The mattress shifted as Griffin sat next to me. "We'll find her," he stated.

"I know." He pulled me up to a sitting position and put his arm around my shoulders. I leaned into him. "I just—"

The phone interrupted me.

"I'll get it," I said. Scooting across the bed, I grabbed the handset.

"Hello, Tru," a familiar voice said in my ear.

I pulled my legs under me. "Pauline?"

"Yes."

Griffin's eyes widened in what had to be surprise. I motioned for him to come closer. We shared the handset.

"I have a proposal for you," she said, her voice flat.

"I'm listening."

"You want the tiles, and I want you to keep your mouth shut about my background."

Her Marian blood.

She continued, "Do I have your word that if I give them to you, both you and Griffin will go away?"

I wanted to believe her, but I wasn't an idiot.

She'd kill us both, given the chance. "How can we trust you?"

"You cannot," she said, and I thought I heard a hitch of regret in her tone.

Or was it wishful thinking?

She continued and her voice was as flat as before. "But you have little choice. Do I have your word?"

Griffin looked at me, silently questioning me.

"You have my word," I said. "Give me the tiles, and I'll go back to Egypt, out of your hair. I swear."

She hesitated. In the background, I could hear what sounded like cars. Something revved its engine, and I changed my mind. No, not cars. Some kind of machinery.

"It is a deal," she replied. "I left a cell phone for you at the desk. Pick it up, then go out the front door. One of my men is waiting there for you in a black limousine. Get in. Once you are on your way, I will call you."

I sensed that now was not the time to argue. "Okay. When do we do this?"

"You must be downstairs in five minutes."

The line went dead.

"It's a trap," Griffin said as I hung up the phone.

"I *know*," I said. "And I'm pretty sure she knows that I know it. We don't have much of a choice." I unwrapped my hair, grabbed my backpack from the side of the bed to retrieve a brush. In a hurry, I yanked the knots out of the wet strands. "Pauline has the tiles, and I need them back. Today. So unless your Leslie can help, and do that in the next few minutes, we're going."

His eyes narrowed. "She's not *my* Leslie," he said.

"If you must know, she's very happily married, and that's why we broke up. She met someone, and I wasn't going to be a jerk about it."

I went back to work on my hair. I hated to admit it, but that tiny bit of information did make me feel better.

He continued. "And you know there's no way she can get the info we need that fast."

"I know." Rising from the bed, I dropped my towel to the floor, put on jeans, a brown sweater, sneakers and my camel coat.

"Difficult, crazy woman," Griffin muttered behind me. "Don't forget your gun."

"I won't," I said, taking it from my backpack and tucking it in the waist of my jeans.

"And this one," he said. He was holding a small Beretta that was just over four inches long. "Put this in your cleavage. When they pat you down, and they will, it might get overlooked."

"Where did you get that?" I was sure it hadn't been in the room before. "And where did you hide it?"

"Don't ask."

I took the gun, checked the clip and hesitated. "Griffin, you say this like you're not going."

"I'm not."

"What?" I asked, stunned.

"Tell them you left me back at the farmhouse. Make something up. I'm going to follow you. If something comes up, I can help, but not if we're both being held."

"If she knows I'm here, she knows you are," I said.

"Good point." He handed me the phone. "Call the concierge and have them locate a doctor who can come to the hotel. Tell them that I need *private* assistance. Her spies should intercept the information."

"And when the doctor arrives and you're gone?" I asked. "What then?"

He smiled. "Doctors never make house calls. It'll be a while. A long while."

It made sense, but I didn't have to like it. "Okay." I made the call, then slipped the Beretta in my bra. It pushed my breasts up, giving me slightly uneven, fake cleavage. I prayed the underwire would hold it in place.

"I've seen you shoot," he said. "So don't, unless you don't have a choice."

I stuck my tongue out. "I'll try."

"I don't like this," he said, putting on his coat and slipping his weapon into his pocket.

I had no idea how much time had passed, but it had to be close to five minutes. No more time to talk. No more time to plan.

Griffin picked up the phone and called the valet, asking that the car be brought around to the side of the building. He stopped me as we closed the door behind us. Standing in the hallway, he caressed my hair. "Don't take any stupid chances."

"I won't," I promised. I'd be careful for him. For myself. For the sake of a Nubian village that needed me to find and return their talismans.

We headed for the lobby. I stopped at the desk. "Any packages for Tru Palmer?" I asked.

A preoccupied hotel manager handed me a small box.

When I got outside, the streets steamed as the morning sun warmed the roads. As Pauline had promised, a black limo sat out front. Standing at the door was a large man, his blond hair pulled back into a ponytail. His gray eyes didn't hold even a hint of a smile. There weren't any obvious scars, but the word *henchman* came to mind anyway.

"Ms. Palmer?" he asked with a hint of accent that was not French. "Where's Mr. Sinclair?"

"In the suite waiting for the doctor. He was hurt in a fire your employer set."

"He must come with us."

"Then *you* go get him." I stared at him, daring him to challenge me.

Henchman hesitated, then shrugged.

Her spies were efficient.

I nodded, and he opened the door, stopping me before I could get in. To Griffin's credit, the guy patted me down, took my 9 mm, and missed the Beretta. I settled into the backseat and began checking out my escape options. Leaning over as if to tie my shoes, I reached under my shirt, pulled the small gun from beneath my bra and slipped it into my coat pocket.

I sat up, comforted by the small pistol.

As soon as we pulled away from the curb, the box rang. I ripped it open and grabbed the cell phone. "Hello?"

"Hello, Tru," Pauline said. "Sit back and relax. Mick will bring you to me."

More likely Mick would take me to a remote area, shoot me and dump the body. "Okay," I replied.

The phone went dead, and I tried to appear relaxed. "Where are we going?" I asked Mick, putting the phone in my pocket. He ignored me.

"Have you worked for Pauline long?"

"That's Mrs. Adriano," he corrected.

"Have you worked for Mrs. Adriano long?" I asked the question again.

And was ignored.

"All right," I muttered. I wished I could turn around to make sure that Griffin was behind me, but managed to keep my nervous curiosity at bay.

We left Paris, heading into the country, turning onto a hard-packed dirt road. We passed empty fields.

I remembered hearing machinery in the background when Pauline called, and wondered where we were driving. If there was a place like that around here, it was well hidden.

Killed and dumped in a shallow roadside grave. The thought flickered through my mind again, and I tried to dismiss it, but it made sense.

She couldn't kill me in Paris—too many potential witnesses.

It was much easier to drag me out to the middle of nowhere under the pretense of giving me the tiles.

I glanced in the rearview mirror and saw Mick watching me. "How long until we get there to where we're going?" I asked. "I want to get this over with."

"Soon."

Maybe it was paranoia egging me on, but that single word sounded like a death sentence.

Mick slowed down. There was nothing in the area that indicated machinery. No house. No warehouse. Nothing but empty fields.

Soon. Paranoid or not, I couldn't take the chance. There was too much on the line.

Up the road, woods came into view. Not much, but they'd give me some cover until I could call for help or until Griffin arrived. If he was following now, I knew he'd be hanging far enough back to remain undetected.

The woods came closer. I looked at the speedometer over Mick's shoulder. The needle was slowly dropping. "Are we stopping?"

"Just for a minute," he said. In the silence, I heard a small *click*. The exact sound of a gun being cocked.

We were at the woods.

I took a deep breath, opened the car door and flung myself out, praying I'd clear the wheels. I tucked and rolled onto the dirt road, bouncing to a stop in the grass.

For a moment, I lay on the cold, wintery ground and worked to catch my breath. I'd jumped from a moving car.

My mother would be appalled. The random thought made me giggle.

My arm hurt. A lot.

I heard the car screech to a halt. There wasn't time to take stock of my wounds.

There was only time to run.

Rolling to my feet, I sighted the woods and sprinted toward the trees, crashing through the low brush on the side of the road.

The winter-bare trees wouldn't provide much cover, but they'd have to do. Crouching low, I looked back at the road. Mick was getting out of the car. I wasn't close, but I could see that his hand wasn't empty.

"Mighty big gun for a quick stop or a friendly meeting," I muttered.

"Ms. Palmer!" he shouted. "We have a schedule to keep."

"Bite me," I whispered, watching as he scanned the trees. He turned toward me, and I flattened myself as much as I could into the dirt. I am invisible.

It seemed I *was* invisible, for his gaze went past me without hesitation. Staying hidden this way wouldn't last forever. At some point, he'd come into the woods, and I'd have to run. Once I did, he'd spot me.

I glanced to the road. There wasn't any sign of Griffin. Had Mick managed to lose him?

My heart pounded as I watched Mick go back to the car, do something, then return to the edge of the woods.

The phone in my pocket rang—a beacon for Mick to follow.

"Damn it!" I fumbled, grabbed it and pressed all the buttons to turn it off. Too late. Mick was heading toward me. Rising to my feet, I dropped the phone and grabbed my gun.

Mick fired. I felt the bullet whiz by my head. Tree bark shattered behind me.

I aimed, fired. I missed, but Mick was near enough for me to see that I'd managed to piss him off by even attempting a shot.

I ran farther into the woods, adrenaline fueling me. Behind me, branches broke as he pursued. Senses heightened, I scanned the forest for points of protections.

I found one. I couldn't see it as of yet, but ahead of me I felt water. A lot of it. It sang in my blood. Called to me.

Cold. Fast.

Refuge.

Bark exploded again. I picked up my pace. There was no time for worry, fear or self-recrimination. There was only survival.

The river came into view. It *felt* freezing. Fueled by the distant mountains, the current looked as swift as I feared.

I didn't hesitate when I reached it, but flung myself off the bank and as far out as possible.

I hit with a splash, and the chill sucked the air out of me. I began swimming toward the center of the river, where the current was strongest. Turning in the water, I watched the bank as I was pulled downstream. Mick came into view, spotted me and raised his gun. I dived below the surface.

And almost didn't make it back up when my coat caught on a sunken tree. Shedding it underwater, I rose, gasping for breath.

By then, I was around a curve and Mick was gone.

I knew I couldn't last much longer in the freezing water. I let the river carry me along for another minute before I headed for shore. My arms were leaden with cold, but just when I thought I might sink, my feet touched the bottom.

I waded out, stumbling and tired.

I started to giggle, and somewhere in the back of my mind realized that I was probably hypothermic.

"Doesn't matter," I said, slurring my words. "Move."

I struggled to my feet and stumbled toward what I hoped was the road. I trudged through a field, over mounds of dirt and dead weeds, all energy focused on keeping my feet moving.

When I reached the road, I dropped to my knees. I was tired. Hurt.

And still freezing.

Mick's car came toward me. "Fuck," I whispered, and fell to my side. I couldn't run, but there was no way I'd go down without a fight.

I balled my shaking hands into fists.

Griffin got out.

I cried.

When I opened my eyes, I was in the car again, but this time in the front seat. There was a coat over me. Beneath it, I was stripped down to my bra and panties.

"Good, you're awake." Griffin sat in the driver's seat, watching me. The car was turned on, but we weren't moving.

He stroked my still damp hair. "You had me worried for a few minutes."

"Me, too." I smiled. "Thanks."

He nodded, and I reached toward the heating vents to warm my fingers. Strips of a car blanket and two sticks acted as a makeshift cast, supporting my left arm. "What happened?"

"You broke your arm."

"I didn't notice."

"That's because you were running for your life."

"Funny how panic seems to kill pain," I said, trying to make light of it.

He didn't look amused.

I glanced around and spotted the same woods. "Why are we still out here? I'm surprised you didn't rush me to a hospital."

He still didn't look amused. "I knew I could take care of you, and we need to decide what to do with the guy in the trunk."

That comment perked me up. "There's a guy in the trunk?"

"The one who was driving."

"Mick?"

"If that's his name. Yes."

Griffin made me nuts. Made me angry. Sometimes made me want to smack him. Right now, I wanted to kiss him. "You are the best boyfriend in the world," I said, grinning.

"Boyfriend, huh?"

I shrugged. "Maybe?"

"Yeah, maybe," he replied. For a moment, we both sat there, absorbing the change in relationship.

A pounding from the trunk caught our attention. "What do you want to do with him?" Griffin asked.

"Use him to find Pauline," I replied.

Griffin sighed and laid his head against the steering wheel. "Can't let that go, can you?"

I shook my head. "No."

He gave a single nod of understanding. "Good cop, bad cop?"

"Sure."

"I'll be bad," he said. "It's hard to take you seriously when you're barely dressed."

He had a point.

"Let's do it."

Pressing a button, he popped open the trunk. He handed me his coat; I slipped it on as we walked to the back of the car. Tied and gagged with the rest of the blanket, Mick was crammed into the small space. There was a bump on his forehead the size of an egg. "Nice," I said.

"I thought you'd appreciate it," Griffin replied.

I glared at the man who had tried to kill me. "Hi, Mick. Long time no see." I punched him in the jaw with my good hand.

"I thought I was supposed to be bad cop?" Griffin said.

I tilted my head to look at him. "How about we both be bad cop?"

"Works for me."

Mick's eyes widened.

"And you thought he wouldn't take me seriously if I wasn't dressed," I said.

Griffin hauled Mick to a sitting position. "I'm going to take this gag off," he explained. "When I do. There will be no yelling. No swearing. In fact, if anything other than Pauline's location comes out of your mouth, I will give you to Tru."

Mick's eyes grew even wider.

I grinned, but I was sure it looked anything but amusing.

"Do you understand?" Griffin asked.

Mick gave a frantic nod.

Griffin pulled the cloth down. "Where is she?"

"I don't know," Mick croaked.

"Wrong answer," I growled, and before I could think, I backhanded him, splitting his lip.

"Wait! Wait! I have a phone in my pocket. You can call her."

"Better," I said. Besides, I was starting to shiver. I shifted from one foot to another, my feet tingling.

Griffin searched him and came up with a cell. He handed it to me. "Get in the car and turn on the heat. I'll be there in a minute."

"Thanks." I hurried back, started the engine, and cranked the heat up as high as it would go.

I called the last number Mick had dialed.

"Well?" a female voice asked. Pauline. "Is it finished?"

"Not even close," I replied.

Chapter 18

"Tru?"

Hearing the surprise in Pauline's voice almost made it worth freezing to death.

Almost.

"It's me. Alive and kicking," I replied. Silence. "Pauline?"

"Yes."

Perhaps it was wicked, as my mother would say, but it felt good to hear the worry in her voice. "We need to talk."

"I suppose we do," she sighed.

Outside, the trunk slammed with Mick still in it, I assumed. Griffin got in the car and I set the phone to speaker. "Did you really think I'd be that easy to get rid of?" I asked.

"I hoped so," she replied.

Griffin and I looked at each other in surprise. "Griffin—"

He shook his head, indicating for me to shut up. I finished, "Would be pissed if he were here. You're lucky that it's just me. I'm more likely to leave you alive."

"Where is Griffin?"

"Back at the suite. He was hurt in the fire *you* set."

"Why would I believe that? He would never allow you to leave alone."

"Do you think I gave him a choice?" I asked. "I'm like you in that way. I do not always ask permission for my actions."

I could almost feel her uncertainty over the phone. She might not believe me but she couldn't be sure. I didn't plan to give her enough time to verify my story either way.

"How did you get Mick's phone?" she asked.

"Element of surprise and a big rock," I replied.

Griffin gave me a thumbs-up.

"Is he—"

"I didn't call you to chat," I interrupted. "I want my tiles back."

"I do not have them on me," Pauline said, but I heard the lie in her voice. "I will need time."

"You have one hour," I said, taking the same tactic she had when she'd called me at the hotel.

"That is not enough time."

I glared at the phone. "I don't recall offering you a choice. You will get the tiles and meet me at a place of my choosing."

"What if I cannot?"

"Then I'll talk to Simon. Tell him everything."

"You would not. If you did, you would expose the others," she said.

I laughed, and it sounded bitter and raw, even to me. "They're not my friends. Efra is." I was on a rant now. "Do you think I care what happens to the others?"

"They are of Marian blood."

"Yes, but they're not family. Besides, I can warn them before you or your people can get to them," I finished, toning it down a notch. "And if that's not enough, I have a suspicion they can take care of themselves. Now, agree to my terms or I will tell Simon you're a Marian."

"He will not believe it."

"I'll make sure he does."

"An hour?" Pauline asked.

She'd believed me. I sagged in relief. "I'll call you," I said, and flipped the phone closed.

"Nice recovery." Griffin kissed me on the mouth.

I leaned into him. They say that when one is close to death, it makes life that much more precious, and right now, time with Griffin was almost as precious as the tiles. Especially since I knew that even though I had the upper hand on Pauline, she was still going to try to double-cross me.

For a few minutes, my whole world was Griffin's hands on my skin and his mouth pressing against mine. We fogged up the car windows like teenagers.

Then Mick began to yell.

"We should get going," Griffin said, starting the car.

"Where to?" I asked. Retrieving my wet clothes from the backseat, I spread them out as best I could, so warm air could dry them.

"While I was following you, I called Leslie, and she used the sounds that you mentioned, a partial trace and a list of Adriano holdings to make a best guess as to where she might be hiding. One of the warehouses on the list isn't too far from here."

"Okay," I replied. "But this time we use my necklace to pinpoint her location. I know you don't like it, but it'll save us a lot of time we don't have."

Griffin glanced over, his gaze sliding from my eyes to the middle of my chest. His eyes widened.

"Tru…"

In that instant, I knew what he did.

My necklace was gone.

We spent five minutes searching the area, but I already knew it was hopeless. The river had taken it, and wherever it was, it was too far away for me to feel.

I patted the empty spot on my sternum. "Let's go," I said, blinking back tears. I'd cried once today and that was enough. "If we get close enough, I'll be able to feel her even without amplification."

Griffin didn't argue, but opened the car door, surprisingly polite. "Are you going to be okay?" he asked once we were a few miles down the road.

"Yeah," I replied, hoping I sounded more sure than I felt.

Taking care not to disturb my broken arm, Griffin squeezed my bare thigh. "Do you need the crystal to do that dowsing thing you do?"

I shook my head. "I just had it so long. It was my lucky charm."

"We'll make our own luck." He pushed my hair away from my cheek. "Since it's gone, is there anything I need to do or say to help you focus and find Pauline?"

"No." The implication of what he'd said washed over me. "You won't fight me on using my talent?"

"No, I won't," he said.

"What changed your mind?"

He hesitated, as if considering his words carefully. "I thought about your gift while I was following the limo. What you are. What I am. If I can trust you to go off with a guy like Mick and take care of yourself, then I'm a fool to not trust you to use a gift you've had your whole life." Leaning sideways, he placed a quick kiss on my shoulder. "I trust you."

"Thanks," I exclaimed, overwhelmed. A simple word, but a complicated feeling.

Another few miles through the countryside, a small town came into view. It wasn't quaint. Wasn't pretty. Wasn't anything one thought a provincial French community should look like.

This was a working town. Factories. Parking lots. A few run-down stores.

And on the outskirts, a multitude of warehouses. It made sense that she was here. She was frightened. Scared. Hiding from the Marians.

Who would look for Pauline Adriano out here?

I closed my eyes as we drew close. *Where are you, Pauline?*

I sank into my breathing and opened my mind. A familiar energy line appeared in my mind's eye. Pauline. And near her, a patch of white.

The tiles. She had them.

I pulled away before they could overwhelm me with their power. I was getting better. My control over tile energy had increased.

My eyes popped open.

"You okay?" Griffin asked.

I smiled. He'd given me a pretty speech, and I knew he trusted me, but I couldn't expect him not to worry about my welfare.

After all, that was his nature. "Fine," I replied. I pointed to the right and a huge warehouse. "That way."

"You sure?"

"Positive." Now that I knew Pauline was there, she shone like a beacon in my mind. Griffin slowed the limo and pulled around to the side of the building. Leaving the sweater and keeping Griffin's coat, I struggled into my wet jeans and sneakers, needing his help with my crippled arm.

By the time I was ready, my arm throbbed.

I took a deep breath, blowing out any thoughts of failure with my exhalation. My eyes locked with Griffin's. This was the moment we'd either win or die, and we both knew it.

He pressed his gun into my palm. "Take this. I saw that you lost yours."

I pushed it away. "Griffin, she's an opportunist. She is not going to kill me. She's going to give me the tiles, and I'm going to walk out of there."

"You don't know that," he insisted. "And besides, I have Mick's gun."

"I'm a lousy shot," I reminded him. "This might do us both a lot more good if you were holding it."

He put it back into my hand. After weighing it on my palm, I jammed it in my pocket. Then I kissed him. "Back me up," I murmured against his mouth.

"Always," he whispered.

We got out of the car and walked to a side door. "Five minutes and I'm coming in," Griffin said.

I didn't argue. A quick hand squeeze and I slipped into the building.

Using a box as cover, I took stock of my surroundings. Whatever action I'd heard earlier had stopped. The warehouse was silent. The floor was crowded with boxes, forklifts and shelving. There were stairs approximately fifty feet away, and at the top, what looked like an office.

Pauline was there. I felt her.

I headed for the stairs. Standing at the bottom, I took a deep breath. Almost over.

Resolutely, I walked up the steps. The top landing was small, as was the office. My heart pounded. I took a deep breath and flung the door open. Pauline was on the phone, and her head shot up as the doorknob bounced off the wall.

I leveled my gun at her and smiled.

She set the receiver back in its cradle. "What a surprise."

"I bet," I said, fighting back the urge to jump over the desk and pummel her. "I'll take those tiles now."

"I don't have them," she replied, looking up at me with her big, lying doe eyes.

I took a step closer. I was on a tight timetable. "One more lie and I'll beat them out of you."

I must have looked as serious as I felt because she jumped up. "They are in the safe."

"So move," I growled.

She smoothed her dress, pleading with her eyes. "You do not understand. I am trying to do you a favor. Simon will kill you if you take them."

"And you are so very concerned with my health." I held up my arm, letting the coat slide back to reveal my bound arm. It throbbed painfully with each heart-beat, and I would have killed for an aspirin. "This was courtesy of your henchman."

"He was not instructed to kill you. Just to keep you away," Pauline insisted.

If I didn't know she was such an amazing liar, I'd have believed her. I shook my head. "Give me the tiles, or I'll blow your little secret."

"You cannot," she begged. "He will never forgive me."

A twinge of pity surprised me. I understood her fear. I'd lived my life as *different* and paid the price. Lost my family. Friends. Lovers. I knew how she felt.

I could even admit that fear of loss kept me from getting close to others, and turned me into almost a good as liar as Pauline.

But it had never driven me to murder. "Then he's not the one," I replied.

Pain played across her features.

"Is that why you took them?" I asked. "For him?"

"Yes."

I was surprised that she admitted her motivation.

"I saw them and I knew he'd want them. He's been searching for them, you know. I thought I could give him all the tiles. I knew the Marians would take me in once they saw my bruises."

"You got him to hit you?" I asked, appalled.

"I asked him to," she said. "Told him that it was part of my plan. My surprise. It worked, did it not?"

The thought made my skin crawl. "Does he know where the farmhouse is?"

"No."

I believed her. There was an aura about her, a

desperation that I felt to be true. "Why not?" I asked, wanting to know.

"I wanted to give him everything at once. Not parcel out my present to him in tiny, insignificant bits." She chewed on her lower lip as if suddenly realizing the folly of her plan. "It was to be a grand celebration. Like Christmas.

"I thought if I could give him everything…." Her voice trailed off.

"That he'd love you," I finished.

She didn't give an affirmation. She didn't need to. Simon wanted the tiles, and she wanted Simon. It was a story that every woman knew, and it never ended well. It didn't help that Pauline was an opportunist, not a planner. It set her up for failure.

"He doesn't know about the tiles, does he?"

She shook her head.

"The other Marians?"

She shook her head again.

I believed her, and if she was lying, I had leverage. "Good. Keep it that way and your secret is safe with me."

The fact that Simon was gathering tiles didn't escape me. Who knew why, but I suspected that a man with that much power craved only one thing. More power.

I didn't know what he would do with that power, and I didn't want to find out. "Hand over the tiles."

She went to a wall safe, taking a few seconds to look back at me with weepy eyes. "Do not make me do this. He knows I planned something. Let me give him these if I must keep the Marians secret."

"You have *got* to be kidding!" I said, stunned at the depth of her desperation.

I cocked my gun. "I'm tired of arguing. Just do it."

She fumbled at the combination.

"I cannot remember...."

I took a step forward. So close to her that there was no chance I'd miss if I fired. I didn't say anything and didn't have to.

"A minute," she said, her voice trembling.

A minute? How much time did I have left before Griffin came in? This was taking entirely too long.

I glanced at the clock on the wall. I was out of time. "Quit stalling," I said.

Behind her tears, a glint of satisfaction appeared.

I realized what was going on. She was stalling, waiting for someone. Making one last effort to save her plan.

Hell! And here I was, letting her do it.

I put the gun to her head. "Now."

She opened the safe and pulled out a red silk drawstring bag.

The tiles. My redemption. My salvation. Their energies sang in my blood, as familiar as my own heartbeat.

Relief would have to wait. Someone was coming, and whoever it was, I didn't want to be there when they arrived. I snatched the bag from her and jammed it into my pocket.

I exited and made for the stairs.

Pauline followed. "When Duke Simon discovers that you have the tiles, there is not enough distance to keep you safe," she shouted at me as I backed down the stairs. "He will never forgive you."

"I promise that if he does find me, I'll make sure he knows you gave them to me."

She paled.

"He already knows," a male voice said, just loud enough for me to hear. The hairs on my neck rose.

Pauline looked past me and took a startled step back. "Simon?"

"You gave her the tiles?" he said.

I glanced over my shoulder. Still halfway across the floor, he walked toward us. "Did you think you could come to one of my warehouses, of all places, and not be noticed?" He shook his head. "I knew you had something planned. Something interesting. I did not think it was betrayal."

"Please," she begged. "I did not mean to be disloyal."

"Yet you are, and now you must be punished."

A shot rang out. I cringed, then realized I wasn't hit.

Pauline staggered backward. A crimson stain emerged on her shoulder and spread out. She fell to her knees, her eyes wide with surprise.

It seemed she was right. Simon didn't forgive anyone. Not even her.

Time crawled to a halt as I crouched low.

I slid on my butt down the metal stairs; it was painful but quick. Another shot rang out, and the air shifted as the bullet glanced past me then ricocheted off the step.

I reached cement. A figure was at the other end of the warehouse. Simon. Another shot echoed through the building. This time from a different direction.

"Run!"

Griffin. Still crouching, I headed toward his voice,

using the boxes and shelving as cover. More shots echoed. I tried to ignore them as I ran. If I paid too much attention, I might never move.

Someone grabbed my coat and jerked me behind a box. I screamed in pain and panic.

It was Griffin. He grabbed my face, shushing me and kissing me. "It's okay," he murmured. "It's okay."

I kissed him back, then shook my head in exasperation. "I almost wet myself," I hissed.

He grinned, and I realized that gunfire was fun for him in a weird, perverted way. Taking a deep breath, I leaned against a box. "I'm a dowser, not a soldier or a freaking spy."

"And lucky," he said. He grabbed the edge of my coat. There was a hole in it.

A bullet hole. Another inch and the projectile would have hit my thigh.

I giggled, then clamped a hand over my mouth.

That wasn't a giggle. It was hysterics.

"I think we better get you out of here." Griffin looked at me as if I was nuts.

"It's a thought," I agreed. "I've had a long day."

He grinned again as if to say *that's my girl.*

I grinned back.

He shifted. "When I start to fire, I want you to run. I'll be right behind you."

"Okay."

I rose a notch and gunfire raked the top of the box. I ducked.

"Gertrude Palmer!"

I recognized the voice as Simon's. I didn't reply.

"Return the tiles, and I will not contact the police."

I guess she was wrong. He did know about the

tiles. *Not contact the police?* The thought that he might try to throw me in jail for taking back property that wasn't his infuriated me.

"You've committed felonies, Ms. Palmer. Breaking and entering. Theft. And wounding Ms. Adriano."

She's alive. As angry and confused as I was at her betrayal of myself and the other Marians, I had to admit I was relieved to know Pauline would live.

"I only want my property returned," Simon continued. "You cannot get away. Men are waiting outside."

"Damn," Griffin whispered.

"Do you think he's telling the truth?" I asked, trying to keep a clear head and not let my anger or worry rule my actions.

Griffin shrugged. "Maybe. Maybe not. But it's a safe bet that he's not alone."

The tiles weighed heavy in my pocket. I couldn't give them up. I also wanted to live, and more important, I wanted Griffin to walk away.

I pulled out the silk bag.

"No," Griffin said.

"But he'll kill us both. Or at least, his men will," I said, wondering just how dirty Simon let his hands get.

"He'll do it anyway," Griffin stated. "Trust me. He's not one to let us go, no matter what he says." He took the bag, weighed it on his palm and then put it back in my pocket. "Besides, you'll obsess, and we'll just have to go after them again."

When had Griffin turned from pain-in-my-ass to partner? And when did he get to know *me* so well?

"When you're right, you're right."

"Yeah. I know. Now let's get out of here."

"What about the men outside?"

"We'll do a Butch and Sundance," he said, putting a fresh clip into his gun. "But without the dying. We go out firing and catch them off guard. Run for the car, and don't look back."

I nodded, ready to fire.

"On three," he said. "One. Try not to shoot me."

"Two," I counted. "I'll be careful."

"Three." We said the final count together and ran for the door.

Bullets pinged the metal side of the warehouse, and we headed toward the light, our guns blazing.

I ran for the car, no sound reaching my ears except the pounding of my heart and Griffin's primal scream for me to hurry.

I dived into the car. Griffin landed in the driver's seat.

The passenger window next to me exploded, spraying glass over my head. Then we were roaring down the road.

Safe. Alive. Unharmed.

So far.

"Are you hurt?" he asked as the odometer hit ninety kilometers per hour.

"I'm okay," I said, letting my head fall back. I glanced over my shoulder. No pursuit yet, but there would be in a matter of minutes. A man like Simon Adriano did not let one simply take something from his vault, then drive away. "We did it."

"For now," Griffin said, sounding surprised as he echoed my thought that our getaway was temporary.

I slid my hand into my pocket, clutching the bag

of tiles. Bits of ceramic that we'd almost died for. That Pauline wanted.

As did Ana, Eve and Catrina. *The Marians.*

I closed my eyes, elation deflating. They needed these tiles. Without them, the mosaic they were building would never be completed.

I wished I could accommodate them. I knew what they were trying to do. Perhaps understood it even better than they did.

But I had a promise to keep, and with that promise, the fate of the tiles in my pocket was no longer mine to decide.

Chapter 19

My gaze flickered to the side mirror. It was only a matter of time before Simon and his goons caught up to us, I knew.

For now, the road behind us was empty. I leaned back. A man like Duke Simon Adriano would not let us go simply because the tiles were now in my possession and we'd managed to keep ahead of our pursuers for all of five minutes.

It was never that easy unless one believed Hollywood.

Our only chance was luck. And Griffin. "Think we can stay ahead of them?" I asked, not taking my eyes from the mirror.

"That's the plan," he said, barely slowing for a precarious turn.

I braced myself and shut my eyes, waiting for the

screech of brakes and the stomach-dropping sensation of a car rolling out of control.

We made the turn in one piece. I unclenched my
fingers from the armrest and looked at the odometer.
We were going almost a hundred and fifty kilometers
an hour. "Griffin?"

He glanced at me, his brown eyes dark and determined.

"We just got the tiles," I murmured. "I'd like to live
to take them back to Egypt."

He returned his attention to the road without slowing.
"If you were driving, I might worry, but we'll be fine."

I leaned against the leather seat. "Is this really the
time for joking?"

"Can you think of a better time?" he asked.

Right now, a sense of humor was one of the few
things keeping me from screaming. "Point taken," I
agreed. "As long as we're close to flying, let's head for
the nearest airport and catch the first flight back to
Cairo."

Griffin shook his head. "Hospital first."

"Excuse me?" I hefted the velvet bag. "We have
to get these to Efra. Now."

"Your arm," he reminded me. "The broken one. We
need to get it set."

What I wouldn't give to have Eve sitting in the
backseat.

I shook the tiles to get his attention. "This is more
important. My arm can wait."

A few hours of pain wouldn't change my life one
way or another, but there was a curse in motion, and
that small amount of time could make the world of
difference for Efra and her people.

"Your arm will *not* wait," Griffin said. "When the adrenaline wears off, you'll be hurting. You do not want that happening when we're in flight."

"I can take a little pain," I snapped, not wanting to argue. Why did he always have to argue? "Just get me to the airport."

"This is different. Trust me."

A thudding from the back caught our attention before our argument could escalate. "We forgot about Mick," I said, weary of the continuing roadblocks that slowed me down at every turn. "Should we let him out or leave him there to suffer?"

"Ladies' choice," Griffin said. I swear I saw the beginning of a smile on his mouth.

More thumping shook the car, and Mick started swearing. In French.

At least I think it was swearing. It was difficult to tell with him gagged and in the trunk. A smile threatened to curve my own mouth. I turned back to the side mirror. The road was clear. "Let him out. We don't need the extra baggage."

Griffin pulled the limo over to the side of the road. The pounding and swearing increased. Sighing, Griffin popped the trunk and opened his car door. "Be right back."

I opened my door, as well. "I'm coming with you."

For a change, he didn't take the time to object. We went back to the trunk, where Mick blinked up at us, his eyes adjusting to the sudden sunlight.

In that brief moment, the atmosphere changed, and I saw a side of Griffin that I'd not been privy to.

Fury.

Unleashed. Unforgiving. And unabashed.

Grabbing Mick's shirt, Griffin yanked him upright and out of the trunk. Pauline's henchman stumbled, weaving on unsteady legs.

Not wanting that anger pointed in my direction, I didn't interfere. Besides, Mick had tried to kill me. It was difficult to feel sorry for him.

His every muscle tensed, as if holding back the worst of his rage, Griffin dragged the man to the side of the road and let him fall to the ground.

Mick glared up at him from the ground.

Griffin looked him over like one might look at a bug on the bottom of one's shoe. "Follow us and I'll kill you."

I smiled and shut the trunk. When I looked up, my pulse leaped. Another car was barreling down the road toward us. "Griffin!" I pointed.

His eyes widened. "Get in and buckle up!"

I ran for the passenger door, then halted.

Right below it was a puddle of water. A growing puddle. "Hell!"

"What?" Griffin barked.

"Water," I said, getting in.

"Radiator?" He put the limo in gear and pulled back onto the road.

"I think so."

"How bad?"

"Bad enough for me to notice." I didn't need to say more. If water was leaking that fast, there's no way we were going to make it to Paris and the airport. We both knew that. All we could do was hope to get to a place where we might either lose Simon and his men or make a stand. "Drive fast."

He floored the accelerator, and as we flew over the

dirt road, fishtailing around another corner, I swallowed a scream even as he regained control.

Hulks like this were made for comfort, not for driving over back roads.

I looked at the dashboard dial. The engine temperature crept upward. It hit the red zone and Griffin slowed the car.

We were still in the middle of the country. "Any reason we're slowing?" I asked. "Because there is nothing around here but dead fields."

"It'll have to do," he said. "When the engine seizes, we don't want to be speeding."

"Okay." I didn't like the answer, but trusted his judgment.

He slowed further. The engine coughed and sputtered. Steam spilled from under the hood. Griffin pulled over and turned the car off.

I looked back. We hadn't lost Simon, and in fact, he seemed closer.

They would be on us in a minute. Griffin checked his clip and I pulled my weapon out.

"How much ammo do you have left?" he asked.

"Two bullets," I replied, knowing it wasn't nearly enough—not with my aim.

"Hopefully, you won't need them," Griffin said. "Get ready."

The car was almost on us, a black sedan with black-tinted windows.

There was little time for planning as it slowed. Griffin and I ducked behind our doors, but even as we prepared for a spate of bullets, the sedan passed us and pulled into the weeds a few feet off the road.

All without a shot fired.

My blood rushed hard and fast, making my arm throb. I forced my breathing to even out, and willed my body to stop hurting.

It didn't work.

The passenger door opened and a pair of loafers hit the gravel. Expensive black loafers that, until now, had probably never seen a dirt road. Simon.

The driver's door opened, as well. The shoes were good, but not billionaire good. Henchman.

"Get. Back. In," Griffin said, keeping his eye on the car.

"Make. Me," I retorted.

He huffed loudly enough for me to hear, but didn't reply as the men emerged.

Both carried guns. That surprised me. Perhaps Simon did dirty his hands on occasion.

"Drop the weapons," Griffin said, his voice calm. Level. As lethal as a chambered bullet.

"You can't get away," Simon replied. His attention on Griffin, he didn't acknowledge my presence with so much as a glance. "We both know that."

"Maybe. Maybe not," I said. He finally looked at me. "But put the gun down or neither of us will get the tiles." I pulled the bag from my pocket and pressed my gun to the cloth.

His eyes widened. "You would not do it."

He was right. Knowing what they meant to Efra and her people, I could never harm the tiles, but I shrugged anyway. "Are you willing to take that chance?"

He frowned, but nodded toward his man. Both bent down and set their guns on the ground. Rising, he motioned for his henchman to stay while he walked toward us.

"Hands where I can see them," Griffin said.

The duke raised his arms and continued. His suit looked obscenely fresh.

"That's far enough," I said when he was ten feet away.

Simon stopped. For a moment, we all stared at each other, the impasse complete. "You realize that I will find you, don't you?" Simon said, breaking the silence and looking down his nose at Griffin, then myself. "There is no place you two can go that I can't follow. I promise you that."

"And your point is?" I asked.

"My point, Ms. Palmer—"

I hated the way he said my name. As if it left a bad taste in his mouth.

"—is that if you do not hand me those tiles, you both will be looking over your shoulder the rest of your lives. The day you stop, I will be there. Waiting to take back what's mine."

Worse than the way he said my name was the smug smile on his lips as he envisioned his future.

"The tiles don't belong to you," I snapped, fighting to keep my temper in check.

"They are more mine than yours," Simon replied, his tone as cool as mine was heated. Then he smiled at me. Unconcerned.

I'd fired a gun on a variety of occasions. To protect. For food.

But never, until this moment, had I simply wanted to kill someone because I felt the world would be a better place without them.

"Keep it cool," Griffin said, breaking through my growing rage.

I realized that I'd chambered one of my two bullets.

"Tru?" Griffin murmured.

I breathed deep and sanity returned. "It's good," I replied.

"Good. Then watch him."

I focused my attention on Simon, steadying my gun hand on the top of the door. Out of the corner of my eye, I saw Griffin stiffen.

That couldn't be good.

"Time to go," he announced. "We have more company about a mile down the road."

No wonder Simon looked so unconcerned, I thought. He expected us to die any minute.

"You can go to the far side of the globe, and it will never be far enough," Simon said as I walked past, motioning for his henchman to step away from the car.

I stopped. Walked back to Simon. Looking up at him, I saw triumph in his eyes, and it ate at me.

Before I could think, I slapped Simon with the butt end of my gun, making his head rock. Simon's man shot forward, but the click of Griffin's gun stopped him in his tracks. I barely heard either of them. All I could think about was Simon. "That's for shooting at me and Griffin."

Simon wavered, but remained upright. "You bitch." He touched his cheek and drew back a bloody finger.

It wasn't enough for me. Might never be enough. He deserved punishment, and not just for myself and Griffin.

I hit him again and this time he dropped to his knees. "And that's for Pauline."

His eyes blazed with hatred as he looked up at me from the dirt, and burned with anger that I'd taken something from him that he considered his by right of might.

Still, a dark part of me wanted him to suffer just a little bit more.

"Let's go." Griffin touched my arm, bringing me back to reality.

As much as I wanted Simon dead, I wanted myself and Griffin alive. I placed the business end of my gun on Simon's forehead. "You will not chase us. You will not bother us. If you do, I will destroy the tiles rather than give them to you."

Simon looked at me, wordless, but there was belief in his gaze.

Good enough.

"Now." Griffin took the gun from my hand, and we ran to the car, leaving Simon and his man in the dirt.

"You okay?" Griffin asked. We circled Efra's village in a rented helicopter, looking for a place to land. Since we hadn't gone higher than twenty thousand feet, I'd actually enjoyed the ride.

Or I would have if circumstances hadn't been so dire. Our arrival in Egypt this morning was as uneventful as our exit from the warehouse had been chaotic. Griffin had used his contacts and money to put my wishes into action.

He'd hired a private Gulf Stream jet to take us to Cairo. Once there, he'd rented a helicopter. I'd learned Griffin had another talent I'd been unaware of. He could pilot a chopper.

I suspected there was a lot about him I didn't know, but questions could wait.

"I'm fine," I replied, putting my hand in my pants pocket and gripping the velvet bag that contained the tiles, drawing strength and comfort from their energy. "Nervous, but fine."

He nodded, and finding a level area outside the village, he set the helicopter down. I stared out the window, wondering what would greet me.

Griffin powered down the bird, and for a moment, I thought he might offer to go with me. Instead, he leaned over and kissed my forehead. "I'll wait here and guard the chopper."

"Thanks." I was grateful for his understanding.

We'd attracted quite a crowd with our arrival.

Wondering at my reception, I hesitated. I didn't expect warmth, but if they tried to stone me we'd have a problem on our hands.

One of the three women who had helped Efra after Pauline hit her scooted to the front and motioned for me to come out. She wasn't smiling, but neither did she have revenge in her eyes.

It was as safe as it was going to get. I climbed out of the helicopter, automatically ducking as the blades slowed overhead. Abraham was front and center, and though he smiled, putting on a brave face, there was a hopelessness in his eyes. His son was next to him, leaning on his crutches and smiling at me with equal parts hope and fear.

They all stared at me with that look. There was an aura of desperation in the people. Despondency. I didn't have to ask what was wrong.

The well was drying up. I felt it. The water level was low. Sluggish. Muddy.

The village was dying because I'd failed.

And Efra?

I looked at the woman who had motioned for me to get out. With sad eyes, she pointed toward the church. I imagined the worst. Pushing through the crowd, I ran into the village, heading for the church. Flinging open the door, I beat a path down the aisle and into Efra's private chamber.

She was in bed, asleep, but at the sound of my entrance, she opened her eyes and smiled at me.

Shocked, I did not return the smile. Pete had said she was fine, but that was days ago. Now her cheeks were sunken, her hair dull. Her body frail. Swallowing the lump in my throat, I hurried to her bedside and dropped to my knees.

"Oh my God," I whispered. "We need to get you to a doctor. Take you to a hospital."

Even though her body seemed to be shrinking, her eyes remained bright. "It looks like you're the one who needs healing," she said, her gaze fixed on my casted arm.

"I'm fine, but we need to get you help."

She shrugged. "Pete came by, and I saw a doctor. Some man from your company sent him."

"What did he say? Did he give you anything?" Panic rose in me.

"What is there to say or to offer? I am old. Much older than you think. No doctor or drug can cure age." She waved the issue away with thin fingers. "We have more important problems. Did you retrieve the tiles?"

I pulled the red bag from my pocket and opened it, spilling the contents onto her bedspread.

She sighed in relief and sagged against the pillows.

"I knew you would find them," she said. "I knew you would bring them back."

"Barely."

"*Barely* is acceptable," she joked, and for a moment, her pleasure at my success was enough.

"Help me up." She pushed the covers back, and my breath caught in my throat. Her nightgown was heavy linen but the thickness of the cloth could not hide her thin legs and sunken skin. "I am dying, and there are things you need to know."

The panic I'd been fighting finally overwhelmed me. "No! Don't say that!"

She hesitated, her dark eyes searching mine. Now they were full of sorrow. "I do not want to leave you, but I cannot live forever. Nor do I want to. Before I go, there are things I must tell you. Important things. Can you listen?"

Whether it was her words or her tone, something in me calmed even as another part of me stuck its fingers in its ears and hummed, denying what I couldn't bear to hear. "I can try," I murmured, my voice breaking.

"Good. There is much about the tiles I have not told you. They have a purpose. An important one."

"I already know," I told her.

Her eyes widened in surprise. "Do you?"

I nodded. "I had a vision. I know the tiles are powerful."

She smiled. "Aleta, she was the Marian you saw?"

"Yes." I was, no longer surprised at the depths of Efra's knowledge. Now that I was talking, I *needed* to tell her everything. "And I met more Marians. They're gathering tiles. I think they're trying to reconstruct the mosaic."

Efra stared at me as if I'd given her the moon. "I never thought it would happen," she whispered, her voice tinged with surprise and disbelief. Her black eyes watered, and she wiped them with shaky fingers. "Yet you brought the tiles back to me." She looked at me as if I'd lost my mind.

"I made a promise."

"So you did," she said, understanding. "And you kept it."

"No," I replied. "I failed. I'm late, and now you're dying."

She touched my face, and I realized I was crying. *Again.* "I have lived an interesting life. More interesting than I wanted sometimes. I am ready to go. Almost."

"But I'm not ready to let you go," I said through the tears. "I just found you."

"You have your sisters now. They are your family."

Ana. Eve. Catrina. "Yes."

"The mosaic is more than a source of power, Tru. When complete, it will align the earth and stop the catastrophes that have plagued the world of late."

I nodded again, barely hearing her. Not caring about the rest of the earth. The woman in front of me was all that mattered.

Her frail hand stroked my hair. "You must take the tiles back to them and help them in their mission. That is where the tiles belong. Where *you* belong."

I sniffed. "What about you? Your people? The well?"

Putting a finger under my chin, she raised my face to hers with an enigmatic Madonna smile. "I do not think it is coincidence that a dowser of great skill was brought to me. You will find my people a new well. One that will not dry up. One that will never go dry."

"What if I can't?" Out of habit, I touched the place above my heart where my amethyst used to rest. Without it, I wasn't sure I could push through the stress to help her people.

Efra shook her head at me, having none of my pessimism. "You are stronger than you think. Stronger than even I thought was possible. You have to believe."

I scrubbed my face. I hated to cry. "I can do that."

"I know." She pushed the covers back again. "There is something I want to show you. Something that belongs to you and your sisters."

I realized that she was getting up, with or without my aid. I slipped my arm around her waist and helped her to her feet.

Her body was light as she leaned against me. Slowly, we made our way to the next room and the Madonna sarcophagus.

Hooking a chair with my foot, I pulled it over and helped her sit.

"Open it," she said, her dark eyes bright and her voice strong despite the fragility of her body.

I pushed the lid up and blackness overwhelmed me.

Aleta lay in bed.

Her breaths were counted now, but she had no regrets for her life. Except one—the mosaic.

Unfinished. She would not live to see it complete. Still, she was leaving it in Maya's capable hands. While that did not end the regret that plagued her, it assuaged it to a degree.

Besides, it wasn't as if she had a choice.

"Daughter," she said, holding her hand out.

Sleeping in a chair across the room, Maya started awake.

"It is time," Aleta told her.

Maya hurried to Aleta's bedside, her dark eyes filled with tears. "Mother," she whispered. Like a child, she crawled in beside Aleta, laying her head against her chest for comfort.

"Your hair is still like silk," Aleta whispered, stroking her locks. "Did I ever tell you that? Like a black silk waterfall."

"Yes," Maya replied. "All the time."

"I shall miss it," she whispered. "Miss you." Her heart was slowing. It wasn't long now.

Maya's shoulders trembled as she sobbed.

"Do not cry, little one."

"What will I do when you are gone?" Her voice broke.

Aleta stroked her hair, knowing there was no answer she could give to assuage her grief, but that was the way of goodbye. It was easy to leave. Much more difficult to be the one left behind. "Do not grieve too long, my daughter. I am off to a new adventure. And it is one I look forward to."

"I know," Maya sniffed.

"And you know that I leave you with an important job."

"The mosaic." She looked up, her black eyes understanding in their grief.

"You must complete what I could not." Her heart slowed even more. A few more breaths...

"I will finish it." Maya nodded, touching Aleta's cheek.

"I know." Aleta leaned back into her pillows. "You

are a good daughter," she whispered, realizing it was
time to leave.
  Her muscles went limp. Her heart stopped.
  She crossed over into a new adventure.

I opened my eyes, and this time there was no confusion or disorientation. I was on the floor. Again.
Lying at the base of the Madonna sarcophagus. A
vessel that housed hundreds of tiles, and not just the
few I'd recovered.

And though the woman on the lid was the
Madonna, I knew she was more than that. It was
Aleta. The piece was an ode to a great artisan, created
by her best student and daughter, Maya, and infused
with the ability to contain the energy of the tiles.

A miracle in a miracle.

I looked at the ceiling, my gaze following a crack
in the plaster. All this time, I'd thought the visions
were about Aleta, the woman who finished the
mosaic. A Roman priestess who left behind the world
she knew, to help the rest of humanity.

They were about her. In a way. Thanks to the
visions, I knew how to rebuild the mosaic. Not all of
it, but enough to get the Marians on the right path.

But the visions were more. They were about
saying goodbye. About duty.

About Maya and what it meant to be the one left
behind.

Knowing what I would see, but still hoping I was
wrong, I looked over at Efra in the chair. She was
slumped forward, her eyes closed. A smile was on
her lips.

Her chest was still.

I rose to my knees.

"I won't let you down," I said, laying my head on her lap. "Good journey, Mother."

I shut my eyes and cried for what seemed like forever.

Chapter 20

"I knew you'd come back," Ana said. "The others weren't so sure, but I knew."

We were walking through the orchard near the farmhouse. Griffin and I had arrived late last night with all the tiles from the sarcophagus.

Perhaps it was Efra's will, or my own urge to please her, but my talent was strong enough to overcome the grief that consumed me, and I'd found the new well for the village within hours of burying my mentor and friend.

My mother in spirit, if not blood.

Then Griffin used his money and my manpower to move the village and sink the pipes. Fresh water flowed within a few days.

When I'd returned to camp, I'd discovered that Dynocorp had terminated my contract, which was not a shock. I didn't care anymore. I was gone within hours, leaving Pete to move our people to the next site.

It wasn't grief at losing Efra or anger with Dynocorp and Simon Adriano that had driven me to return to the Marians so quickly. Finding oil was just a job. There would always be villains. And loss was a part of life.

I had a duty now. A purpose.

The Marians needed me. They needed the tiles. I had a promise to keep.

"How could you be so sure we'd come back?" I asked, kicking a pile of wet leaves. "I didn't even know that until later."

"I had a feeling." Ana smiled.

Looping my arm through hers, I laughed, but then stopped as something niggled at my dowser senses.

I had a *feeling,* as well. It had nothing to do with friendship.

"What's wrong?" Ana asked, disengaging her arm from mine. "You look weird."

"There's something here. Close by," I said.

"What?"

I held my hand up, indicating she should be quiet. Shutting my eyes, I reached out. "Something Marian, I think." Whatever it was, it was weak. So faint I couldn't get a bearing on it. Perhaps if I had my crystal, I could locate the source of the energy.

I'd tried a few other crystals since losing mine, but none gave me the intensity and the focus of the one I'd lost.

I opened my eyes.

"Well?" she asked.

I shook my head, disappointed. "I don't know. I can't get a bearing on it."

"Could it be the temple?" she asked.

"What?"

"The temple," she explained, "where the mosaic was built."

My heart started pounding at her words. Aleta's temple? The cavern where she worked on the Madonna mosaic?

Ana continued. "We've been looking for it. We know it's close, but we can't find the opening." Her gaze bored into mine. "Can you?"

I shut my eyes again, willing myself to find it. To be strong.

I was rewarded with another niggling feeling in my head that was almost undetectable. "Sorry. It's close, but the energy signature isn't strong enough. Not anymore."

Ana sighed. "It's okay. We'll find it," she said, continuing down the path. "Eventually."

Lost in thought, we walked in silence. Ana stopped when the path ended and the orchard opened up to a view of the rocky, rolling foothills. "She would have loved this," she said.

"Who?"

"Scarlet." Hands on her belly, Ana looked over the wild land before her. "That's the other reason we're so eager to find the temple—not just because we want to rebuild the mosaic. We didn't bury Scarlet. That was simply show for the public and the Adriano family." She said the Adriano name like a swear word. "Scarlet was cremated. When we find the temple, we'll put her ashes there. A place of honor."

She laughed to herself. "It sounds funny to say that

aloud. *A place of honor.* She was such a free spirit, and that sounds so stuffy." Ana sighed and leaned against me. "But it still feels right."

"I wish I'd known her," I said, putting my arm around Ana's thickened waist.

"What do you think you're doing, so far from the farmhouse?" a voice shouted. We both turned at the interruption, to see Griffin and Robert walking toward us. "It's freezing," Robert called again.

Ana grinned at the admonishment. "I'm pregnant, not stupid. And I'm wearing a coat."

Her husband frowned, but the anger didn't reach his eyes. "Still, you're gong to catch your death," he scolded. When he reached her side, he pulled her to him, wrapping his arms around her expanded waist. "Come back to the farmhouse and get warm. I've made you hot chocolate."

Ana's grin broadened. "Marshmallows?"

"Of course."

Ana shrugged a goodbye, and I knew that my company was no match for marshmallows and chocolate.

Especially when shared with her husband. "See you back at the house."

The pair walked away, arm in arm.

Griffin joined me, and we walked in silence over the hills, with me following my feet and Griffin keeping me company.

We rounded a large grouping of stones, and before us was a waterfall, steaming in the cold air. Taking care on the mossy rocks, we made our way to the water's edge. I dipped my hand in. "It's thermal," I said, pleased with my find.

"Maybe later, we can go skinny-dipping," he said, enveloping me in his arms.

With my back against his chest, I snuggled into him.

"Happy?" he asked as we watched the water flow and splash.

"Very." I missed Efra, but there were no regrets. Though it seemed absurd, I knew that everything had unfolded just as it should have, and there was some small comfort in that.

Destiny.

"When this is over, come with me to Cairo," Griffin whispered.

I turned in his arms to face him, and as always, his hand cupped my cheek. His eyes filled with expectation. "I don't want to lose you, Gertrude Palmer."

I stuck my tongue out at hearing my given name.

He grinned. "It seems the only way to make sure you don't shoot someone, and they don't shoot you, is to stay by your side." He kissed my mouth. "Close by your side."

I swiped his bottom lip with my tongue. "Will you let me drive?"

"Never."

I sighed. "You are such a man."

"So, Cairo?" His other arm slid around my waist, and his eyes looked into mine. Questions. Eager. Hopeful.

I knew I had everything that mattered and more.

A mission. A mosaic to reconstruct. A legend to bring back to life. A family. Love. And the only answer I could give.

"Yes."

* * * * *

*More secrets will be revealed as
THE MADONNA KEY continues.
Don't miss the next thrilling adventure,
VEILED LEGACY by Jenna Mills
on sale December 2006
wherever Silhouette Books are sold.*

*And be sure to look for Sharron McClellan's
next exciting Bombshell novel,
coming your way in March 2007!*

New York Times *bestselling author*
Linda Lael Miller is back with a new romance
featuring the heartwarming McKettrick family
from Silhouette Special Edition.

SIERRA'S HOMECOMING
by Linda Lael Miller

On sale December 2006,
wherever books are sold.

Turn the page for a sneak preview!

S oft, smoky music poured into the room.

The next thing she knew, Sierra was in Travis's arms, close against that chest she'd admired earlier, and they were slow dancing.

Why didn't she pull away?

"Relax," he said. His breath was warm in her hair.

She giggled, more nervous than amused. What was the matter with her? She was attracted to Travis, had been from the first, and he was clearly attracted to her. They were both adults. Why not enjoy a little slow dancing in a ranch-house kitchen?

Because slow dancing led to other things. She took a step back and felt the counter flush against her lower back. Travis naturally came with her, since they were holding hands and he had one arm around her waist.

Simple physics.

Then he kissed her.

Physics again—this time, not so simple.

"Yikes," she said, when their mouths parted.

He grinned. "Nobody's ever said that after I kissed them."

She felt the heat and substance of his body pressed against hers. "It's going to happen, isn't it?" she heard herself whisper.

"Yep," Travis answered.

"But not tonight," Sierra said on a sigh.

"Probably not," Travis agreed.

"When, then?"

He chuckled, gave her a slow, nibbling kiss. "Tomorrow morning," he said. "After you drop Liam off at school."

"Isn't that…a little…soon?"

"Not soon enough," Travis answered, his voice husky. "Not nearly soon enough."

Silhouette

nocturne™

**Explore the dark and sensual
new realm of paranormal romance.**

HAUNTED
BY LISA CHILDS

**The first book in the riveting
new 3-book miniseries, Witch Hunt.**

DEATH CALLS
BY CARIDAD PIÑEIRO

**Darkness calls to humans,
as well as vampires...**

*On sale December 2006,
wherever books are sold.*

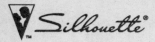

HARLEQUIN *Romance*®

**From the Heart.
For the Heart.**

---

*Get swept away into the Outback
with two of Harlequin Romance's
top authors.*

Coming in December...

Claiming the
Cattleman's Heart
BY BARBARA HANNAY

And in January don't miss...

Outback Man Seeks Wife
BY MARGARET WAY

TAKE 'EM FREE!

2 FREE ACTION-PACKED NOVELS PLUS 2 FREE GIFTS!

Strong. Sexy. Suspenseful.

SBOMB06

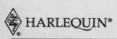
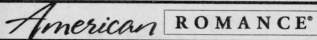

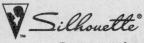

Silhouette®

BOMBSHELL™

COMING NEXT MONTH

#117 DAUGHTER OF THE BLOOD—Nancy Holder
The Gifted

For New Yorker Isabella de Marco, serving as Guardienne of the House of Flames in New Orleans was a birthright she still hadn't come to terms with. The ancestral mansion was in the midst of dangerous transition, and powerful demonic forces were aligning against her. With her partner and lover both wounded, Izzy comes to rely on a mysterious new ally for help…but does he have a hidden agenda to bring about her eternal damnation?

#118 VEILED LEGACY—Jenna Mills
The Madonna Key

Adopted at birth, Nadia Bishop never knew her roots—until she came across what seemed to be her own photo on the obituary page! Was this the lost sister who'd appeared in her dreams? Tracing the murdered woman to Europe, Nadia discovered the key to her own life—her blood ties to an ancient line of powerful priestesses made her a target…and her child's father might be part of the conspiracy to destroy her.

#119 THE PHOENIX LAW—Cate Dermody
The Strongbox Chronicles

The biggest threat in former CIA agent Alisha MacAleer's new life was babysitting her nephews—until an ex-colleague showed up on her doorstep, dodging bullets and needing her help. Suddenly she was thrust back into the world of double agents, rogue organizations and sentient AIs, while also helping men who'd betrayed her before. As avoiding death grew more difficult for Alisha, could the phoenix rise from the ashes once more?

#120 STORM FORCE—Meredith Fletcher

Taken hostage by a gang of escaped prisoners during one of the worst hurricanes in Florida history, Everglades wilderness guide Kate Garrett was trapped in a living nightmare. Her captors were wanted for murder, and though one of them might be the undercover good guy he claimed to be, it was up to Kate to save her own skin. For the sake of her children, she had to come out alive, come hell or high water…or both!

SBCNMI1106